The Joining: Bound By Blood

by

Erika Sands

The Joining: Bound by Blood

Contact Information: info@thewildrosepress.com

Cover Art by *Angela Anderson*

The Wild Rose Press
PO Box 708
Adams Basin, NY 14410-0708

Visit us at www.thewilderroses.com

Publishing History
First Scarlet Rose Edition, January 2010
PRINT ISBN 1-60154-763-3

Published in the United States of America

"Remember. One taste."

She smelled of sunlight and sweet herbs, yet he knew only darkness. A line of blood dripped from the wound created by the stiletto. His lust for blood slammed into him. "I think," Ariel responded, "that I'd better take care of the wound myself."

With the gentlest of intent, D'Nar lifted the hair off her shoulder. He leaned in, forcing her back against the wall, then braced one arm against the stone. Careful so as not to touch any other part of her body, his tongue snaked out toward the thin red stream.

"Will you allow me?" Once he tasted her blood, he would want her, for a vampyr's need for sex and blood couldn't be separated. Perhaps she feared that she would want him back.

"My Lord?"

He could understand her trepidation as she backed up closer to the wall. "I suppose I should find your attraction to me flattering." He followed her retreat, not quite understanding why his need for her should outweigh the social dictates he sought to protect.

He slid his lips along the strong line of her jaw. The metallic scent of her blood was driving him crazy. But he couldn't lift his head as fierce urgency gripped him. He leaned closer to her.

"My Lord," she hesitated. Her hesitation told him she feared her reaction to him as much as his to her. "Remember. One taste."

His head swam with the essence of her. He reared back, knowing he could become just as bad as, if not worse than, the two young vampyrs he'd saved her from. But he refused to apologize. He would never apologize for what he was.

Dedication

To my very own K'Mera
Alexis Daniele and Nicole Patrice.
I love you guys.

Chapter One

D'Nar wondered at the balance of nature as he walked the deserted streets of the marketplace. Two suns graced the sky—one red as fire and the source of their strength, the other yellow, rotating with their planet, signaling day and night, the change of seasons, the cycle of life and death. Yes, theirs was a complicated planet, with its hot, harsh climate and the rains that only came twice a year. Enough to sustain life, the life he needed to survive. His sustenance came from the blood of humans.

Humans needed the yellow sun and the water to grow crops, feed animals, and feed themselves. In the same way, vampyrs needed humans. A chain linked them all together. A chain that could be broken at any moment.

D'Nar shivered, his skin rippling with the strong, swirling wind. A storm was coming. As always, storms were dangerous for all who lived and tried to survive.

"D'Nar. D'Nar."

Whirling at the sound, D'Nar found a young noble racing toward him, gasping for breath as he skidded to a halt. D'Nar held up his hand, motioning for the young man to catch his breath. "Slowly. Breathe."

The crest on the youngster's tunic marked him as a member of the B'Shir family—wealthy merchants. What would cause this young male to panic so? "Now speak."

"Alleyway," the young man choked out. "Two hundred paces. There." He pointed. "They are—" Guilt and shame oozed from the vampyr. His gaze fell to the ground.

D'Nar knew the tale without the telling. He took

off at a full run, reaching the scene in seconds. *"Rista!"*

Two young vampyrs had cornered a human female. One pressed a feeding stiletto deep into her neck. The other had her pinned against the hard brick wall of an empty building. Aghast, D'Nar cried out again. *"Rista!"*

The male who held her whirled at his cry, blanching in recognition. The other turned ever so slowly to see who dared to interrupt his fun. As he did, he withdrew the stiletto from the woman's neck, centi by painful centi. Once the gleaming silver, now drenched in red, was free, he slid the blade with tantalizing care across his tongue. In spite of his horror, in spite of his disgust, D'Nar could taste every precious drop. "Arrogant little blood sucker," he hissed at the young vampyr.

"That's what we are, my Lord."

D'Nar kept his anger in check. "Have you no shame, T'Meric?"

The young man snapped the stiletto back into its case. The sound echoed off the wall like a death knell. "Actually, no."

A death knell, D'Nar thought, to all that was good and proper about their race. "They are living, breathing beings."

"They are food," T'Meric countered. "They are pleasure."

D'Nar deliberately dropped his gaze to the obvious bulge in T'Meric's pants. The young male swaggered a step or two so all could see his erection. "So," he bit out. "Flaunting your feeding habits for all to see is proper behavior? How dare you! Especially for a noble of your rank."

"At least it's honest," the young man snarled back. "Do we change simply because we feed and make love behind closed doors?"

"No," D'Nar replied, swallowing his impatience. "But we needn't revert back to our dark ages either.

2

We're civilized beings, not barbarians. We created laws to show right and wrong. You come perilously close to breaking them."

At that moment, the female, sensing their attention was not on her, tried to bolt. With a lightening quick grasp, D'Nar caught her. "Hold," he cried.

The woman struggled, but she would never break free of his grip. "I won't harm you. Neither will they."

She lifted her gaze to glare at him. His first thought was shock at her insolence. Then he barked out to the two young men. "Does she belong to you?"

A flicker of uncertainty crossed T'Meric's face. The young vampyr hesitated and a wave of fury slammed through D'Nar. "Is she your property?" he repeated.

"No."

Moving the hair from the woman's neck, he saw the mark of a free bond woman. "You dared to touch this woman? A free bond woman!" he shouted. "You won't be so cocky once your father hears of this." He turned to the other young noble, who paled. "Nor yours."

D'Nar centered his attention once again on his captive. "You don't fear me, woman?"

She swallowed, but refused to break his gaze. "No."

"You should." D'Nar eased his grip, but did not completely let go. "These two have insulted you. Since they won't apologize, I will do so for them. They shouldn't have touched you."

She seemed to relax once she realized he would place no blame on her. "Thank you, Lord."

"Do you have a punishment in mind for them?" he asked.

Was that a flicker of delight in her gaze? Could he blame her? Then again, she held no fear. That made D'Nar very uncomfortable.

"Nay, Lord. I leave that in your hands."

D'Nar guessed she had many punishments running through her mind. But as a free bond woman, he had no right to probe her. "Very well." He turned to the young men. "Your families will be notified. I'll make sure of it personally. See then whether your arrogance is warranted. Now go. Both of you."

T'Meric opened his mouth to speak, then thought better of it and skulked away. The other young vampyr followed.

Once they were gone, he turned to the woman he held captive in his arms. "Now I ask again. And this time, you may speak freely. Are you all right?"

She nodded. "And I repeat. Yes, I am."

"Your name?"

"Ariel, my Lord. I'm a fourth generation healer."

Ahh, he thought. That explained her status. But not her beauty. The top of her head came just to his chin. The wind whipped an errant strand of her red-gold hair across her face, reminding him of the streaks he sometimes saw bolting across the sky from the red sun. Her high cheekbones accentuated a heart-shaped face. A strong chin enhanced her stern countenance. But her gaze caught him, emotion swirling like clouds in the sky waiting for the tempest to erupt. She was angry. He couldn't blame her. "I beg your forgiveness for their behavior." He bowed, knowing he didn't have to.

She returned his bow, and he knew she didn't have to either. "I won't forgive, but I'll try to forget."

He frowned at her answer. Even as a free woman, she bordered on insolent. And yet, wasn't that his point? His race was becoming more and more open in their acts of violence. That violence seemed to be pushing her race toward insurrection. "You're bleeding," he told her, trying to turn his thoughts from his fears.

"I'm a healer." She smiled, but the smile didn't reach her angry gaze. "I can heal myself."

4

D'Nar shook his head. "And we both know there's a quicker way to accomplish that."

She smelled of sunlight and sweet herbs, yet he knew only darkness. A line of blood dripped from the wound created by the stiletto. His lust for blood slammed into him. "I think," Ariel responded, "that I'd better take care of the wound myself."

With the gentlest of intent, D'Nar lifted the hair off her shoulder. Spun red gold, he thought, even in the darkening gray of the oncoming storm. He leaned in, forcing her back against the wall, then braced one arm against the stone. Careful so as not to touch any other part of her body, his tongue snaked out toward the thin red stream.

"Will you allow me?"

He sensed her indecision. Once he tasted her blood, he would want her, for a vampyr's need for sex and blood couldn't be separated. Perhaps she feared that she would want him back.

His breathing labored in his chest. The craving for the tangy taste of her blood careened about the edges of his lips. His cock became engorged, filling with desire. D'Nar closed his eyes as he shuddered, trying to rein in the lust created by her blood and her beauty.

"My Lord?"

Opening his eyes, he read shocked disbelief in hers. He understood her confusion. He was a grown male vampyr, not a youngster in heat. He had no business subjecting her to this public display. "I ask your pardon. I haven't fed recently."

Given what had just occurred, he could understand her trepidation as she backed up closer to the wall. "I suppose I should find your attraction to me flattering," she told him. He followed her retreat, not quite understanding why his need for her should outweigh the social dictates he sought to protect.

He slid his cheek against hers, inhaling deeply. Her scent, mingled with the coppery tang of her blood, became an intoxicating combination. "I'm as much at a loss as you. But you must know that you're extremely beautiful. Whatever possessed you to enter the marketplace and travel by yourself?"

There was something about her, something that called to the darkness inside him. He didn't want to give in. He didn't want to let go. She must have sensed the war within him.

"I needed some herbs for a salve," she replied, pushing at his shoulders with her hands.

She had to know how useless her efforts were. He slid his lips along the strong line of her jaw. The metallic scent of her blood was driving him crazy. But he couldn't lift his head as fierce urgency gripped him. He leaned closer to her. A power, a force deep within him, kept driving him, driving his need. "You take your healing obligations seriously."

"I do."

"Perhaps you would consider healing me?" Her breath caught, but she didn't answer. "One taste? To seal the wound?"

The next several seconds were sheer torture. He hadn't realized how much he needed her to nod. When she did, the dam of control broke as, with a rush of pleasure, he lapped up the fluid on her neck.

"My Lord," she hesitated. Her hesitation told him she feared her reaction to him as much as his to her. "Remember. One taste."

His head swam with the essence of her. He reared back, knowing he could become just as bad as, if not worse than, the two young vampyrs he'd saved her from. But he refused to apologize. He would never apologize for what he was.

"I thought you were under control," she accused without much conviction.

Her words knifed through him. He'd thought so, too. His blood had answered a call of its own, rushing straight to his cock, making it strain to reach her.

"So, after saving me from those two young men, you put me in the same predicament."

He sighed. Nothing but the touch of her hand would ease the tension in his groin. But he wouldn't ask. "I have tasted your blood. Would you have me deny that I'm aroused?"

"Of course not. I'm a healer. I understand your response more than most."

He watched her gaze fill with a hidden knowledge, one she probably didn't even want to know. She'd awakened a sleeping I'man, touching the beast within him. And she was responding to that need. He sensed that something surreptitious, something daring, called to him from within her. The forbidden nature of their public union stirred the primitive side of his nature. And hers, it seemed. Desire simmered between them. But D'Nar wanted more than a mere sip. Part of him wanted the wound to open again. He imagined her blood running over his tongue and all sanity flew from his mind.

He bent down to her neck and scraped the skin of her neck with his incisors. She flinched even as her neck arched toward him. Her eyes became hooded as sparks of desire flew between them, making him forget that all could see them and their passion.

"One touch of your hand."

He reached up and pushed his fingers between hers. He groaned as her soft skin slid over his. As a healer, she didn't have the calluses of a field hand, but rather the hands of a courtesan.

"I dare not," she stammered.

"Ahh. I see. Something tells me you've never done this before." He leaned back for a moment to look into her eyes. "Am I correct?"

"My skills lie in other areas," she replied, her breath catching in anticipation.

He laughed softly as he bent down to nuzzle her ear. "No, that's where you're wrong." D'Nar took the hand wrapped in his and kissed the palm. "So small, yet filled with such power."

The wind swirled around them, making him shiver. The storm would not be denied any more than the passion growing between them. The public alleyway intensified the forbidden nature of their union. Did she want him enough to throw propriety to the winds swirling around them?

"What is it you desire, Ariel?"

Her eyes widened. Her lips parted. Her breasts rose and fell in time with the rapid beat of her heart. He could smell her arousal. Even though her woman's scent was driving him insane, making him do things he'd never before done, he hesitated. He wanted her to have a choice.

"Tell me," he insisted, knowing that she was free to say no if she chose.

His mouth hovered over hers and he breathed in her breath. No longer two, somehow they'd become one with the same purpose. Her hands pushed at his chest, but her fingers fisted in the fabric of his tunic. Even though she was obviously fighting herself, fighting the secret craving of wanting to make love to a vampyr, she didn't move away.

"Shall I leave?"

"No," she whispered, reaching up to kiss his lips. "I want you."

His mouth engulfed hers, their tongues twisting and twining. He took her hand in his and slid it inside his pants.

"Touch me," he begged. He wrapped her fingers around his cock. She withdrew as if her fingers had been burned. D'Nar gentled her hand, coaxing her where he wanted her to be. He let her fingertips trail along his steel tight erection, showed her how to use the fluid from the tip of his cock to lubricate his shaft, showed her how to lightly cup his balls and roll them inside her hand. Her inexperienced strokes told him she was very new to the play of lovers. Her innocence caused molten heat to run through his veins. The more aroused he became, the more he wanted to sip from her neck again. Instead, he focused on her pleasure. His free hand reached up and brushed the outline of her breast. She gasped. As her mouth opened, he plunged his tongue inside. Her kiss fired his senses, making him forget who he was. And where.

D'Nar struggled for breath as he released her mouth. His hair had come loose from the tie at the nape of his neck, creating a silken curtain that surrounded them. Her chest heaved. His hand spread over her heart as if it wasn't enough simply to hear its wild beat. He needed proof.

"My Lord," she choked. "We shouldn't be doing this."

He laughed softly as his teeth brushed against the soft skin of her breasts.

"That's where you're wrong."

He wanted so very much to make love to her, to bite her soft skin, to show her the meaning of pleasure. But he couldn't. Just around the corner, people passed by them.

His heart beat wildly in his chest in answer to hers. How incredibly arousing. D'Nar lost control as a rush of pent up desire and bloodlust flooded his system. He pushed his throbbing rod into her fist as if he were inside her core, warm and moist. His cock became so hard that he thought he would never come. Then she bared her neck to him. He couldn't believe she was giving herself to him of her own free will. Her body softened in his arms, pliant and willing.

"Yes," she whispered.

He wanted nothing more than to sink his incisors into the soft skin and let the tangy taste of her blood fill his mouth. The river of her life sounded in his ears. Her heartbeat became his. Pounding. Pounding.

"I need—I need to," he choked out.

He ground his hips into her fist. But he didn't drink. Instead, he exploded, convulsing in great shudders until he thought he would never stop coming. The world roared, or was that his roar of conquest? He wasn't sure.

Leaning his forehead against hers, he waited for the thunder to subside. He pulled out a hand cloth from his pocket and with exquisite care, he wiped off her hand before cleaning himself off.

But their tryst was far from over. Now that he was fulfilled, D'Nar wanted to pleasure her as well, hear her cries of pleasure. His fingers slipped underneath her tunic-dress. His hand reached up to caress the soft skin of her belly. She sucked in her stomach at his touch, her breathless cry reaching inside him, stirring his passions again. But this was her time and he wanted her to know the pleasure only a vampyr lover could give. His hand slid down the soft skin of her belly to tangle in the soft thatch of her pussy. Her hips jumped as his fingers weaved their way lower. She was warm and moist and so ready for him that he had but to slide his finger into her core for her to cry out in pleasure. He swallowed her cries with a kiss and teased her. She moaned softly as he flicked at her clit. Her entire body shivered. She sucked on his tongue as she drew in a strangled breath. D'Nar slid his finger down her slit and inside her core over and over again until she convulsed all over his hand. The image of T'Meric's tongue sliding across his feeding stiletto filled D'Nar's mind as he brought his finger to his lips. He lapped up the taste of her, unable to get enough.

She stared at him. "I can't believe this just happened."

"Vampyrs are a strong race, Ariel," he explained, stepping away at last. "We do what we do because we must. Yet we're no more passionate than you are. And no less."

She blushed, not quite able to meet his gaze. "As a

healer, I understand the physical necessity that drives each of us. I was as much at fault as you."

"There was no fault."

"Yes, there was. My mind understands your need for blood." She lifted her face to his. He read confusion and hurt and the remnants of desire in her gaze. "Yet my heart cannot understand your actions. Vampyrs treat humans with no respect, as those two young men demonstrated today.

I know you told *them* we're not things, yet *you* use us without thought because you *need* to survive. Just now, you used me."

"Shall we talk about survival?" he asked, not wanting to admit she was right. "Without vampyrs, humans couldn't survive either. Or can you defeat an I'man?"

"You know I can't. Nor can I change what is at the moment. But sooner than later, vampyrs must change. We take better care of our animals than you do your humans."

"In some cases, yes. As you witnessed today. But not all, Ariel. Not all." He stepped back from her, allowing her to leave. He was rather surprised when she didn't bolt. "May I escort you to your dwelling? The storm is almost upon us."

"I would be grateful."

He took her elbow, guiding her into the marketplace before letting go. He moved with swift determination, pleased to find she matched him stride for stride. They reached her home in short order. "Thank you, my Lord."

He nodded. "Ariel?"

"Yes?"

"Ponder this. The animals upon which you feed don't realize their ultimate purpose. You do. Would you wish to be without that knowledge?"

She caught his gaze, her own level and open. "No, Lord. I only wish to be free. Really free."

****

Ariel closed the door to her home and heaved a sigh of uncertain relief. Had she just planted a very dangerous seed? Or perhaps prodded one already growing inside him?

How would he react? Would he tighten the yoke of servitude or try to understand, perhaps bring about a measure of change?

Of all the strokes of fate, could she have devised this one? Or foreseen the consequences of how the day played out? Ariel touched her neck where his tongue had caressed her flesh, where his teeth had played with her skin. What was this bond that so tightly bound their species together? The bond of blood?

Ariel shivered. Her core heated in memory, her nipples tightened with her thoughts. The touch of his hand had sparked through her insides. She couldn't believe his boldness, making love to her in an alleyway. She didn't want to acknowledge her response. Thank goodness the storm had come upon them, otherwise the entire city might have witnessed something forbidden.

Shaking her head, she stalked to the shelves that held her medicines and added the herbs that had nearly cost her so much. She would not dwell on him or the memories he invoked. Her life would go on unchanged.

A knock on the door startled her. She looked down to see that she had pulverized the herbs she'd been crushing. Shaking hands pushed the bowl away. "I'm coming," she called.

She threw open the portal expecting an emergency, not a young messenger dressed in the black and red colors of the Viceroy's house. "Yes?" she questioned, a thousand thoughts running through her mind and yet not a single one coherent.

The young man handed her a missive. "My Lord awaits your answer."

She flipped open the note. An invitation. To dine with him. On the morrow. "Tell him," she began. A shiver ran through her once again. "Tell him," she tried again as the memory of his tongue against her skin threw her thoughts to the wind. "Tell him that I thank him for his offer. I'll be there."

Chapter Two

With the storm long past and their red sun a fiery ball in the night sky, D'Nar found himself at the compound of his old friend, M'Nem. Tonight was the coming of age ceremony for M'Nem's youngest son M'Net who had just reached the age of eighteen annums. Tonight, M'Net would become a vampyr.

For most vampyrs, the ceremony was a sacred rite, cause for great celebration. Yet D'Nar pondered the evening with mixed emotions. Tonight, M'Net would take his first taste of blood. He would also take his first woman. For vampyrs, the two acts could not be separated. Once the change was complete, M'Net could only survive on the blood of humans, leaving D'Nar to wonder if this was such a cause for joy.

They were so tied together, he thought. Vampyr, human. Human, vampyr. Although those like T'Meric would scorn their beginnings, vampyrs began their lives as humans. Leading to the great question: why do vampyrs change at the coming of age and humans do not?

Of course, he knew the intellectual answer. Because vampyrs were warriors, they were the protectors. They were charged with destroying creatures, such as the I'man, who threatened the welfare of all the people on the planet. They were also the hunters. Their planet was not a kind place to live; as such, the creatures living on it were tough and fierce. Humans might have domesticated certain animals, but they still needed meat to survive. Hunters provided that meat. They also died providing that meat.

D'Nar closed his eyes and shook off these dark thoughts. He resolved to set aside the burdens he carried and simply enjoy the night. He drank in the sounds of the guests assembled, the laughter, the ribald comments, the excitement in the air, and he smiled.

He opened his eyes to see a servant carrying a tray of goblets. He took one and found the dark red wine spiced to perfection with herbs and a hint of blood. Leave it to M'Nem to make sure his guests were well cared for.

"D'Nar."

Turning at the sound of his name, D'Nar smiled as his host approached. "Salutations, M'Nem," he said, bowing low with respect. "The storm was a good omen. May M'Net remember always."

M'Nem bowed in return. He looked around in satisfaction. "Yes, tonight will go well." M'Nem chuckled. "He is more than ready."

D'Nar nodded. All vampyrs, male and female, remembered their rite of passage. The night was engraved upon their souls. Nothing could ever compare with that first taste of blood and ecstasy.

"Damn near had to lock the poor boy up these last few days," his host continued with a chuckle.

D'Nar smiled. He remembered the edginess, the irritability, the loss of appetite. But most of all, he remembered the frustration at being constantly hard, but unable to find release. "The change is always difficult."

"Yes." M'Nem sighed, a shadow crossing his face. "You witnessed for M'Nir. He should have been at his brother's side as an honored family member, the one chosen to help M'Net through the change."

D'Nar reached out to squeeze the elder man's shoulder in sympathy. M'Nir had been found near the outskirts of the city, torn apart nearly beyond recognition. No one could understand what caused such destruction. M'Nir was a grown vampyr and a skilled hunter. D'Nar had been the first vampyr on the scene, and he'd never seen anything like it. And he never wanted to again.

"Make yourself comfortable," M'Nem insisted. "At M'Net's request, I've asked only a few to witness the ceremony."

D'Nar bowed again. "You do me great honor, old friend. As does your son. Think only of your blessings and partake in the joy of life."

M'Nem sighed, then smiled with determination. "You're right. As my wife has also been trying to tell me. At the sound of eight."

"At the sound of eight," D'Nar repeated.

Following his own advice, D'Nar immersed himself in his surroundings. Torchlight flickered against golden walls causing flaming shimmers that caught the eye. Strips of gauzy material—some creamy in color, some blood red—reflected the light, creating leaps of flames around the room. A thread of excitement ran through the banter of the guests. No, that wasn't right. More like tension. Everyone in attendance knew the outcome of the evening.

Strains of the k'ettes, the stringed instrument of their people, reached his ears. The musician plucked the strings with the finesse of a lover, coaxing a response as one would from a woman. The music would grow soon, in pace and intensity, in time with the experience.

D'Nar made his way through the crowd, stopping a few times to speak with nobles he held in esteem. Those who knew D'Nar knew that he did not show affection often. He was Viceroy to the city, and the scrabble for power left him little choice but to be reserved. But tonight, he chose to leave the burdens of his office behind. He kept walking, preferring the night air to the incense filled chambers. Once he reached the balcony, he gulped in the clean scents of the evening.

Time seemed to stop when he saw her. Ariel must have sensed him for she turned to stare directly at him. He couldn't fathom her being there on the balcony any more than he could fathom his reaction to her. Immediate, swift, pulsing with power. His gaze locked on hers. Her lips parted ever so slightly, begging for his touch. Her shoulders straightened, and she held her head high. But heat radiated from her gaze, telling him that, as proud as she might be, he could bring her to her knees with a simple look.

Torchlight framed her hair, creating a golden red halo around her head. Her hair sparkled as if touched by the stars. Her eyes reminded him of the sea, sometimes blue-green, sometimes all green, but tonight dark as jade and just as mysterious. His feet brought him to her without conscious knowledge. "Ariel."

"My Lord," she replied, bowing. Politely, properly, as a woman of rank should. Suddenly, D'Nar found he had no use for proper or polite. He wanted that moment again.

"What brings you here?"

"M'Nem. He requested the services of a healer, just in case."

Although infrequent, the smell of raw sex and blood could drive any of them mad. "I see." D'Nar wanted to reach out. Touch her neck. See if his scent still lingered upon her. "I didn't expect to see you here."

She smiled. "I fully expected to see you here."

Yes, she would have. "That doesn't mean I'm going to let you decline my invitation now."

She looked surprised. "I hadn't considered the possibility."

A thrill ran through his veins. Then he realized that power might have motivated her choice more so than the man. "Excellent. We have much to discuss."

This time she chuckled, although he wasn't sure of

the reason for her laughter. "Discuss? Do you always talk while you make love?"

He laughed, glad she understood. "That depends. We'll have to see, won't we?"

"Indeed we will."

D'Nar bowed and turned on his heel. He looked forward to verbally sparring with her almost as much as he looked forward to the nights they would share. "Fascinating creature," he muttered to himself.

****

The platform was prominently displayed in the center of the inner chamber for all those chosen to see. M'Net lay writhing in the center, strapped down for his own safety and for that of the concubine who would service him. The young man twisted and turned, bathed in his own sweat and the scented oil the concubine had used to stimulate his every cell.

For a young man, M'Net was well endowed. His erection tented the loose fabric of his loin cloth. The same seemed to be true for every male in the room, Ariel noted. M'Nem beamed with pride as his son lay on the threshold of manhood. He gasped, he twisted, but he never broke his bonds or gave in to the incredible fever in his blood. The ceremony was also a test. Violent vampyrs were destroyed without hesitation for they could turn on anyone in their blood lust. And their lust for lust.

Lamps were extinguished until only the dais remained lit. The concubine was young and well schooled. She was naked, her breasts full and ripe. Even from her vantage point, Ariel could see that her nipples had become tight pebbles. Her pubic hair had been removed, exposing labia that were dark, curved, smooth, and very, very wet. The room smelled of sex— raw, uninhibited sex.

The concubine removed the strings of the boy's loincloth with sensual grace. Her fingers trailed a fiery path along the boy's skin and Ariel stared in fascination. One could hardly remain unaffected, yet she knew only private frustration. As an innocent, she had never found completion in the sexual act. That is, until she'd met D'Nar.

Ariel bit her lip and wondered again at her temerity. Her gaze constantly returned to D'Nar. Although the blatant act upon the dais was incredibly stimulating, the heat between her legs exploded more at the sight of the virile vampyr.

D'Nar was handsome in a rugged, masculine way. His jet-black hair was tied back from an angular face. There was nothing soft about him. His thin nose ran straight to a strong chin, while his cheekbones accentuated the length of his face. But they were all forgotten as she looked at his eyes. Brown velvet. Eyes a woman could drown in.

The concubine ran her tongue down the boy's chest and he moaned. His erection jerked in reaction to the flowing strands of her hair as the girl slid lower and lower. Ariel reached out to steady herself against the doorframe she stood next to. Did she really have the courage to go through with her plan?

The temperature within the room grew steadily. Not one of the witnesses breathed normally. If she closed her eyes, Ariel was certain she would hear the thunder of the men's hearts beating in time to the lust upon the dais.

The young woman knew her work well. A lick here, a taste there. Her mouth danced everywhere but where M'Net wanted. In one swift motion, she straddled the young vampyr's chest, bringing him closer to her woman's scent.

As the changes began, his face was no longer that of a boy or that of a man, but somewhere in between. M'Net growled and Ariel watched as his face became more angular, sharper. All in the room knew his incisors grew in anticipation of his first taste of blood. A murmur of approval ran through the room.

The concubine settled her dripping core over his mouth. M'Net growled even louder as the rest of the change occurred. Ariel stood at the ready, for the blood fever was hard to control. But M'Net merely reached out to lap at the concubine's core, assuring she was ready for him.

The young woman slid back down the boy's chest until she straddled his erection. A single gong rang through the heavy air. At that signal, concubines glided into the room on silent feet to service the witnesses' pleasure.

Ariel walked with them. For better or worse, she had set for herself a course of action.

****

D'Nar couldn't understand the fire in his blood this night. He'd attended many of these ceremonies, yet never had his need for release seemed so strong. The concubine caring for M'Net was good, energetic, enthusiastic. And M'Net was behaving as a noble of his rank should, with dignity, in spite of the mindless need to mate.

As was custom, a concubine slid silently before him. She kneeled and parted the folds of his pants. Her touch. God, her touch was agony, ecstasy, fire, and blood, all pulsing between his legs.

She slipped his enormous cock free with ease. Her fingers worked magic with their gentle persuasion. She would milk him for all he was worth.

D'Nar opened his eyes to watch the concubine slide up and down on the boy's shaft. The woman on her knees before him took him in her mouth, moving with the same rhythm. Oh, the sweet heat. The incredible suction. He could have spent himself, even as he heard several cries of release in the background.

But tonight, D'Nar wanted more. He wanted star-lit hair and jade green eyes. He wanted Ariel.

M'Net neared his end. The concubine leaned over at the same time they released his arms. He gathered her to his chest and sank his incisors into her neck. She cried out with mindless pleasure as M'Net slammed his massive prick into her warmth. His cries joined hers in raw animal lust.

D'Nar put his hand on the woman's head. As he did, the veil fell away and he stared in shock at the color. He then saw a pair of swirling green eyes as they lifted to his.

The knowledge released something primitive inside him. He drove his throbbing member into her mouth. He was the hunter, she the hunted. When she lifted her wrist for him to drink, he threw her hand away. He needed no blood tonight. She was all the fire he needed to come. He stared into her eyes as his hips drew his erection out to the very tip then heaved inside, totally filling her mouth. He pumped and pumped, losing himself in the furnace her mouth created. He could feel his orgasm building, climbing, and reaching for more than just release. He wanted to explode. He wanted… "Arrhhh," he screamed as he spent himself inside her mouth.

****

Once the pulsing stopped, D'Nar lifted her off her knees, pulling her tight against his chest. His gaze tore through hers and Ariel read a thousand questions, all superseded by the only one that really mattered. "Do you think to hold minion over me now?" he asked her, his arm a steel band around her waist so she could not run away.

Ariel fought against his arm. The arm only grew tighter. "Never."

"They why? Why do this?"

"To repay my debt to you."

He didn't answer at first as his gaze searched her face for the truth. "Then allow me to repay mine."

Confused, Ariel wasn't sure what he meant. She didn't have to wait long to find out. His free hand nudged her gown apart, finding one of her breasts. A

21

streak of fire ran down to her core as his fingers pinched her nipple. "My Lord, please—"

Her protest died as his lips covered hers. She struggled again, but perhaps more against herself than him. She broke the kiss as her gown was lifted above her hip. "My Lord. D'Nar."

He stopped to stare down at her, a question in his gaze. "Is this your first time?"

"At a ceremony? Of course not."

"But you've never made love, have you?"

Embarrassment heated her cheeks. He lifted her chin and she read only concern on his face. "No, Lord."

A strange fire lit his gaze. Feral and proud. "I'm honored."

His lips grazed the skin of her neck and she knew how tempting her flesh was to him. Yet he did not try to drink. Instead, he trailed light kisses down her neck. This wasn't the time or place to make slow, sweet love to her and she knew that. But as his mouth made its way down her chest to find her nipple, she was certain he wanted her to experience only pleasure. He wanted to give to her, not take.

Exquisite sensations shivered through her as he tongued her nipple. The ceremony was all about sex and blood, but he was making it more than that. D'Nar cared about her.

As his mouth played and sucked on her breast, his hand lifted her gown higher and parted her legs. "You're more than ready," he whispered, against her chest. "I could bed you right here and be well within my rights," he added as he lifted back to look straight into her eyes. His gaze darkened with pleasure, his and hers. "You gave yourself to me willingly."

Ariel moaned. That was the chance she had taken. "Yes," she gasped as his fingers entered her weeping core.

She bucked against his hand as he found her nub. "Your first time and our first time together will not be in a sex-filled room with others watching."

One finger, two, he slid them in and out as his mouth captured her breast. So much heat, she thought. She couldn't breathe. A yearning, a craving centered between her legs.

She buried her face in his neck, licking the salty sweat from his skin. Her hands gripped his shoulders, her fingers digging into them to ground herself in a sea of sensation. She mewled in desperation, the need to feel more of him.

"Yes, sweet. Smell the lust in the room. Think of my shaft plunging into you. Harder. Deeper. That's it."

Short staccato moans flew from a voice she didn't recognize as hers. She pumped her hips against his fingers, coating them with her own hot juice. A fine tension built between her legs. She bucked and heaved, searching for the pinnacle of love. Just as she reached the edge, her gaze caught his. Then his mouth crushed hers, catching her screams of completion. She couldn't believe the incredible sensations of pleasure flowing through her.

Her knees collapsed, but he held her tight until she could support her own weight, then stayed close. Ariel let her head fall against his chest. "I had no idea," she murmured.

His hands lifted her head. "You're very beautiful. But as I stand here right now, I must tell you. You don't."

"There's more?"

He smiled down at her. "Much more. Will you still come to dinner tomorrow evening? We have much to, ahh, discuss."

She nodded and his smile changed. "Tell me."

At first, she didn't understand. "Tell me," he urged again.

Tell him that her body pulsed with passion? Tell him that she should have been well sated, but deep inside she knew only emptiness? "Tell me," he whispered, the words a lover's caress.

"I want you."

His expression never changed. But she could read pride and satisfaction simmering along with the hunger. The same hunger she felt. "Good," he breathed, his breath mingling with hers.

His lips were so close, his incisors brushed her skin. "Because I want you more."

Chapter Three

D'Nar paced across his private study. Sometimes he wished he were a merchant or a baker, not Viceroy. A half smile came to his lips as he imagined directing the placement of a loaf on baking sheet in the fire instead of directing the placement of soldiers along the walls of the city. What would he do if he didn't have mountains of correspondence to answer, disputes to settle, buildings to build, roads to fix, people to satisfy?

A knock on the door broke his thoughts. "Enter."

"You sent for me, Lord?"

He nodded. For a moment, he wondered what he would do without this man who had been with him for so long. "So many problems plague us, Toby."

"Sir?"

D'Nar looked at the man and then down at his right hand, knowing he could not survive without them both. "Do you hate me?"

"Hate you, D'Nar?" Toby asked, obviously surprised by the question. "Of course not."

"Why?" D'Nar wanted to know. Why could they work together so closely, at times sharing each other's thoughts, yet seem to exist so far apart.

Toby frowned, tilting his head to the side in an attempt to read D'Nar's expression. Only Toby could. "What troubles you, my Lord? The woman?"

D'Nar shook his head. He walked over to Toby and touched the man's forehead just above his temple, showing him graphic scenes of the devastation he'd just witnessed. "Another death. Even more horrible than the last. A young vampyr, fully capable of defending himself and schooled to do so. Torn to shreds."

D'Nar let his hand fall along with his heart. "I can't imagine who or what could do such a thing," Toby answered.

"You can't? Stir enough hearts and revolution comes easy," D'Nar told his friend, his tone bitter.

Toby's face turned grave. "We've existed for so long by believing we benefit each other."

"We've existed with one race dominating the other," D'Nar replied, giving voice to his fears.

Toby shook his head with an odd smile. "I'm human. Yet I'm as powerful to my people as you are to yours." The elder man walked over and poured out a measure of water into a cup. After he took a drink he said, "Is this cup half empty or half full? Are humans the lesser race, D'Nar? Or perhaps the stronger. Can you exist without us?"

"No, nor can your race exist without ours. You could not survive."

"Thus, you see the way of the world."

D'Nar was silent for a moment. "Have you ever wondered why there can be no blending of our races?"

Toby threw him a quizzical look. "Genetics I would assume."

"Yet we both start out as human."

"There are those who do not like to be reminded of that fact," his advisor sighed. "And yet, we share two suns. You could not survive without the red and we would perish without the yellow. You will never see the blending of those, Lord."

"No, I suppose not. And still I wonder. Must we always remain separate?"

"Somehow, I'm thinking that your thoughts rest elsewhere besides the death of this young vampyr," Toby replied with an enigmatic smile.

"Yes and no. We're so different yet so alike. We need each other so much, yet humans yearn to be free. I took an oath to protect and defend. And yet, I have no way to defend when I don't know what to defend against. These deaths are causing great unrest within the city. Vampyrs believe it is the work of a marauding band of humans."

"Balance is the key," Toby answered. "You know this. You keep no slaves, yet your household thrives. Surely all the people can see that yours is the way of the future."

D'Nar only wished they would. He tried very hard to lead by example. Those that wished to see walked with open eyes. Others did not. "The young don't care. The incident in the marketplace was a perfect example."

"Then it's time to shake some sense into both our peoples."

D'Nar felt the crushing weight of his responsibilities ease. "Thank you. I knew you would stand beside me in this. We'll need to carry our message carefully but firmly. Also, the other Viceroy's need to be warned. No one travels outside the city without a full escort."

"I'll make sure all is arranged."

D'Nar smiled. "I'm in your debt. Now, let us plan for a more pleasant time."

Toby chuckled. "Is she as beautiful as your face tells me she is?"

Pure excitement flowed through his veins at the thought of Ariel. "I shudder each time I think of those young pups with their hands on her."

"Then don't dwell on the past. Think of the future."

D'Nar paced, unable to hold back the thrill riding through his veins. "I want to, but I'm unsure of myself, Toby. I want to bind her to me, yet I don't."

"That's because you want her to desire you for yourself, not the bond."

"Once I mate with her, I'll never know the truth in her heart."

Toby walked over to him. The reassuring squeeze on his shoulder meant more to D'Nar than words ever could. "Trust in yourself and in her. Trust in the ways of our people and the design behind our world. Most of all, remember that change is as much a part of evolution as time."

D'Nar didn't realize Toby had left the room until he heard the door click shut. Toby's words rang true but they also frightened him. Change might be a part of life, but it could also be very dangerous. For all of them.

****

Ariel wished her heart would stop its wild dance inside her chest. She tried to concentrate on anything that might help calm her, such as the rocking motion of the horse that carried her to her destiny, the elusive scents in the dry night air that would cool their sweat-soaked bodies after—she dared not think about it. She could barely make out the stars because of the light of the red sun in the sky, the red sun that fed the man she was about to make love with. "You're very silent, my Lady."

"You do me great honor, Master Toby. But I'm not your Lady. I'm simply a healer."

She heard the man chuckle, drawing his horse closer to hers as they walked. "There's no such thing as 'simply a healer.' Nor do I think the word 'simple' applies to you any more than it did your mother."

She threw the man a look. "You knew my mother well?"

Toby shook his head. "No one knows another being well. We think we do, yet there are always pieces others will not see. But I was honored to call her friend and Lady. As I do you."

Ariel inclined her head in acceptance. "Then I thank you for the compliment."

Toby chuckled. "No wonder he's fascinated by you."

Twin spots heated her cheeks. "I find myself equally as fascinated."

"Yet he frightens you."

"D'Nar? Oh no, he's the one thing I'm not frightened of."

"Good," Toby replied. "For if you were, I would turn this escort around immediately."

"We'll never really be apart once the bond is complete," she confessed. "Yet I'll never really know if it's the bond that speaks or him."

Toby didn't answer right away. "Are you so sure of that?"

"You ask an unfair question. The bond is unbreakable."

"And that is so terrible?"

"I don't know," she sighed. "I'd always dreamed of..." Ariel let her voice trail off.

"What?" Toby asked. "Somehow I think that if you really listened to your heart, you would admit that this is what you dreamed of."

When Ariel first learned the ways of their society, the thought of a vampyr's touch excited her beyond imagination. As she grew older, the thought became forbidden. She was too necessary to her people to become bound for a lifetime. And yet here she was, on her way to do exactly what she had tried so hard not to do, as helpless as a newborn babe to stop the hand of fate. "I owe my people my life."

"Only *your* people?"

How arrogant she sounded. "Forgive me, Master Toby. You asked what frightened me. Change frightens me."

Toby reached over and patted her hand. "Your heart is pure, child, otherwise we wouldn't be traveling this night. Yes, change is frightening. Yet it comes whether we ask it to or not. So as a counselor, I must caution you. Don't step into this relationship with preconceived attitudes. Keep your mind and your heart open."

Ariel nodded. "I'll try, sir. I'll try."

****

Sendara stared at herself in the mirror, wondering at the passage of time. The image that stared back carried strength and wisdom, and with it the knowledge that she had no right to be jealous. She'd always loved D'Nar much more than he loved her.

Black flowing hair with only a strand or two of gray, she thought. No sags or wrinkles, except the tiny laugh lines about her eyes. She exercised daily and her breasts were still as firm and tight as when she'd first entered this house.

Still beautiful. But not to the eyes of the one she craved.

"My Lady. My Lady. My Lord D'Nar is here."

D'Nar? Here? Could the rumors be false somehow? Her heartbeat sped up. She swallowed, forcing her mind back to logic instead of false hope. She'd done nothing but listen to the rumors of a new concubine entering D'Nar's home.

"Then see to his welfare, child. Have wine and fruit brought to my sitting room. And tell him I'll join him in a moment."

Sendara turned to stare at her image once again. Not quite steady fingers reached for a brush as golden eyes darkened in memory. And confusion.

What was he doing here? The question followed her from her dressing room to the sitting room down the hall.

"My Lady," he bowed before hugging her and kissing both cheeks.

She smiled, but she'd never been able to hide anything from him. So she didn't try. "My Lord. Come. Sit."

They both reclined on soft cushions. Spiced wine for him and a tray of fruit for her rested on the table in front of them. "So the rumors are true."

"Rumors travel faster than the truth."

"Oh come now, D'Nar. Remember with whom you speak."

He inclined his head. "I didn't want to hurt you, Sen. That's part of the problem."

She tilted her head to read his expression. She found fondness and regret in his gaze. Not what she'd hoped for. "Your business is your business, D'Nar. You haven't shared my bed in a long time."

D'Nar sighed. "You're still very beautiful."

Just not beautiful enough anymore, she thought. "Thank you."

"Tresim came to me a few days ago," he continued. "She told me P'Lat made overtures."

"You change the subject well, my Lord."

"True."

"Do you release her then?"

"Easily done. She seemed genuinely happy when I told her. But you knew that already."

"Of course," his concubine laughed. "What else is left to an old woman?"

"You're not old," he retorted.

"D'Nar, my lovely lying vampyr. You have eyes in your head. Do you think I don't?"

"And you have the sharpest mind I've ever encountered."

She bowed. "My mind isn't what you came here to discuss, is it?"

"I don't want to bind her to me. At least not right away."

At first Sendara didn't answer. She couldn't. Then she gave him a bittersweet smile. "Oh my, D'Nar. You're truly smitten."

"Then you know what I ask. I must feed before I go to her."

A knife-like pain stabbed her heart. "You ask a great deal from an old love."

D'Nar dropped his gaze. "Can you forgive me?"

"Only if you allow me to be selfish. One last time?"

"I cannot," he whispered, hoping she would understand.

She nodded. "Forgive me for testing you."

Lifting her wrist, he grazed her soft skin with his incisors. Her heart began to pound in excitement. She knew he could smell the sweet river of life beneath her skin, hear the fluid rushing through her veins. She shivered as D'Nar bit down and warm, tangy blood flowed from her body to his. With her other hand, Sen caressed the full swell of one breast then the other, teasing the budding nipple. She moaned and tried not to think about how important it was to him not to break the promise in his heart—fulfillment with another woman.

As he sucked at Sendara's wrist, she rolled her nipple between her fingers. Fire filled her hot, wet, heat-slicked core. She released one tender breast to favor the other, not to have one become jealous. He slowed his pace to small pulls with each beat of her heart. But the damage was done and her passion soared. She writhed as her hand slipped down between her legs. Her clit throbbed with need.

Sen could still feel his fondness for her. There was no doubt she returned those feelings, perhaps even more, for she loved him in her own way. But what they'd shared was the thrill of youth. And that time had passed.

D'Nar bit down for one last taste of blood from Sendara's wrist. As he did, she slid first one, then two fingers inside her core. She was so hot for him, dripping her juices all over her fingers.

Her unique scent must have reached his nostrils, for he growled and reared back away from her. As he tore his mouth from her skin, Sendara bucked her hips against her hand. The call of the blood took over and Sendara screamed her release.

He'd been true to his word. He'd taken nothing but

her blood. Now he would be surfeit, sated enough so that when the time came, he would not drink from this new concubine and bind her to him. Sen thought her heart would break.

"Forgive me," he choked in remorse.

"Already done, my Lord." *I will cry my tears in solitude later.* "May you only know joy."

As he wrapped his arms around her to say goodbye, Sen closed her eyes and wished she could have one more night alone with him. She let go, knowing her time with him had come. And gone.

****

Bathed, perfumed, and barely adorned, Ariel's heart seemed ready to jump outside her chest. Breath refused to stay inside already overworked lungs. Limbs wouldn't stop trembling. Waiting for him to come to her was torture.

"You're very beautiful, my Lady."

Ariel whirled around. She hadn't heard the door open. Her mouth opened, yet words wouldn't come. He stood before her, his bronze chest gleaming in the lamplight. His muscles rippled as he walked to a small side table. "Thank...you."

He poured out two goblets of wine and brought one to her. "You intrigue me. Where is the brazen woman who dared so much last night?"

"Here," she answered, pointing at her chest. "Along with the woman who wonders if you will be a gentle or selfish lover."

He smiled. "Both." Taking a sip from his own goblet, he reached out and tipped hers toward her lips. The wine was sweet and spicy. "For me to be gentle, I must now be selfish."

He took her free hand and let her feel his problem. "I won't bind you to me this night."

Stunned, Ariel could not believe what she was hearing. "I don't understand."

"I want you to be certain of your choice when you

cleave to me."

"You...you're not going to love me?"

He laughed. "Oh no, sweet. You will not walk out of this room a virgin. That I promise. But I won't drink from you."

She'd never heard of such a thing. "I don't believe you."

"Perhaps what's lacking between our races is respect. I respect you too much, Ariel. I won't force you to become mine until you want to."

"But, I thought..." She let her voice die. She didn't know how to answer. "I thought you couldn't do one without the other."

"Many, I do not believe, would be able to do so. But I made certain I was surfeit before I came to you."

Stung, Ariel turned away. "So you go from one bed to another."

A strong hand on her shoulder pulled her around. "Does this feel like I have been in another's bed?" he growled, pressing his pulsing flesh against her stomach. "That's why I need your help. I must now be selfish or rape you."

His hips pumped the steely shaft hard against her. She felt his need, knew the urgency of which he spoke. Yet all the while, she wondered what he was trying to do. She lifted her gaze to watch as anger faded and fire took its place. Her hand wrapped around his distended flesh as he groaned.

Did he really think they could join together without the bond of blood? "One kiss," he begged.

Ariel lifted her face to his. He engulfed her mouth, his tongue thrusting deep inside. Her bones melted as they fenced. As much as she wanted to continue, she knew she had to break away or she wouldn't be able to do as he asked.

She also wanted to explore. She knew anatomy, of course. But not sensuality. She'd never had the chance to examine a man's body like this before. Her hands

34

roamed at their own will, following the contours of his muscled chest. He was both hard and soft, his skin sleek with moisture, as her fingers slipped over ridges of muscle and tendon. She trailed her fingertips lightly over his flesh until it rippled with desire. His nipples hardened into tight peaks and she played with them as he had hers. "Not now, woman," he moaned, pushing on her shoulders to go lower.

Ariel smiled. If she'd been more daring, she might have resisted, but she couldn't imagine the fever in his blood right now. So she slid his pants down slim hips, allowing him to step out of them. His musky scent, now familiar to her, created a heat in her pussy that nearly matched the fever in him. She marveled at the beauty of the man, so hard yet so soft. She also marveled at her power over him. One finger running along the underside of his shaft and he jerked with need. A lick here, a kiss there. His hands gripped her shoulders. "Ariel, please."

Yes, she liked that a lot. She licked the tip, then rolled her tongue over the head. Letting his rod slide slowly inside her mouth, she sucked and he growled in pleasure.

D'Nar soon took over the rhythm. He moved faster, but seemed aware that he could hurt her if he wasn't careful.

"Lick my balls," he urged, as she ran her hands up and down his erection.

"Like this?" she asked, sucking one softly into her mouth.

"Yes," he groaned.

Ariel pulled his shaft into her mouth and swallowed the length of him. When she let go, she asked, "Am I pleasing you, my Lord?"

He growled in answer.

He tried to thrust, but she released her hold on him, telling him without words that she held the power. Once he remained still, she took him into her mouth again. She sucked down to the base, then let go to swirl her tongue over the tip of his cock. She did this several times, feeling his cock twitch and grow beneath her lips. Realizing he was nearing his limit, Ariel licked the tip of his cock and then swallowed him whole one last time. All of a sudden his body straightened. He took over and thrust once, twice, and screamed in pleasure as his seed poured into her mouth.

Ariel swallowed until he was spent then released the root of his pleasure. He gazed down at her, his look still hungry, but now tempered with tenderness. "Trust me, my Lady. My debt to you will be repaid ten-fold."

Chapter Four

D'Nar couldn't believe he was still standing. His knees shook with the effort to remain upright. He wanted nothing more than to sink into the fluid feeling of aftermath. But his word meant more than his life, and he was going to make sure Ariel knew the same pleasure he'd just experienced.

Lifting her by the arms, D'Nar gazed down at her face. "You're so beautiful," he whispered. His heart skipped several beats as she looked up at him with such innocence and trust. Yet a woman still lurked in that gaze, for he could see her hunger for him. He wanted to go slow—not frighten her, not overpower her—yet he couldn't get enough of her scent, her taste, the feel of her body against his.

Bending down, D'Nar grazed her lips with his. He growled as he caught his own scent, his body responding to the primal instinct to mate. He wanted her, now, immediately, with a mind-blowing surge of lust. How in the name of their two suns could he be gentle as he'd promised?

He slid his hands to the sides of her face and thrust his tongue deep into her mouth. She hesitated at first, then touched his tongue with hers. Their tongues fenced for a few moments before he released her to nip and play with her lips. She learned quickly and soon they were sparring passionately. D'Nar thought his heart would pound right out of his chest.

Without thought, he slid his arms around her lush femininity. So soft, so pliable, while he was so hard, so ready for her. But this time was about her. He would be her first lover. She deserved all the respect he could give her and more.

What the devil?

D'Nar broke away from her at the pounding on his chamber door. "My Lord. My Lord."

Toby? Daring to interrupt? D'Nar snarled, feeling the feral change inside take place. His features became hard, angular, almost animal-like. The need to kill coursed through his veins and he knew he could no more stem the tide of this change than he could stop his need for blood. He turned away before Ariel could see his face. He didn't want her to see his killing face. "You dare to interrupt me?" he cried, throwing the portal open, oblivious to his nudity.

Toby only stared, his thoughts hard for D'Nar to read. But even in his agitated state, D'Nar admired the man's calm. "Life or death, nothing else would bring you to my doors at such a moment."

"Death, my Lord."

"How many?" he choked out as realization hit him.

"Two, possibly three. The bodies were just discovered and one hangs on to life. I've been told not to hope."

D'Nar wanted to rail, scream. His fingers clenched at his sides. His body shook with need, but his mind was already clear from the horror of Toby's tale. "I'll need a moment. Get two horses ready."

"Three."

He whirled. Then he realized his error. His face was still filled with the forceful need to kill. Yet Ariel didn't flinch. Her eyes widened and she stared back at him with what he read as curiosity and pity. "No."

She gave him a half smile as if she expected his answer. "I'm a healer, my Lord."

"They are already dead."

"Possibly three, or didn't I hear correctly? If one is alive, can you save him, my Lord? You, Master Toby?"

Damn her logic. "You know I cannot. Nor can he."

"I'll be but a moment."

D'Nar turned to Toby. "Three horses." The man bowed and hurried away.

D'Nar shut the portal and turned to her, his face now back to normal. "We're far from finished here, Lady."

Her gaze held sympathy and hunger, concern and determination. "Right now, we have other problems to attend."

"Rest assured, I would rather have a choice."

"So would I."

He reached out to pull her to his chest. His reaction to her was swift and hard to deny. "And when the time comes?"

"I'm your captive."

His kiss left no doubt as to his intentions. "You didn't say willing."

"I thought that was obvious."

She pushed at his shoulders until he broke his hold. "Alas, you're right. We must go." He strode to the door ready to call for heavy clothing. When he opened it, he found the items waiting for them.

He handed Ariel's to her and said, "Meet me at the stables when you're ready. But be quick."

"I will. And D'Nar?"

"Yes?"

"We must stop this senseless killing."

"I know. We can but try."

She nodded and he turned to dress, starting a journey he had no wish to make.

****

The ride wasn't long, and Ariel came to appreciate the chilly wind as she grew warm from the unaccustomed exercise. Their horses kept to a gallop, racing against the wind. The desert floor glowed with fire in the light of the red moon. Six vampyrs were already waiting for them, standing guard over the bodies. Ariel jumped from her horse as she reached them.

Blood stained the desert floor crimson. Two bodies lay unmoving beneath battle cloaks. But one young vampyr still lived, though as they'd been told, just barely. The gaping wound in his neck seemed to have sealed itself, but he'd lost a great deal of blood. She took a flask and touched a drop to his lips. His mouth parted. Lifting her patient, Ariel found that he was quite young. Her heart broke at the thought of one being cut down so early in his life.

She put the flask to his lips, allowing his incisors to grow so he could drink. At this point, she wasn't sure if the infusion of new life into his body would help or not.

Once he was finished, Ariel set about stitching what she could. "I've done what I can," she finally announced.

D'Nar came to her side. "You've done well, all things considered."

She listened as he started barking orders, imploring the guard to be slow and gentle as they took the boy back. Then he told Toby to take the other bodies to the city and make arrangements for their funerals.

Toby looked askance at both of them. "You're not coming?"

"In a moment," D'Nar replied. "Whoever did this won't return tonight."

Ariel nodded. "I agree."

"I'd like to inspect the area. Perhaps find a clue as to what might have caused such loss," D'Nar explained. "See if I can put a picture to what happened."

"Very well, but take care," Toby replied. "I don't trust anyone outside the city gates anymore."

Once they all rode out of sight, D'Nar turned to her. "Come with me."

He led her through an opening between two rocks to a small hidden spring. The area around the spring was rich with plants. "I fear that this is some sort of place the young come to. Perhaps to be out from under the eyes of their families. I smell the root of the Tarba bush."

Ariel closed her eyes. Yes, she did too. Tarba was a powerful drug to the vampyr and forbidden unless for medicinal purposes.

She also sensed something else. Something strange that she'd never felt before. "My Lord, do you sense something, I don't know, other than the Tarba?"

He shook his head. "No. What is it you feel?"

"I'm not sure. Come," she replied, moving toward a thicket of high grass at the edge of the spring.

Ariel let her mind go free. She ran her hand over the grass, walking through the stalks over and over again. She walked for several moments seeking the area with the strongest pull. "Here, my Lord. Come here."

She watched D'Nar walk toward her. "What do you sense?"

"I'm not sure. Something of this world, but not a force, a feeling. I'm not sure how to describe it. Don't you feel it?"

He shook his head. "I'm vampyr. I have one purpose. To protect our races from any being that threatens. I would know if danger were present."

Ariel agreed, for his face would have responded to a danger the mind might dismiss, but nature never would. "And yet, someone or something has caused this carnage."

"I know. But what?" he asked.

Ariel answered, unsure of what the answer would be. "I can sense things. This sense has been handed down through generations of healers." She stopped in a thicket of thigh-high grasses. "Here. Yes. Here it is again. Sort of like a thrumming inside my hand. Some kind of energy."

Ariel ran her hand over the plants again. As she

did so, she reached out to take D'Nar's hand, bringing him closer that he might also experience the feeling.

At the touch of their skin, the world exploded. Images flashed through her mind in a collage she struggled to follow. She saw marvelous buildings, tall and not made of brick but of some other kind of smooth stone; towering trees with huge green leaves made her gasp with their beauty. She knew mountains, but the ones before her eyes made her wonder if they could touch the sky.

She felt no pain, but found herself on her knees, collapsing under the onslaught of a power she could never have imagined. Images she had no way to describe—strange things flying through the air— moved too fast through her mind for her to really understand them, but they left an impression of an old age. The remnants of the power tingled through her nerves like the touch of ice against the skin, biting at first but numbing thereafter.

When she could, Ariel opened her eyes. She saw that D'Nar was on his knees also. As he looked up at her, she knew he seen the same pictures she had. "D'Nar?"

He looked bewildered. "Are you all right?"

"I don't know."

"What just happened?"

"Again, Lord. I don't know." Ariel struggled to rise and found herself on unsteady legs. She watched D'Nar rise and weave as well.

"Come," he ordered, leading her to the spring where they both drank from the pool. The water was sweet and soothed her parched throat.

He took his coat off and spread the garment on the bank so they could rest against a large boulder. He reached for her hand and when they touched, her skin tingled. What was this incredible power flowing between them? "Do you feel that?" she asked.

They sat for a long time before the intensity

subsided. But the underlying feeling never left her. Her hands shook and she clasped them together in the hopes that it would stop.

"Yes, though I'm at a loss to explain how this has happened or what it all means," he answered, covering her hands with one of his.

"I'm not sure either, but I believe there's a purpose to this night and we'll know soon enough."

"Close your eyes," D'Nar suggested. "Can you see the images?"

"So many pictures, as if someone gave me their thoughts and memories combined," she told him. "But one I remember vividly. It was of Mount C'eres."

He paused for a moment. "C'eres? That's very interesting." He pulled her against him and she reveled in the warmth of his body. Strange after all they'd just witnessed, that she would feel so safe. Her logical mind cried out for caution, told her to flee to the safety of satin chambers and high stone walls. But her heart told her otherwise. They belonged here, together, at this place in this moment.

"Do you feel it as well? The rightness of being here?"

"Yes. We're meant to be here, now, in this place, together."

A strange lethargy invaded her body. Although she never closed her eyes, Ariel slipped into some kind of dream state. The pictures she couldn't comprehend before filled her vision, slowing so that each became clearer. In her mind, Ariel was going back in time.

She had no idea how long the process took, but once she reached her destination, Ariel found herself on a world that was hers, yet not. Instead of two suns, only one orb graced the sky. Bright yellow, impossible to look at as it fed its fire directly to her. Her first thought was that she would burn to a cinder. Then she realized that the orb merely enveloped her in great warmth, not in fear.

The sky was a color she had never seen before, the kind of blue that hurt the eyes, and the clouds seemed to have been painted by a child, hit or miss with a randomness that made all the sense in the world.

Wrenching her gaze from the beauty of the sight, Ariel noted the same mountains in the distance that she'd seen only moments ago. But before her spread fields of life, some golden, some green, so immense she wondered how many people they could feed. An incredible contrast to the barren desert of her world.

Dwellings dotted the horizon, strangely built structures, very tall, with thatch upon their roofs. Certainly not the brick and mortar homes of her people. And not necessary, for there was no constant wind to kick up dust and stones that would bite the unwary traveler. No lightening storms to send shards of death down onto the ground, burning any fuel nearby.

Ariel gasped in wonder as beings approached. Human, but the height these people's dwellings had to be at least seven decans or so, maybe taller. They moved with graceful ease for ones so tall. They were as fair in their looks as they were in their movements, silver-haired and bronzed by the sun, yet not nearly as dark as D'Nar or herself.

As they neared, Ariel caught her breath in rapture. She should be frightened by this dream. But how could she, when she heard the laughter? True laughter. As joyous a sound as she'd ever heard. Then she realized that little ones, if she could call them that, followed. They scampered and danced behind the older ones in complete abandon. How incredible to feel so safe, so secure.

Ariel reveled in the sound, the smell of the fresh air, the warmth of the bright sun and watched as the family gathered water from the pool before her. They were just about to turn away when the earth began to tremble, then shake violently.

Frightened for these happy people, Ariel tried to cry out. She tried to focus, shift the vision, but the vision wouldn't let her go. That was when she realized that she couldn't change what had already happened. Pain knifed her chest at the thought of all this beauty being destroyed.

She started, coming out of her dream state to find D'Nar holding her tight. Tears gathered in her eyes. She wanted to go back, warn them, and tell them to stop the terrible fate that awaited them. She buried her face in his chest, her heart rending with pain. "Hush, my sweet. You must let go."

"So beautiful, D'Nar."

"I know. I shared your vision," he replied.

"You did? I thought I was alone." He nodded and she wondered why she hadn't sensed his presence. With a shrug, Ariel realized it didn't really matter. "The legends don't speak of the time before the two suns—The Before Time. Could that have been what we saw?"

"I'm not sure, but I believe you're right," he answered, his tone thoughtful.

"Then we were brought here for a purpose," she announced with conviction.

D'Nar pulled her tighter against him. "Why do you say that?"

"Because it's up to us to repair the damage that's been done."

"I'd love to do so," he replied with a small laugh. "But I fear I have no idea how to make two suns one, no way to make the heavens release water back to an arid planet. So, what is this miracle you speak of?

"Life."

Chapter Five

At first, D'Nar wasn't exactly sure what she meant. Her meaning became crystal clear, however, when she took his hand and brought it to her breast. As much as he wanted her, he wouldn't take her under duress. "No, Ariel. Not this way. You're reacting to the carnage you saw here."

"No, I'm not," she insisted.

Her hand reached for him and he caught it just in time. He had only so much willpower. "Ariel, I can't answer to what has happened between us. I need to give everything a great deal of thought. But I won't allow you to react to something you don't understand."

She shook her head. "*You* don't understand. I understand perfectly."

A sigh escaped her lips as if he were a two-year-old needing patience and understanding. "Woman," he growled. "You're beginning to try me. Love needs to be made in love, not in death or in some sort of vision. Come back to me, to D'Nar, and tell me that it's the flesh and blood being you want, not the vision or the response."

She rose and walked over to the pool. With anger still vibrating inside, yet feeling a helplessness he'd never known before, D'Nar followed. She drank and bathed her face then motioned for him to do the same. The water refreshed him.

"There's a reason the young come here D'Nar, and it is not just the Tarba root. This water," she hesitated a moment. "I can't answer why, but you just felt its power. But there's more here."

Ariel took him by the hand to the tall grasses

where he'd felt the explosion of power. The air sizzled between them, each touch a spark turning into flame. Very slowly, she unbuttoned her coat and let it slide to the ground. She had knotted her hair behind her head and now released the glowing strands, to the detriment of D'Nar's ability to breathe.

His heart accelerated to the point of breaking. New visions filled his mind, ones of their bodies entwined in ecstasy. But they were only visions. Before him stood breathtaking beauty. On his land, in his world. His limbs trembled with need.

The light of the red sun didn't do her justice. Her skin gleamed a rich copper color that would never darken to the color of his, yet he found it much more fascinating. He wanted to reach out, take her, and crush her to him. But her game was irresistible, especially as she opened her blouse and bared her breasts before him.

"Feel the wind caress my skin," she murmured, her words sending heated shards dancing along his spine. She bent down and pulled off her boots then unbuttoned her trousers. She had no idea that her movements were more enticing than those of a courtesan. "There's an ancient blessing here, one that's asking us to make love. Now. Upon this grass."

Who was he to deny her? He was a simple, hapless male feasting on the beauty shining before him. "Once I touch you, there'll be no going back," he choked out, barely able to control himself, wanting to push into her body right then and there.

"I know."

All coherent thought ceased except the need not to hurt her. His fingers shook as they caressed her face, his erection screamed with need as it grew heavy, full with seed. His lips touched hers and he drank as a bee to a flower, sucking the sweetest of nectars while his hand found her breast, also heavy and full.

He played with her nipple, bringing it to a

hardened peak as she moaned into his mouth. He released her to rip his tunic off, throwing it aside. Her hands, once released from his neck, spread over his chest, searching his body and causing his knees to buckle. But he straightened them, for he was determined to taste her before they were done.

D'Nar lowered his mouth and suckled at her breasts, but only for a moment. Time was of the essence, for he no longer had control of his body. Kneeling down, he nipped at her belly then moved to the feminine crease between her legs. He wanted the taste of her on his tongue and found her already moist with need.

"D'Nar," she cried out.

"Not yet, my sweet." He smiled as she collapsed, unable to take her own weight. He settled her back onto the grass and parted his pants, pushing them down to his knees. "See me now, Ariel. A helpless male filled with desire only for you."

Her legs parted at his words, the invitation he sought. She shifted beneath him, seeking that which she did not know how to fulfill. But he needed to make this night easy on her, and settled his weight softly over her first.

Spreading light kisses across her face, D'Nar shifted to allow his fingers to enter her core. Her moist heat bathed his skin, surrounding him in succulent fire. First one, then two fingers. He wanted her to yearn for the next step, be so ready to orgasm that his entry wouldn't be noticed. But he also had to stretch her tight channel or he would hurt her badly. As he thrust his fingers in and out, she cried out.

"I need you," she begged, thrusting and thrashing beneath him.

****

Could there ever be such sweet torture, she wondered. A heat such as she had never known centered in her core. She wanted him inside her, filling her, the joining of their two bodies.

Ariel tried to push onto him when he finally gave in to her silent demands. He rolled her on her back and spread her legs with his. His cock waited just at the entrance to her core, but he wouldn't slip inside. Ariel wanted to cry out, beg him to end this exquisite torture.

At first, she felt no real difference as he slowly penetrated her virgin flesh, then the stretching began. Piece by exquisite piece, he pushed his engorged erection into her core. Then he stopped. "I must hurt you now, my sweet. Forgive me."

One sharp thrust and he tore past the barrier of her innocence. She bit her lip at the pain, but marveled at his control. He'd stopped moving, giving her time to adjust to his size and weight. She now had exactly what she'd wanted—they were joined and could never be parted.

Ariel let one of her arms fall into the grass. When he began to move, she clutched the blades in her hand. As she did, flashes of fire filled her mind. On one level, her body knew the soreness of entry. On another, she knew the wonder of sex, but more than that, the completion of male and female. Now, she knew even more. They'd touched in a way that seemed to bring the world together.

She reveled in her womanhood. Soon the soreness dissipated and intense pleasure took its place. He spread her hips even further, using his body to tease and torture her. Then, it seemed, he could hold back no longer.

D'Nar became who he was, a vampyr. His teeth grazed the skin of her neck, ready to bite. He growled, uttering pleas for fulfillment and pushing himself into her until he could go no further.

Her own orgasm built. He pulled his hard erection all the way out then rammed into her weeping heat time and again. She wanted more. She was greedy.

She kept seeking and rising, reaching for something she wasn't sure she could attain. Then she felt the pinch of his teeth sinking into her neck. The pull of his lips beat in time with the thrust of his hips, forcing her to rise with him even further.

As he pulled back, Ariel opened her eyes and sank into the depths of his gaze. The bond was based on the physical, a sharing of blood, but this sharing went far deeper. They would always be a part of each other, more than two bodies joined in ecstasy, more than two bodies becoming one.

Suddenly, she felt lifted out of herself and the world exploded. D'Nar cried out in ecstasy, releasing his seed deep into her womb. Ariel reached the plateau a moment later. His hips kept moving in time with hers as she screamed with him. Her body shook in rapture, her heart beat madly in time with his. Pleasure coursed through her veins as his tongue lapped at the blood dripping down her neck.

She came down to earth slowly. Her heart still pounded and her limbs still coursed with tiny aftershocks of pleasure. When she could finally catch her breath, he asked, "Did I hurt you?"

She felt opened and exposed, sore but not hurt. "No. Although I'm not certain how I'll be able to walk again."

He seemed loath to break their bodies apart, but did after spreading tiny kisses all over her face. He rolled to his side and leaned over, smiling down at her. His next kiss made her think of a fine wine, sweet at first then sharp and tangy going down, leaving the connoisseur with the desire for another sip. "I couldn't help myself. I'm sorry. I wanted satin and spice for you this night."

What she got was much better. "I'm not complaining."

"I know. Still—"

"You worry without cause, D'Nar. And I'm still

open to satin and spice should you wish to continue." Then her thoughts turned to the reason they were there. A chill shivered up and down her spine. "But I must see to my patient first."

He nodded and rose, pulling her with him. He helped her dress, smiling again as her fingers refused to be nimble. They walked at first, while Ariel tried to ease some of the stiffness in her legs, and D'Nar tried to mark the ground where the attacks had taken place. Then they mounted their horses for the ride home. "I'm afraid I've overdone everything tonight. I'm no more used to riding a horse than I am to..." She let her voice trail off because she could not find the words to describe the wonder of what she felt.

"Riding a man?" he quipped. They both laughed as only lovers can.

"You won't let the events of the night color our time together, will you?" He sounded so uncertain.

She tried to reassure him. "Never, D'Nar. Not ever."

He reached out to take her hand and bring it to his lips. "What we shared can never be described as anything but beautiful. You know that, don't you?"

Ariel nodded, knowing what they'd shared was beyond description. "What we shared transcended more than we may ever know, my Lord."

****

Weariness tried to steal D'Nar's fortitude. He sat listening to the leaders of his city bicker among themselves without purpose and wondered why he bothered. Not one of them wanted to address the scope of the problem, only how fear and mayhem would affect their tiny worlds.

"Enough!" D'Nar thought of the young vampyr fighting for his life and his stomach soured. "Have you all heard nothing that I've said?"

The head of every major family filled his dining hall. Many were annoyed at being roused in the middle of the night, but D'Nar wanted them to understand the urgency of the situation. "My Lord," his friend M'Nem spoke. "We agree there's a great danger lurking that must be taken care of. And we agree that our young men are not behaving as proper nobles should. We all know a deep sadness for the families of the slain young men and are willing to do what is necessary to keep them from straying away from their true paths. But what you describe, well, I fear I just don't understand."

D'Nar motioned for Toby to bring T'Meric into the room. When the young vampyr swaggered in, D'Nar knew he must convince these men that there was more than just wayward behavior being discussed this night. "T'Meric."

The young man barely bowed. "My Lord."

T'Meran, his father, spoke next. "He has been suitably punished, Lord. You can rest assured of that."

D'Nar shook his head. "This meeting isn't about punishment." He wanted to say more, but telling these men about the sickness in their society wouldn't work. They needed the young to demonstrate. "But it is about our laws, our society, and our beliefs."

"All because I decided to feed in public?" T'Meric sneered.

T'Meran opened his mouth to reprimand his son, but D'Nar held up his hand. "No. Because you believe you have the right to do so."

"And I say again, Lord. Humans are food. What difference whether we drink in public or behind closed doors?"

A small murmur of assent ran through the crowd, sending a chill down his spine. So, the sickness had already spread more than he cared to know. And yet, that was the purpose of this meeting. To see how far the cancer reached. "We're not animals," B'Shat cried. "And neither are humans. We're civilized beings with laws created to keep us that way. Have you forgotten who you are?"

T'Meric held up his hand to silence the reaction of the group. Arrogant young pup, D'Nar thought again. He holds no fear. He'll think differently when he faces his first test of courage. "We're vampyrs. We're the superior race. I say it's you who have forgotten who you are."

Again a murmur of agreement ran through the crowd and sickened his heart. "Silence!" D'Nar roared, anger threatening to overtake him. He drew in several deep breaths before trying to continue. "And I say," he challenged, "that you have all forgotten the true way of our world. There's a balance that must be maintained. Arrogance will not fill you with the fluid of life, but it will destroy the source if you let it. Go ahead," he told the young vampyr. "Be superior. Challenge the humans. And when they rise up in anger, forcing our race to defend itself, who among us lies dead? The very beings we depend upon for survival." He swept his hand across the room. "Is this what you want?"

Silence greeted him, for which he was grateful. At least they were thinking. "Now you see why we need the laws we have created."

"And my friends?" T'Meric cried. "The ones we've lost? Every vampyr in the city wonders in secret as I wonder now. Who else could have done this? The humans, whether or not you want to believe the truth, are fighting back."

"T'Meric. All of you," D'Nar countered. "Do you really believe that a human, even a group of humans, could wreak the destruction we've witnessed? Against a group of young vampyrs? Even drugged as they were this night, instinct would have caused them to destroy those that attacked. We train from birth to defend ourselves. I don't believe this terrible devastation was caused by humans. Otherwise we would have seen a great deal more carnage—human carnage."

"If not them, then who, D'Nar?" one of the nobles asked.

"I can't answer that now. There's no evidence, no sign of what happened. At least, nothing that makes any sense to us at the moment. But luck seems to be in our favor and that of the young vampyr who has survived. If he lives, he may be able to tell us what happened. Until then, I'm asking all of you to comply with my orders. No one travels unless absolutely necessary and then with no less than a company of armed vampyrs. Within the city, we set a curfew at the sound of twelve. I didn't have to ask you all to come here tonight to make these declarations. However, I ask you now. Do you agree?"

A chorus of agreement greeted him. "T'Meric."

"Yes, Lord?"

"Since you seem to be a spokesperson for the young, I charge you with this responsibility. See that no one sneaks out of the city after curfew."

T'Meric didn't seem too sure he wanted this task but in the end knew he had no choice but to accept. "Agreed."

"I don't want one more drop of blood on my hands."

Chapter Six

Ariel knew she had only a few more steps in her before she collapsed. She'd returned to D'Nar's home rather than her own, feeling a bit at odds with herself. The sun would be rising shortly, bringing an end to a terrible yet incredible night—one filled with life and with death.

The young vampyr had held on. Every moment he did moved him further away from death's door. Now his life's thread hung on time and fate, she could do no more.

Yet her own life soared inside her. Making love with D'Nar filled her heart.

As she entered the chamber, D'Nar turned to look at her. His smile of greeting changed to an expression of alarm. "Ariel," he gasped.

"I'm just weary, my Lord."

He helped her off with her coat then lifted her into his arms. "No, you're completely exhausted. And I'm as much to blame as anyone."

"Blame? I say again, you don't hear me complaining, do you?" She grinned at him as he set her on her feet in front of his bed.

"No, my Lady. Nor do I believe that I would ever hear you complain. Of course, that would be my job, now wouldn't it? To keep you from complaining?" he quipped, while removing her clothes. When he was finished, he wrapped her in a gown made of a very light silken material.

"Hmmm. You've given me a true dilemma, Lord. How will you take my silence from now on?"

He lifted her once again and set her down on the

soft cushions of the bed. Then he sat next to her so he could look at her. "That you are silent because of this." With that, he bent down and covered her mouth with his.

Once he released her, Ariel smiled. "I thought as much."

He rose and she settled herself under the covers. The next thing she knew, the bed shifted and he climbed in beside her. She'd never slept beside a man before. "No more talk. You must rest." Safe and sound in his arms, how could she not?

****

Ariel awoke surrounded by a furnace of heat. At first she couldn't understand the weight pinning her down, then she realized D'Nar's arm held her tight against his body.

What wonder was this? That she could feel so secure in someone's arms. She thought about the events of the night before. He seemed to truly care about her without the full bond of blood between them. A sip, a taste. The bond wouldn't connect them until he truly fed off her life blood, when he would take enough to sate his hunger. She couldn't think of anyone else who would consider such a thing. Most vampyrs would drink first and think later. Yet he went out of his way to prove that he cared, about how she felt, about how he felt.

A light breath tickled the back of her neck. "Did I awaken you, my Lord?" she asked.

"I wish to be neither lord nor master in my own bedroom, Ariel. Can't you call me by my given name?"

"Old habits. I beg your pardon, D'Nar."

She felt his body shake with laughter. "That's better. For a moment, I had visions of stately ceremonies and Viceroy duties in my own bedroom."

She laughed with him. "I'm not so sure I would appreciate you being so stiff."

He threw his head back and roared. "My sweet,

you will always appreciate my being stiff."

She could feel the heat rise in her cheeks. This by-play between them was new to her as well. "I—"

He kissed the top of her head. "Come. You must never be embarrassed by pillow talk. What goes on between a man and woman is theirs and theirs alone."

Of course, what was between them at that very moment was a very hard erection, which gave her a true taste of the power she had over him. And would give another taste of the pleasure that only he could give her.

A moment later, she was lifted out of the bed. Damn if the man didn't read minds as well, for the next thing she knew, she'd been disrobed and carried into a private bath chamber. As she sank into the heated water, she moaned in delight. All of her muscles were stiff as boards. "Oh, D'Nar. This is heavenly."

"I know, my sweet."

"I'm not used to riding."

"Nor being ridden." He said the words as if she belonged to him.

A bit affronted by his attitude she asked, "Am I then a mare to be taken at will by a randy stallion?"

"Would that be so bad?" he whispered, sliding his body beneath hers as she floated on her back against his chest.

She seemed ready to resist and his arm tightened around her waist so she couldn't move. "Easy, Ariel. I'm only teasing. Or had you forgotten my concern at the way our society exists?"

Society indeed, she thought. "I care not for society. This is between you and me."

"And didn't I prove my loyalty and honor to you last night?"

"You did."

The arm that held her slid up until his hand covered her breast. "Do you believe that I can do such a thing twice?"

"That would be a feat indeed."

D'nar shifted his body until he was resting against the wall of the bath. Then he used both hands, running them up and down her limbs. Between the heat of the water and the heat of his erection against her back, Ariel thought she would melt.

His hand rose to her breasts and sparks flew through her limbs. What a strange sensation to know lightening inside and out. For each time their bodies touched, he would pump his hips against her back in search of fulfillment.

Of course that couldn't compare to the heat he created once his fingers started to play with her nipples. But this arrangement of their bodies was way too impersonal for her likes.

She flipped over quickly and pushed on his shoulders, seeking his mouth. When she did that, however, he lost his hold on the side of the bath and his head sank under the water.

He came up sputtering and laughing and lifted her in his arms high above his head. He let her slide down in slow motion, stopping to suckle on the very nubs he'd held before. But they both wanted more. His kiss seared her soul, his tongue sought hers and they mated, following a dance lovers had performed for hundreds and hundreds of years.

Without letting go of her, D'Nar turned and walked over to the edge of the bath. He set her down on the tiles and Ariel gasped at the cold touch of the stone even as she reveled in the heat of the mouth that traveled her body.

She lay fully exposed to him and he took full advantage. His tongue grazed the soft skin of her belly then swirled around the soft mound of hair between her legs. He made sure she was more than ready for his entry by tasting her core and then sucking at her nub.

There was that intense pressure again. And the need. And the loss of reason except for the feeling between her legs. Only this time Ariel wanted more. She wanted sex between them without pain, with only pleasure. She got more than she bargained for.

He gripped her hips and slid them to the edge of the bath. Funny, but the height was perfect and he readied himself for entry without moving more than her body forward. So positioned, he placed the head of his shaft to enter, but went no further.

"Please, D'Nar," she begged.

"Yes. That's it. Tell me what you want."

"All of you. Inside of me. Oh, D'Nar, don't tease. Not now."

He pushed the head in. "Tell me, woman. What is it you want?"

"You. Only you. I want you to fuck me."

That seemed to push him over the edge. He shared her desire and buried himself inside her in one searing movement. Ariel clenched her muscles around him, trying to draw his seed into her body.

He withdrew only to thrust again. His hands held her hips so she felt the blow of each of his thrusts. She opened her eyes to see his body sway side to side as if the sensations he felt were too much to bear.

Of course, that sent her emotions spinning wildly. Once, twice, he bent over to suckle at each breast, but this was not easy loving. They both wanted the power and force centered at the joining of their two bodies.

The volcano that built was more than she could have imagined. He began to growl, thrusting in and out with a force even she wondered about. Her own cries matched his and they both climbed higher and higher, seeking fulfillment.

When they both reached the summit, her world exploded. She convulsed around his shaft, sending him toppling over the edge with her. The room echoed with their screams and they shook with the waves of pleasure that washed over them.

When she finally came back to reality, he had his arms braced on the tiles by her sides. D'Nar's seed filled her womb and his mouth was buried in her neck. Yet he never drank—a true testament to his honor.

His arms shook as he lifted back away from her. "Have I fulfilled my promise to you?"

"In more ways than one."

****

D'Nar was certain he would never catch his breath. His limbs trembled from the force of their lovemaking, yet he refused to leave the molten refuge of her body. In fact, his own body surprised him when he felt no diminishing of his erection. What was this incredible magic between them that he could love her and not drink from her, yet remain so entranced as to want more right after release?

Of course, that was when he became aware of the weakness in his legs. He swayed, nearly staggering as he tried to lift her up. He had to break the connection and pulled out of her with regret.

"My Lord. D'Nar," she cried in alarm.

"I'm all right."

She led him by the hand away from the pool and dried both of them off. Then she pulled the hair off her neck, baring the lovely pulse of her artery to his gaze. "You must drink, D'Nar. You have proven to me all I need to know. I don't want this with another, but only you and me from now on."

He had no choice. She would never know the frenzy of bloodlust that consumed him. How could she? She was human. He was vampyr.

His teeth nipped at the skin of her neck, but the image of the mare and stallion stuck in his mind and he knew exactly how he would take his first taste of her.

Of course, just acknowledging permission caused the bloodlust to roar through his body with all the emotions and passions that went with it. He pulled her over to the bed and threw her down on top of the cushions. Their last lovemaking was child's play to this. D'Nar knew only one response to her offer, fast and furious, without thought or care, seeking only the fulfillment of his nature.

He flipped her over and lifted her hips, spooning himself behind her. Her breasts hung down, heavy and full and he played with them as his lips and tongue grazed the skin of her neck and shoulder.

His erection grew heavy and full, but this lust was different. Every thought centered on his need for blood. His lust was simply a by-product of a greater lust, one drawn from the centuries and the red sun resting high above their world.

He pushed into her without request. She accepted him without invitation. His hands continued to play with her nipples then reached down to her core. He found her nub and began to play with it, all the while pulling out and thrusting in, a true stallion in that his only thought was for his own fulfillment.

His incisors grew until they ached. His teeth grazed her skin until he found the exact spot he wanted to drink from. Her pulse beat beneath his lips as his own heartbeat matched hers.

His hips pounded into hers. Innocent flesh or not, he didn't care. One hand held her tight, the other worked furiously at her clit. He felt her passion rise and just before she reached her pinnacle, he sank his teeth into her neck.

Great river of life. Sweet warm fluid, tangy in the aftermath but sweet again with the next drink. A rush of energy filled his limbs, heightening his senses, making him aware of the muscles of her core clamping around him. But even more.

At first, he thought only of quenching his thirst. But then something extraordinary happened. He became one with her. On one level, his shaft plunged in and out of her with no other need than completion. But on another level, he sensed her need, too. She wanted him just as much as he wanted her—with a softness that was foreign to him, but just as intense.

He drank as a man starved for both food and tenderness. She opened her neck even wider to him and his insides melted. Then all thought ceased as they climbed higher toward the crest of love.

"Give me more," she cried, begged him for release.

He pumped his hips in time with the pulse in her neck. The urgency in her cry fed him more than her blood, for he knew her desire as his own. He reached for the pinnacle of release as a prize just beyond his grasp.

A guttural cry roared from his mouth as he pulled away from her neck. Strong, fresh blood coursed through his veins. Power surged through his body. He climbed higher and higher, drinking in the power of feeding. But even greater than that was the knowledge that she wanted him just as much as he wanted her. In return, D'Nar gave her everything.

"Harder," she screamed. He complied. "Yes, that's it."

He could feel her heat wrap around him, milking every sensation out of his thrusts as his hand worked at her clit. Her muscles clenched and for a moment time stood still. Her breath hitched and then she screamed in attainment. His own moment in time stopped with her. Then his entire body exploded in the most intense orgasm he had ever experienced. Shock upon shock, wave upon wave, he thought he would never stop pumping into her body. All thought ceased as he passed out.

Chapter Seven

She was being crushed. Ariel came to only to find that D'Nar had collapsed on top of her. She struggled to push him off, concern flooding her. "D'Nar? D'Nar?"

He came around slowly. "What happened?"

"I don't know. We seem to have knocked each other out. I've never heard of such a thing happening before."

"I have. In the tales of my youth from other young males."

"But the same happened to me."

Awe filled her at the moment they'd shared. "Ariel. What have I done?" Horror filled his voice. "I lost control. Did I hurt you?"

She had been out of her mind with ecstasy and he was asking if he'd hurt her? "No, D'Nar. You didn't hurt me. You couldn't. I asked for you to be rough. I was begging for it, as I recall." She could sense he wasn't really listening to her, so she shifted up onto one elbow and stared straight down at him. Of course her annoyance didn't last long, especially when she realized how sincere he was. "Have you—?" She wondered if she had the right to ask. "Have you ever wanted something like this to happen with another?"

His gentle smile gave her his answer. "Never."

Pleased, she flopped back down and let his arms close around her. Unfortunately, her stomach was speaking to them both. A loud growl issued from her mid-section and she started to laugh. He joined her mirth with his own and long moments went by before they could stop. "Come, you're hungry. And I fear I didn't allow you to finish your bath."

He helped her up and they washed off quickly. A table was set in the next chamber where she found meats, cheese, fresh baked bread, and fruit. More than one person could ever consume. However, she did try. "I was as hungry as you, my Lord," she told him. "I didn't eat yesterday."

"Did the thought of making love to me frighten you?"

"The unknown is always frightening," she answered as honestly as she could. "That's what trust is all about."

"Do you trust me now?" he asked, his gaze sincere.

She gave her reply a great deal of thought. "I don't know how to answer without seeming selfish. I trust your honor and your loyalty to that which you believe to be right. I don't believe you would ever harm me. But how can I say yes or no when I don't know you? We have much to learn about each other."

"Although your words wound, at least you're honest. And you're right. Sharing a bed doesn't automatically create trust nor does the bond of blood."

"I didn't mean to wound you, D'Nar. I would never want to hurt you. But this trust you seek must be built with time or the foundation will falter. Would you want that?"

"No." He smiled at her. "You're wise beyond your years and I see we can learn much from each other."

He rose and came around the table to stand before her. "You must rest some more."

"I can't. I must see to my patient."

"I'll check on him for you. I need answers only he can give."

"He needs to gain his strength."

"He'll speak to me," D'Nar replied, confidence flowing through his words.

A great sadness flowed through her. "He will not speak to anyone ever again, my Lord."

"What do you mean?"

"His voice box was torn out."

****

D'Nar bowed as he entered the home of the young vampyr C'Cin. His uncle, C'Cir, greeted both of them for he couldn't stop Ariel from accompanying him. "I hear there is great fortune within this house, although it comes with a great price."

"Many thanks to you, Viceroy, and your healer. C'Cin still lives and for that, we're very grateful."

"That's why we are here, C'Cir," D'Nar continued. "We need—."

He was cut off by an upraised hand. "You do me a great honor, D'Nar, by your visit and your care. I would be remiss if I did not show like in return. Please. Take a moment to refresh yourself from the dust of the journey. You, also, Lady."

The offer warmed D'Nar's heart more than the older gentleman would ever know. At least someone cared about the rules of their society. "Our thanks for your generosity," he replied with a bow.

D'Nar ushered Ariel into what was known as a public chamber, a place where guests were greeted and refreshment served. Sometimes the room was even used for small informal gatherings of family and friends rather than using a larger, statelier chamber. "C'Cin?" Ariel asked as they were seated.

D'Nar watched as C'Cir sighed, grief ravaging his features. "Drank more of the mixture you brought. There's more color to his skin today and he breathes easier. But I fear he'll never breathe normally again."

"I'm a healer, Lord. I can only repair the damage done," she answered, her tone grave but hopeful. "He has done the rest. But I fear you're right. He'll never breathe normally again. Nor will he speak. That which gave sound to his voice is gone."

"I know," the elder vampyr replied, pain filling his face. "But he's alive. And though I'm only his uncle, I'm extremely grateful for that. I don't think his mother, strong woman that she is, could have borne the sorrow of losing her son so soon after losing her husband. "

"Your brother was a good man, C'Cir," D'Nar commiserated.

"Yes. And wise. Just blind where his son was concerned," the elder vampyr replied. "Perhaps now it's too late for the boy to change."

"Not if I have anything to say about it, Lord," Ariel announced with conviction in her tone. "Where there's life, there's always hope."

"And that's why we're here, C'Cir. I ask your permission to probe your nephew. He may not be able to speak, but he might be able to give me the answers I seek anyway. We must know who or what has done this terrible deed."

C'Cir's countenance turned grave. "I feared you would ask this of me. But the right isn't mine to give."

"It's mine," a voice replied from the doorway. D'Nar turned to see an older vampyress enter the room. Strands of silver streaked her dark rich hair, yet the woman stood straight and tall. Fierceness flashed in her gaze as she approached and D'Nar knew she would stand beside him in any battle. Funny but that fierceness, that aggression, made them allies in battle but unable to be comfortable living together. The males and the females of the vampyr race were both alphas; they sought supremacy through competition, which made them great warriors but competitors in bed. Both male and female of their race took human concubines. They might need to mate to procreate, but living with a human was far easier than living with another vampyr. And though they were slighter in stature, he was sure the females of his race were sometimes the stronger. They bore the pain of childbirth, something he would not wish to endure.

"Lady." D'Nar bowed in respect.

B'Den bowed, returning that respect. "Viceroy."

"Much hinges on your answer, my Lady."

To his chagrin, she turned to Ariel. "What say you, healer?"

Ariel bowed. "That more is at stake than one life. False information and misconceptions could tear away at the very fabric of our world. We must know the truth, whatever that truth may be."

"And you're certain no harm can come to him?"

"No, Lady. I can never be certain. But I wouldn't be here now if I didn't think it all right."

B'Den sighed and D'Nar saw a weary woman, terribly frightened of losing her son, carrying the fresh wound of losing her husband. "Let it be done. But at the first sign of distress, you must stop."

"That's why I am here," Ariel replied. "My first duty is to my patient."

"Be gentle, Lord," B'Den pleaded.

"I will."

****

Many were the times that Ariel wished she were more than human. How she yearned to heal with a single lick of the tongue. But now, more than ever, her human helplessness showed. What happened now, only a vampyr could accomplish.

D'Nar sat still as stone on the edge of the bed, his fingers touching the temples of the young vampyr, C'Cin. She could read no expression on his face, nothing that would give even the slightest hint that he'd made contact. Sometimes, as she well knew, it couldn't be done.

She hovered over both lover and patient, while the two elder vampyrs stood silently in the room. Without thought, Ariel reached out to touch D'Nar's shoulder. A swift hand pulled hers back and she found B'Den shaking her head. "No. They must do this alone."

Then it occurred to her that B'Den might not be correct. "Lady, I know this may sound strange," she said in a soft, hushed tone. "But I feel that I'm

67

somehow connected to them both. I'm the key that will unlock the door. You must let me join them."

B'Den looked skeptical, C'Cir simply looked horrified. No human had ever dared to invade the sanctity of their traditions. But B'Den was a perceptive woman. She must have sensed that there was more going on than just circumstance.

"I've trusted my instincts before, I must rely upon them now." She nodded for Ariel to continue.

Now that she'd gotten what she'd fought for, Ariel hesitated. What she was about to do would change much between D'Nar and herself. Still, she knew she had to forge ahead.

Ariel reached out and touched D'Nar upon the shoulder. She closed her eyes. Nothing. Only the thrum she felt whenever she touched him.

She moved her hand up to his temples in the same way he was touching C'Cin. Still nothing.

Then, with a force that nearly knocked her off her feet, D'Nar moved one hand to her temple. She staggered and found a chair placed beneath her just as she collapsed.

A conduit. Wasn't that what she'd been trying to explain all along. She was a conduit. So was D'Nar. And what she saw petrified her.

There was no name for the thing that touched her. But the frisson of fear that wormed its way down her back made her shiver. She couldn't make out an exact shape, but the creature's touch made her think of a reptile, cold and devoid of feeling. But she sensed it carried the stealth of an I'man. How could these pictures be so nebulous, yet so menacing? The shimmering images horrified her like nothing she'd experienced before? Was that from the effects of the Tarba root? Ariel couldn't tell.

The three young vampyrs were laughing, joking, innocent of the evil nearby. Their instinctive response to danger, dulled by the drug, came too late. They had no real chance to defend themselves. The shadow creature had circled the spring before the young vampyrs realized their predicament. They attacked, and seconds later...

Ariel jerked back to break the connection. Breathing hard, she choked, "They had no chance, Lady. But what they encountered I cannot say, for the likes of it I have never seen before."

She watched D'Nar lift his head after rubbing his face with his hands. "I'm not certain either," he agreed. Yet he flashed her a look that she didn't understand.

B'Den nodded and sighed, her gaze fearful. "I accept your word and am simply grateful to you both for saving his life."

A moment later, C'Cir caught his breath and B'Den whirled. C'Cin had opened his eyes. Ariel and D'Nar were no more than an afterthought, as mother and uncle rushed to the young vampyr's side.

As they worked their way back to D'Nar's home, Ariel bit her lip. She wasn't sure if she should speak or not. She'd expected D'Nar's concern, perhaps even fear, for an enemy they might not be able to defeat. But not anger. And certainly not directed at her. Finally, she could stand the silence no more. "D'Nar?"

At first, he didn't answer and wild thoughts flew through her head. He was angry that she was usurping some of his authority. She was too involved in affairs that were none of her concern. She was a hero for saving the young man's life....

"I must know," he choked out.

"Know what, D'Nar? You're angry, yet I don't understand why."

"Did you see anything while I probed C'Cin?"

Puzzled, Ariel asked, "You didn't?"

"I felt a wave of power the likes of which I have never known. But I saw nothing."

Comprehension dawned with a terrible clarity. "What I saw cannot be described."

Hurt pride laced his voice. "Must I beg you for the information?"

So that was it. A situation clearly out of his control and the one person who had answers was a mere human. And female. "Must you let your pride get in the way?"

"My pride?" he roared. "This isn't about pride. It's about death and destruction."

And being helpless, she thought. A state so foreign to his nature that D'Nar couldn't accept what was happening. "I don't know the way of things right now, my Lord. But what's going on seems to be beyond our control."

"Control," he echoed with bitterness riding his tone.

Ariel sighed. "It gets worse, D'Nar."

"What do you mean?"

She took a deep breath. "What I saw will destroy us all."

Chapter Eight

What was happening? Had the world suddenly gone mad? A few days ago, he was the Viceroy of a city—his city. Now he had no idea what he was or what was happening to life as he knew it. A few days ago, he was a vampyr in control of his life with powers that were his alone. Now he had absolutely no idea about anything.

D'Nar took a deep breath and let the air out slowly. "What's going to destroy us all?"

"A terrible shadow, far more dangerous than anything I could describe. A shadow creature straight out of my nightmares. I would call it a demon from some of the texts that I have read. The writings speak of a shadow creature with no fear, no regard for any kind of life."

"I haven't read of any such creature," he scoffed.

She frowned at him. "I didn't think you'd accept my words. The tomes of which I speak are healing texts."

"Healing texts?" What manner of books were these? The writings for their world existed in the Great Library, and he had studied there extensively as part of his schooling.

"The art of healing has always fallen to humans, D'Nar. The art of protection falls to vamyprs. It's the way of our world. My ancestors wrote many recipes to heal the sick. They also wrote of the dark arts, healers who tended to the darker side of our nature. You asked about human hatred. There have been many throughout our history who have wished to conjure a deliverer."

D'Nar had always suspected as much. "Ariel, I hold dominion over you. That is the way of our world. How many years has this been so?"

"Too many, my Lord," she replied with a wry smile.

He agreed. "Would you have me perish, then? For that is what would happen if you refused to give me your blood."

"True. But I'm sure you would find more humans your allies than your foes." He watched her hesitate, then bite her lip in consternation. She was clearly unhappy with the direction of their conversation. "I couldn't be a part of that kind of destruction any more than you."

"I know." This time, he hesitated. One word, one small word, loomed larger than both of them. Trust. Could they trust each other? "But you would tell me if such a plot existed, wouldn't you?"

A world of hurt simmered in her bright azure gaze. "Are you asking me to betray my people?"

"No," he replied with a swift shake of his head. "But by your reply, you assume that helping me is a betrayal."

A shaft of sadness ran through him. Their conversation tugged at the fragile bond growing between them. She sighed, acknowledging the trap he'd set for her. "I straddle the fence between our races. As a healer, I find myself forced to remove the fence altogether."

He watched as she took a deep breath then let the air out once more. "However, there's still right and wrong. A plot such as this would hurt everyone, kill many, but also create an unbridgeable gap between our races. I couldn't be a part of that."

"I had to ask," he told her, sorry that he'd hurt her, wondering if they could overcome such a hurt. "You understand why."

She barked out a bitter laugh. "The world is more

72

important than the two of us, D'Nar. So yes, I understand."

Funny, but he didn't. His life was not his own and had become inundated with obligations and responsibilities. It belonged to the people. Not to him.

"I must call a Great Council," he decided.

"Are you certain, my Lord? You have no tangible proof that a shadow exists."

"C'Cin isn't proof?"

"Yes," she answered. "And no. People hear what they want to hear, believe what they want to believe. We would be asking them to believe in a nightmare. That's not something anyone wants to do."

He frowned. "I can't simply stand by and wait until someone else gets killed."

"True, but think of the panic it would create if this thing really is what we think it is."

Indeed, he thought. She was right. So how did one catch a shadow? "We need proof. And we need to know what this thing really is. We can call it a shadow, but I can't bring a shadow to the Council. Come. We must go back to the palace. I'll have Toby send riders to the other cities."

"And then what, my Lord?"

He grinned. "Then you and I are going back to school."

She gave him a perplexed look that then filled with dismay. "School, my Lord?"

"Yes," he insisted. "School. We go to search the Great Library."

****

The Great Library stood as a testament to endurance. Neither wind, nor sand, the incessant heat of the yellow sun, nor the cold of the night could mar its beauty. Each block of stone had been perfectly formed to fit the next. Tall columns flanked the entrance and majestically announced to all who entered that great deeds rested in higher learning. The building dwarfed all others in its size and scope. Thousands of books and scrolls resided within its walls, waiting only for those who wished to discover them.

Of course, Ariel had thought D'Nar was kidding— at least to a certain extent. School. Instead, she found herself the captive of a hard taskmaster. The captive part she didn't mind. The hard part she thoroughly enjoyed. The books she could do without.

Ariel had never been one to learn from a book. She enjoyed doing. She could learn more with her hands than her head. But she knew the books they had to start with and he didn't. So he kept pushing her to search. Text after text, tome after tome, scroll after scroll, until Ariel wanted to scream.

Instead, she sat back and rolled her neck to loosen the knot that had formed there. "D'Nar. May we have a moment? I fear my brain is ready to explode."

He looked up with a frown at being interrupted. But her words must have reached him for he rose and stretched. Then he walked around behind her to knead the muscles in her shoulders. Ariel purred with delight.

"I didn't know you were so easy to please," he quipped.

"Usually, I'm not," she admitted. "You have magical hands."

"Indeed," he replied, his tone full of smug satisfaction.

Men, she thought. Give them an ounce of praise and they strut like peacocks. She was about to tell him so when she gasped. His hands, tired of her neck, had found their way down her chest and beneath the fabric of her blouse.

"Not here," she whispered, mortified by his intention.

"And why not?" he answered. She could hear soft laughter threading through his reply. "This is a house of learning, isn't it? We have much to learn about one another, Ariel."

She struggled to get away. "This is a *public* house of learning, D'Nar. Have you no shame?"

He didn't answer right away. He was too busy playing with her nipples. "I'm the Viceroy of this city. By my order, I can close this Library and force everyone to leave. Of course, then the whole city would know why."

"You wouldn't dare."

"Oh, no?"

Damn the man, she thought, flames shooting through her veins and ending deep inside her core. She began to take short shallow breaths. Her hands trembled. God, she wanted him.

"You don't play fair."

"But I love to play. Don't deny me."

Did he think she would say no now? "But how? Where?"

"Come with me."

Ariel rose and followed as he led her by the hand through a maze of shelves. At the end, they stopped in an alcove of sorts. D'Nar swung her around to face him so that her back was to the shelves. His mouth engulfed hers. He tried to inhale her. One hand wrapped around the back of her neck, pushing her face hard against his so neither one of them could breathe without the other.

Instead of being frightened, Ariel simply let her passion go.

As soon as she did, he groaned. He guided her hand to his erection. He was huge. No, more than huge. Engorged. Fierce. Hungry for her.

There would be no foreplay between them. He undid his pants and let them fall to the floor. He lifted her skirt until her lower half was naked before him. She watched as his face shifted into a sharp almost feral mask. He gathered her in his arms and braced her buttocks against a shelf. Then he stroked his staff, centered himself at her entrance, and rammed himself inside of her.

Ariel screamed and came immediately. Huge wracking shudders coursed through her, yet she wasn't satisfied. Something was missing, as if she'd tasted a first course in a meal but the best the cook had to offer was yet to come.

She felt the pinch as he bit her neck, yet even more, felt his cock grow inside of her. How could that be? He was already larger than she thought a man could get.

He licked her skin, the rasp of his tongue sending shivers down her spine.

She wanted more. She got more than she ever bargained for.

He growled and bit down again. This time he drank. And as he sucked, her blood surged in answer to his vampyr call.

Ariel's body writhed in ecstasy. She moaned as the need built again.

He answered. His hips pulled back and he thrust his rod into her so forcefully the shelf shook.

Pain mixed with the need. He filled her, grew until she thought she would burst from his strength. He reared back and thrust again. And again. His hands held her steady, otherwise she was sure she would have gone right through the wall.

"More," she begged.

He stopped. Lifting his mouth from her neck, she watched him lick the blood from his lips as if she were a delicacy. He savored every drop.

"Say that again."

"More. Harder," she demanded.

He thrust into her again. "Like this?"

"Yes."

He did it again. He rotated his erection so that she felt every inch of his steel shaft. "And this?"

She moaned. "Oh God, yes."

"Beg."

"What?"

"Beg me for it. Plead with me to finish you."

He pulled all the way out until just the tip of his erection remained inside her feminine heat. At first, she'd wondered if he was trying to prove his power to her. Then she realized it was making him crazy. The more she wanted him, the more he wanted her. Emboldened by his request, Ariel whispered, "Fuck me."

He shuddered. His breathing doubled. His arms trembled. "I need to hear more," he pleaded.

"Fuck me harder. Harder."

His restraint snapped. Physically, he was so much stronger than she, but she knew in her heart he would never really hurt her. He pounded into her like a battering ram and she reveled in his strength. "Can you feel me?" she whispered. "Am I hot inside?"

He moaned. With each stroke, with each thrust, feeling of her muscles wrapping around his cock, he groaned. He kept reaching. She kept reaching.

Ariel's insides tightened. "Yes. That's it. Keep—"

She never got the rest out. D'Nar cried out. He screamed as if his orgasm began all the way down in his toes. He shot his come deep inside her womb and as the hot fluid fill her, her insides melted. This wasn't just falling off a precipice, this was an explosion. No, many explosions.

Her screams joined his, echoing off the walls.

So much for anonymity.

Ariel had no idea how much time passed until she could catch her breath. The wood of the shelf dug painfully into the cheeks of her buttocks. Her newly opened core felt raw and sore. Yet all she could think of were the tiny aftershocks of pleasure still coursing through her body. And how she wanted them to go on forever.

"Did I hurt you?" he asked with seeming remorse.

"Of course you did. I asked you to, didn't I?"

"But—"

"No buts, D'Nar. Except that next time you need to find a softer place for mine."

He roared with laughter. "That can be arranged."

He pulled out of her, much to her chagrin. "We need to get back to work," she reminded him.

He grinned, quirking his mouth so that her heart did a funny kind of flip inside. "I thought that was what we were doing. Looking for information."

"About each other?"

"Very educational," he replied, his tone husky and full of meaning. "But you're right. We must continue our search, though I'd much prefer my exploration of you, not some dusty old scrolls."

Ariel hid a smile as she put her clothes back in order. Her heart skipped a beat at this new and intimate D'Nar. "It's said that good things must come to an end so they may begin again."

"True," he agreed. "However, I've never been a patient man. Can you blame me?"

Ariel laughed softly. Even as sated as she felt, she still hungered for him. And, it seemed, he felt the same way. "No."

She watched him straighten his clothes and felt a light blush creep up her cheeks as her gaze dropped below his waist. As her eyes shifted to greet his, he gave her a warm smile and ran his palm across her cheek in a quick caress. "Come. No matter how we feel, we have responsibilities to fulfill."

He turned and walked down the corridor. Ariel followed. As she did, she marveled at the knowledge stored in this majestic building. Her head rotated from side to side in wonder. Then a flash of light caught her eye. She stopped and walked toward the source. "D'Nar. Wait."

He halted and then joined her. "What is it?"

"This is unusual," she murmured, looking down at a box on shelf near her knees. It was surrounded by scrolls and covered in dust. She lifted the box and brushed away the dust to find the treasure of nanjir wood beneath her fingers. Dark in color with a fine but distinct grain, the box was also banded in polished gold.

"Very beautiful," he remarked.

Ariel stared at the piece in awe and delight. Then curiosity followed. "This is very strange, D'Nar. Such a beautiful box in the Great Library? Overlooked for many, many years judging by this coating of dust?"

"Indeed," he agreed. "I wonder what writings are so important that they should rest in such beauty."

"I do, too. I'm almost afraid to open it."

His mouth quirked in amusement. "It's a box, Ariel."

Men! She reached out to open it and a jolt ran up her arm, a frisson of fear. "D'Nar," she whispered.

His face filled with concern. "What's wrong?" he asked, alarmed.

"I'm not sure. I think this is what we've been searching for."

"But," he paused, his tone skeptical. "How do you know?"

"Too much coincidence," she replied. "It doesn't make sense that this treasure should be sitting on a shelf all this time without being discovered."

"No one looked," he quipped, trying to lighten her mood.

She threw him a razored glance. "Be serious."

"All right," he sighed. "I don't know. Perhaps it wasn't meant to be found. Until now."

Ariel's hands shook as they caressed the wood. If that were the case, then were they simply being used by fate? "I'm frightened, D'Nar. Frightened and excited."

"So am I. But we came here to learn. We can't

simply deny the answers because we don't like them."

"Are we being set up, I wonder? Or are we being led down a path?"

"I don't know."

"Could this have anything to do with our vision in the glen?"

"Again, I can't say yes or no."

"So many questions, D'Nar. Ones we have no answers for."

D'Nar covered her hands with his. "We won't know until we look inside."

Chapter Nine

Excited yet frightened, D'Nar helped Ariel lift the lid with trembling fingers. He felt the same way, and not just about the box. "Look at the parchment, D'Nar. I've seen ancient scrolls before, but never on paper this fine."

He agreed. "And the writing seems to be very old. Yet meticulous. Can you read the words? They look to be in a much older script than what I'm used to reading."

"Yes," she replied, but he caught hesitation in her reply.

"What bothers you?"

"I feel we're puppets on strings. That if we'd never—" She stopped and blushed.

"Never made love?" he finished for her.

She nodded. "We'd never have found them."

Her features turned serious. A hint of fear lurked in her gaze. "And now that we're being led down this path, we won't be able to stop."

D'Nar reached out and enveloped her in his embrace. "I know. But we have to keep going. Planned or not, if there's one more death, violence may erupt between our peoples."

He kissed the top of her head and gave her a single hard hug. When he let go, she reached into the box and lifted the first scroll as if it were made of spun glass. She unrolled the parchment then made to hand it to him. He shook his head, embarrassed to admit he was not as learned as she. "You go ahead."

So she began.

"I have placed this last scroll on top of the others.

As important as those scrolls are, I wanted my own words to warn any and all who come after me. There is not much time. Even now, the earth splits along with the sun. I pray that my beloved planet, E'randor, endures."

Ariel paused. "The earth splits along with the sun?" she repeated. "Can it be that the vision we had was of The Before Time? Could it really be true? That there was only one sun, not two?"

"Yes," he answered. "I think the vision was true. It certainly is logical. Remember your science. One small shift in the alignment of our planet would be catastrophic. I can't imagine what would happen if the sun were to split. Keep reading."

"They came without warning. We were unprepared. We never thought anyone capable of reaching our world through space. We never thought such wondrous visitors would want to destroy us."

"Through space? Oh, D'Nar," she cried with wonder. "Think of the possibilities."

He was, but beyond the wonder of their abilities, a cold dread seeped into his bones. "Continue. Please."

"We welcomed them. Marveled at their technological advances. Showed them ours as well. And all the while they were sizing us up to see if they could take over our world and make it their own."

"Oh no," she exclaimed. "Those poor people. What kind of beings could be so heartless to devise such a betrayal?"

"An enemy," he answered. "A diabolical enemy."

"You will never know," she continued reading, *"never understand their single-minded purpose; their belief that they had the right to simply take over our world and absorb us. No, assimilate us. Nor their willingness to sacrifice as many of their own fighters as necessary to achieve their purpose. They cannot, no, will not be stopped."*

"They?" she asked him.

"Keep reading," he suggested. "Perhaps we'll find an answer."

"Here. I think. Yes," she said, running her finger down the paper.

She cleared her throat. *"They call themselves the Inistrari. I call them plague. They conquered our world in less than a month. Two million souls. Gone. We fought with every weapon we had, but they learned well. They knew how to defeat us. They kept attacking, decimating everything in their way."*

Horror filled D'nar's soul. "Two million people? Dead?" he whispered. The number was inconceivable to him.

She nodded, her eyes filling with tears. He could offer only small comfort before he gestured for her to go on in spite of their breaking hearts.

"I ask forgiveness for what we have done. The Inistrari made us like them. All or nothing. Kill or be killed. We decided we would rather die than let their plague destroy another world. Those who can travel to the caverns deep within Mount C'eres. With my beloved gone, I have nothing left, only my son K'hlil. I pray with all my heart that he finds a way to survive. Then I pray that he does not. For I have no idea what kind of a future I have left him."

Ariel's voice trailed off. "What's he talking about, D'Nar?" she asked, eventually. "Do you know?"

He shook his head, now more afraid than ever. "Is there more?"

"I don't know." He watched her scan the page. "I don't recognize this word. Do you know what a *sinquatira* is?"

A drizzle of cold dread snaked its way down his spine. "I don't recognize the word either, but I have a feeling I know what happened." She threw him a quizzical glance. "From the way this is written, I think they used this *sinquatira*, as they call it, to split the sun."

"Could a *sinquatira* do such a thing?" she asked, her tone hushed in disbelief.

He wasn't sure. "Everything is balance, Ariel. Throw one thing out of balance and anything can happen. What else does it say?"

"Only an apology." She read. *"May God forgive us all, but it is done. Fare Well."*

He watched her face fall. "What is it, Ariel?"

She didn't answer. Not a word. He removed the paper from her hand and read the signature. His stomach fell to his feet. "It is signed, A'Shar D'Nar."

****

With a heavy heart, Ariel squeezed D'Nar's hand. "Am I responsible for the way the world is today?" he asked her in a strained voice.

"How can you be? The scroll says nearly everyone was already dead."

"No, Ariel. The sun. When they split the sun, our races split in two."

She thought about that for a moment. "How can that be? How can you be sure?"

"Because we are halves of a whole. We cannot survive without each other."

Ariel wished that could be really true. But D'Nar was wrong. "No, we can't," she agreed. "Several humans together wouldn't be able to bring down an I'man. We're not fast enough or strong enough. You have a hunting instinct inside you I'll never have. Your senses are sharper, your reflexes swifter. But would you know the difference between astrea and firling?"

He shook his head no. "I'm not a healer."

Ariel laughed. "That's a good thing because I was talking about grains for making bread and beer, not herbs to heal with."

He laughed with her. "Point taken."

"D'Nar," she said, sobering. "No one can be responsible for decisions made in the past. Or who made them. Our world is what it is. All we can do now is be responsible for what we do with our world now. We must learn from the past and use that knowledge to shape the future."

"Which is why we're here," he agreed, smiling at her. "Come. Let's see what else we can find."

They both searched the nearby shelves for more scrolls. They found several that confirmed the words of A'Shar, D'Nar. Listen to this," Ariel cried as she unfurled yet another scroll.

"We live deep inside the mountain. How I long to see the Sun. What I would give to see the blue of the sky again. Or the green of the trees. And feel the wind upon my face. But there is no Sun anymore. None that we can see. Only a red glow in the sky. And sometimes we cannot see that for the atmosphere swirls with gray ash. And the air is so cold it steals the heart from the unwary soul.

"We must grow what food we can. Stores that once seemed as though they would feed us forever dwindle at an alarming rate. But we are learning. Just recently, we were able to get seedlings to grow by pulverizing the cooled lava and adding nutrients. So there is hope. There is always hope."

Ariel smiled up at him. "Now you know the real reason we've survived. Our ancestors never gave up hope."

"I wonder if I would have had such fortitude," he murmured.

Ariel put that scroll down and continued to open others to read. Many were lists of names, families, made in remembrance. "What a shame," she agreed. "That they gave up so much only to have us squander it away."

"Squander?"

"Isn't that what we're doing when we fight against each other? They sacrificed themselves so that we might have our lives and our world."

"Such as it is," he finished for her.

"No," she replied, her faith steadfast. "They knew the alternatives. A piece of a world is better than none at all.

"Wait," she added. "Here's another scroll. This looks different. The writing looks to be that of a woman." Ariel read a few lines then continued out loud.

"We are outcast. No one knows why our children have become this way, only that they cannot live without human blood. It is as unthinkable as eating human flesh to most of us. Many mothers cannot accept the stigma and they abandon their children to our small group. Some cannot cope at all and kill their children, sometimes themselves. The change seems to come just before adulthood. Instead of the joy of seeing our children grow into adulthood, we know only fear. This metamorphosis is very strange and follows the emergence of the red sun. Many have wondered if this is not punishment for destroying the Inistrari."

She dug into the box again and pulled out yet another scroll.

"The fever is upon me. The darkness calls. I try not to answer. But resistance is futile. I go through the motions of eating, but food tastes like dust. At first, being different, being outcast meant nothing to me. I don't mind being used. I'm proud of my abilities. I'm faster, stronger, a better tracker than them all. I bring back meat, which feeds us all. So I am tolerated."

She skimmed down the page. *"My heart pounds as I dream of each precious red drop. Rich, tangy, so sweet. As I stand next to L'Iara, I smell her desire, her woman's heat. She cannot withstand this onslaught any more than I can. Her skin, soft as the fur of the Chekchi, ripples as I touch her. Her eyes glaze over with animal lust when I draw my fingers down her neck. I can see the pulse there, throbbing just below the surface of her skin in time to the throbbing of my manhood. But L'Iara is different. She's gentle. I have no wish to hurt her, no matter how much I crave her blood."*

Ariel paused to slow the beat of her own heart. How incredibly erotic. Especially with D'Nar cradled against her back, his incisors scraping the skin of her neck, his desire evident in his short, shallow breaths.

"Great wonder of joy, she has given her consent to feed me. I tremble in awe at her beauty, at her acceptance of me. I'm so tired of being hated, feared."

"Keep going," D'Nar whispered into her ear.

"Her skin is as white as the snow, nearly translucent in places. Her breasts are rich and full. I had thought my first tasting of her would be from her neck, but as I suckle on her nipples, I bite, and her breasts give me tiny bursts of life. As they will one day to a child. I would that this child be mine, but that is impossible. It seems the distance between us grows more and more. Perhaps, someday, that will change.

"I do not wish to cause her pain. I will have to learn to be more careful of hurting her in the future. She is so much smaller, so much more fragile than I. But her breasts are so exquisite, and as I bite down, I lathe each nipple and she cries out in ecstasy."

"Pain and pleasure," D'Nar murmured, his incisors scraping the skin of her neck. "Keep reading," he begged as his hands kneaded the very globes that were being described.

"Her hips fit my hands to perfection and her woman's core calls to me. I have never tasted nectar so sweet, not even compared to the river of life. She is all that I have ever dreamed of. She is more.

"My flesh rises and turns to steel at the thought of her heat. Her mouth, as it closes over my manhood, threatens to make me lose control. She is beyond compare. She is trying to make me come. She wants to taste my body as I taste hers. But I will not let go. Oh, sweet torture. Her tongue licks up and down my shaft, making me shiver all over.

"I tremble at the thought of entering her. She will

draw the life out of me and I will gladly give it, only to be able to give her the same pleasure in return."

Ariel smiled. D'Nar could no more resist the call of the words on the paper than she could. She pushed back from the table and leaned over, bracing her hands. He lifted her skirt once again and swept a trembling hand over the soft skin of her ass. He grazed his lips across each rounded mound and then lifted up to enter her in one swift thrust.

"With each thrust of my body into hers, I climb the mountain of pleasure. But the pinnacle cannot be reached without the joining of our hearts as well as our minds. I taste the river of her life as I give her the river of mine. She sings through me, the sweet song of ecstasy."

D'Nar did the same, pushing into her with the same need. He slid in and out, taking sips of her blood from her neck as he pulled on her nipples. Shots of fire streaked through her as the pressure mounted.

"More, D'Nar. Let the pleasure take the world away. Let our lovemaking heal the wounds. We are bound by more than desire and blood. We are bound because we choose to be bound. There can be nothing more right in this world than making love."

He kissed the back of her neck and shots of fire ran up and down her spine. She yearned for release, but for some reason, the climb was slow. Yet the struggle was worth every step. His erection rotated inside her core, pulling out, thrusting back in. But this time, Ariel felt every movement.

His hands held her hips, grinding into her core as if he wanted his whole body inside hers. She wanted the same. He moaned and she knew he'd reached his highest threshold. But she wasn't quite ready to join him there. He must have known for his fingers began to stimulate her nub.

Every time he entered her, she felt his erection touch her womb. Never before had he been so deep inside her, so much a part of her. His fingers continued to play with her clit and she lost all sense of thought and fell into feeling. "Yes," she cried. "That's it."

She rose to reach his plateau and they fell together in the most intense orgasm yet. D'Nar screamed out his release and pumped shot after shot of come into her. His fingers pushed her off the ledge and she screamed out as well, her insides shaking with the force of her orgasm. Her body throbbed with aftershocks.

D'Nar collapsed onto her back and Ariel steadied herself against a shelf. He pulled out of her and lay there, trying to catch his breath. His seed dripped out of her core and down her leg, a testament to their joining.

"How many times does this make, oh virile one?" she quipped.

He lifted back, but she could feel his body shake with laughter. "I've lost count, my beauty."

They dressed slowly. "It seems as though we're not the only ones to share incredible lovemaking."

"And, it seems," he sighed, "not the only ones to deal with prejudice."

"We survived," she reminded him.

He nodded. "True. But that was the past."

Ariel hugged him hard then picked up the box with the scrolls. "I must read more of these. I believe the more we know, the better off we'll be."

D'Nar didn't seem to share that feeling. "I hope so. If what has happened in the past is happening now, I can only wonder about the future."

Chapter Ten

D'Nar walked with Ariel back to his home, his emotions in turmoil. Vampyrs were once treated the way humans are treated today, used for their value, a necessity. Funny, but Ariel must have known his thoughts, for she linked her arm in his and squeezed his hand in support.

In an open display of affection, D'Nar lifted their clasped hands and kissed the back of hers for all to see. He could almost hear the buzz of gossip that gesture would create throughout the marketplace.

But as they walked, D'Nar opened his eyes—really opened them. He watched an adult male vampyr receive a wide berth from the humans he passed as he swaggered down the street. Covert glances followed the man and D'Nar recognized the caution that a human jewelry vendor used as the man approached.

"Can you feel the tension in the air?"

"Yes," she sighed. "I've never felt such mistrust before."

He nodded. "Or perhaps we have a different perspective after what we read."

A bell tolled the sound of three. "I must leave you. I have been asked to attend N'Son's funeral."

She stood in front of him, sadness filling her features. He marveled that she cared so much. "Kiss me."

Taken aback he asked, "What?"

"Kiss me," she insisted.

He frowned. "In public? I know that you think my enjoyment of making love in public is somewhat naughty, but you know our society. You know public displays of affection are frowned upon."

"Kiss me anyway. Perhaps what we need to do is shake up our society a little. Perhaps what we need is a display of caring to calm the currents roiling beneath the surface. What better way is there to express our trust in one another?"

He thought for a moment and found she was right. The opposite of fear and mistrust would come through caring and acceptance. Besides, kissing Ariel was his second favorite pastime—consummation came in at number one.

With a gentleness he didn't know he possessed, D'Nar covered her cheeks with his palms. Her skin felt soft as the whispering wind. The world fell away as he gazed into her eyes. They became one as he bent his head and gave her the sweetest kiss he could. In it, he hoped all would see how he felt about her, his need for her, his respect, and his pride. Perhaps this was the way to get a message to his people.

He let go and smiled. She smiled back. He watched her walk away with a strange fullness in his heart. She was his L'Iara.

He turned to find two of his men waiting for him on the corner, ready to escort him to his duties. "You are fortunate, my Lord," one of his guards told him as they turned in a different direction.

In this wondrous woman he had found? Indeed. In the ceremony he now had to be a part of? Not at all.

A vampyr funeral was held without emotion. D'Nar realized the tradition must have grown from ancient times, probably because emotions were viewed then as a sign of weakness.

Wood was probably the most precious commodity on their planet aside from water. With limited rainfall, grasses grew in places where water pooled, but trees fought long and hard to survive. *Just like the people of their planet*, he said to himself.

Most of their structures, except for a few great

buildings like the Library, which were made out of stone, were built using a mud mixture made from dirt and tubus, the milky glue that came from the tubor plant.

With wood being so precious, the higher the funeral pyre, the greater the family's status. N'Son came from a wealthy, titled family.

N'Far greeted him. "Salutations, my Lord. You do my family great honor by attending. I thank you for coming."

"Salutations, N'Far. And to you, F'Den. You both have my deepest sympathy."

D'Nar bowed to both of them then took his place for the ceremony.

After that, no words were spoken. Only the plaintive sounds of the k'ettes mourned the passing of this young man. D'Nar stepped up when it was his turn, bowed low, and threw oil on the wood four times to symbolize the four directions of the soul's journey. Then all turned to face Mount C'eres. Although the prayer was silent, it was taught to every vampyr child. The wish was for the soul to fly to the red sun and be born again inside the great mountain. For inside the mountain rested their strength, their spirit.

Once the fire was lit, D'Nar's duty was done and he turned to leave. The rest of the night was private and belonged to N'Son's family. However, as he began to walk away, N'Far stopped him. "My Lord. A word? In private?"

He nodded and followed N'Far into his home. "I'm terribly sorry for your loss."

N'Far sighed and D'Nar knew the man would never really get over the pain of his son's death. "I thank you. But that's not why I wished to speak to you in private."

D'Nar frowned. This boded ill. Obviously N'Far did not trust his words to be said anywhere else but in private. And directly to him. "Go on."

"F'Den's sister's husband is G'Rakor."

"I see."

"There has been talk of rebellion and retribution. As Viceroy of T'Emba, he considers declaring martial law as well, then using martial law to his own end."

Dismay surged through him. He'd only made the declaration to keep people safe within the city, not to punish anyone, certainly not as an excuse to murder humans.

"Have you heard if there have been any deaths there as well as here?"

"No, my Lord."

He nodded. "I thank you for the information. You were right to come to me in private. Say nothing to anyone else, I beg of you. And your wife. I don't want a spark to fan the flames of disaster. Not until I have time to reason with everyone first."

He shook N'Far's hand, then reached out in salute. "You have my gratitude and my heartfelt sympathy. Let us both pray no one else dies."

On his way home, D'Nar wondered. G'Rakor wouldn't think twice to use this emergency for his own gain. He'd coveted I'Stara for a long time. Should D'Nar die in a rebellion, how sad. Then G'Rakor could step in as the new Viceroy, for he would have the knowledge and the leadership to take over since T'Embra was the second largest province on their world.

Of course, now that D'Nar knew the nature of the threat, he could plan for it. But he feared that the other Viceroys might back G'Rakor. Although he was an expert at government affairs and had earned his rank through hard work, G'Rakor carried no allegiance to anyone but himself. He would stop at nothing to further his career.

D'Nar hoped the cost would not be the lives of his people.

****

The days passed in a flurry of activity. Ariel deferred to Sendara as the senior concubine, for she had little experience planning state functions. But she wanted to learn and Sendara didn't mind teaching her. At first, Ariel thought Sendara might be cold, and though she sensed the woman's envy, Sendara was warm and welcoming.

D'Nar's days were filled with meetings in addition to his already overburdened schedule of running the city. He came to bed long after she fell asleep and was up before she awakened. He drank from her, but promptly fell asleep unfulfilled, leaving her feeling empty inside.

She did have one pleasure though. She visited C'Cin several times, the last to make sure he was fully recovered. He communicated by writing on a tablet and told her more than once of his gratitude. He was an engaging young man and Ariel hoped he would be able to overcome his handicap. Her heart broke for him, for as she sat with him, she would catch a moment of sadness in his gaze. His only crime, it seemed, was to be young.

On her final visit, B'Den came to the door to say good-bye. "I wish to thank you, healer."

Ariel knew what the admission cost the elder vampyress. She bowed. As she stood back up, she gave B'Den a knowing smile. "I am sworn to heal all who need me, mistress," she said, using the term with the utmost respect.

"There is no need for formality between us, Ariel. And it is I who should be showing respect to you." With that, B'Den bowed to her. If the moment had been any less serious, Ariel would have jumped up and down for joy. If caring could win one battle, mutual respect might just win the war.

"As a healer, you are bound to perform a job. You did your job well. My son lives," B'Den told her. "But you have gone beyond your duty, shown that you care about him in a way that transcends the differences between our races. When the time comes, you will find many who feel the same way."

Ariel bowed back and turned to depart, her heart soaring. The bell tolled and she started to run, knowing she was late. She reached D'Nar's home only to find him already gone. She washed and dressed as fast as she could, arriving at the ceremony just in time.

To D'Nar's very great displeasure.

She started to apologize, but he shook his head with tight-lipped disapproval. He motioned for her to stand beside him, but she could feel his anger. Her delight at B'Den's acceptance faded and she fought within herself. True, he had the right to be angry. But she also had the right to be heard.

And then it struck her. Wasn't their disagreement a microcosm of the sickness that threatened their society? She'd started to get angry in response to his anger, defensive in spite of feeling contrite. He didn't want to listen, falling steadfastly back on his right to be right. How easy to put a flame to this tinder, fuel the fire, then let it burn until none could stop it.

Ariel sighed.

The ceremonies passed faster than she expected and she was grateful. Each Viceroy rode in the center of his entourage between six guards mounted on white horses. Each guard was dressed in the uniform of his house and carried his colors on banners that swirled in the breeze. The spectacle drew nearly the entire city out to watch.

But one thing was missing. Usually the city cheered and celebrated when the Viceroys visited. Today seemed subdued, with an underlying cloak of fear, as if the people were afraid to be happy.

Once each Viceroy reached the steps of the Great Hall, he dismounted, and was escorted inside by two guards. The guards stopped on the platform in front of the door. At the end of the ceremony, the guards flanked each other with their banners, declaring to one and all the importance of their meetings.

Once everyone was inside, Ariel was able to share a brief private moment with D'Nar.

"D'Nar, I—"

He placed his finger on her lips. His gaze, normally open to her was shuttered and distracted. "Not now. I must gather myself for the Council."

"I didn't mean to be late."

He nodded, but she had no way of really knowing if he accepted her apology or not. "Just make sure that tonight's festivities are a success." Then he kissed her long and hard.

Ariel wished there were someone she could talk to. But Toby was at D'Nar's side and Sendara was busy making sure all complied with D'Nar's wishes. When she reached the ladies' quarters to dress, Ariel had decided there was another sickness in their society—men who thought miracles could be accomplished with a wave of the hand.

"You must stop frowning, you'll get wrinkles."

"Sendara," Ariel laughed as she put the hand mirror she was holding down on a table. "What are you doing here? I thought for sure you would be in seven different places at once, trying to get tonight just right."

Sendara laughed with her. "That's why I have seven young women to help me. And seven more to oversee them."

"I hope nothing goes wrong. D'Nar was upset that I was late for the welcoming ceremonies. He made it clear he didn't want any more mistakes."

"Men," Sendara sighed. "Such children. They stamp their feet, beat their chests, let us take care of the details, then take all the credit."

"I know," Ariel giggled. "Their bark is worse than their bite."

Sendara waggled her eyebrows at Ariel. "I don't mind their bite."

"That's not what I meant and you know it."

The elder woman sobered. "I know. But it's good to laugh about them sometimes. Don't take D'Nar too seriously, Ariel. His heart is pure. But he's a man and a vampyr."

"An impossible combination."

"Exactly."

"Thank you, my Lady."

"Now come, we need to get you dressed in something special tonight. Take a little edge off that bark of his."

Arial was surprised, as she hadn't expected to wear anything special. But Sendara had taken care of this detail along with all the others they'd laughed about.

Ariel gasped at the sea green gown. "The color matches your eyes," Sendara told her.

"It's beautiful," she cried, running her hand over the satiny material. "I've never worn anything so wonderful."

Sendara smiled, obviously pleased with her choice. "D'Nar is a Viceroy, you know. He must keep up appearances."

Ariel's smile faded. "Am I just an appearance, then? A token to grace his arm?"

"Of course not," Sendara answered, her tone stern. "You must never think like that. Whether they want to believe the truth or not, we are their equals, even though we are human and we are women. Never believe otherwise, Ariel."

Ariel nodded. In her heart and mind, she was more than D'Nar's equal. The challenge and urgency was to make him understand her role, not only in his life, but also in their world. If D'Nar could accept her as a true equal, then others would as well.

Would he be able to see beyond her role of

concubine? "D'Nar is an exception. As you well know. But I fear even he can only accept so much."

Sendara agreed. "Our household is a prime example of what can be achieved with reason and respect."

Ariel smiled, pleased that Sendara had included her in the statement. How could the woman not be jealous? And yet, she had made all the preparations for a state dinner and was helping to dress Ariel for the evening. Sendara had picked up a brush and begun to comb Ariel's hair, lifting strands this way and that, deciding upon a style. Ariel hadn't had her hair brushed by another since she was a child.

"Yet change must come," she replied, reminding both of them of the task at hand. She thought about telling Sendara about their discovery in the library but thought better of it. The scrolls only proved that the sickness of their world had to be cured. All living beings existed with a kind of inner harmony—a balance. The longer their world remained out of balance, the more painful the cure. Of this, Ariel was certain.

"Fear breeds mistrust," Sendara answered, pinning sections of her hair to her head with decorative combs. "Mistrust breeds more fear. Until only the cycle remains."

A chill ran through Ariel. "I'm frightened it'll be even worse than that," she explained. "The other viceroys, the vampyrs, even the humans; those in power have the most to lose. They'll do anything to protect their positions—even fight—to keep what they have."

"True," Sendara agreed, putting the finishing touches on her hair. Ariel admired Sendara's skill. Her hair cascaded in soft curls down from the top of her head to frame her face. The hairstyle was perfect for the dress Sendara had given her. "Change is a process. I'm afraid this process will be long, painful, and costly for both races."

"Does it have to be?" Ariel wondered out loud. "Don't the people who hold the power understand how much they have to lose?"

Sendara didn't answer right away. "I was about to say no, they don't. But I'm not sure. Perhaps they do. And that's why their only recourse is to gain. Think about it for a moment. The only way not to lose territory in a war is to win battles and take more territory. The same applies to power. In order not to lose power, one must gain power. Domination benefits the winner, not the loser."

Sendara's sigh reached deep inside Ariel. "Perhaps we're like a pendulum," the elder woman continued. "Perhaps we have to reach one extreme in order to swing back to the other. I don't know."

Ariel agreed. Because of what she'd read in the scrolls, she knew it had happened before. "Thank you for my lesson tonight."

Sendara threw her a quizzical look. "Lesson?"

Ariel laughed. "I like my hair this way."

"And?" Sendara asked, laughing with her.

Ariel was glad this woman, who had become her friend, understood. She needed an ally. Vampyrs, even one's as open minded as D'Nar, could be a handful. "Racism is wrong. Prejudice is wrong. Domination is wrong. And none of them will be able to exist indefinitely. Eventually the fuel that burns the fire will run out."

"I hope so," Sendara whispered.

"You had the choice," she continued. "Of whether or not to accept me into your household. You used reason to make that decision. I believe reason and time will counteract the fire."

Sendara shook her head. "You give credit where there is none. I did what I did out of love for D'Nar."

"I know. But you made a choice. You used reason. Logic dictated that sharing was easier than fighting.

Because you knew that if you chose to fight, you might end up with nothing. The ultimate end of a fight, no matter who wins, is simply loss."

"Not everyone will use reason," the elder woman warned Ariel.

"I know. And that's what I fear the most."

Sendara smiled and reached out to give her hand a reassuring squeeze. "Then we must not let them. We must make our strength, their strength."

Ariel smiled. "You're right. We must."

"Now go," Sendara ordered. "Dazzle him. Dazzle them all. Show them what it means to be human. And a woman. Show them who we really are. Plant your seeds."

Ariel reached out and gave Sendara a fierce hug. "I will. And I'll keep planting them until they bear fruit."

"And beyond," Sendara whispered. And Ariel heard the hope of their world in her voice.

The fate of their world now rested on reason. Would both races listen? Would they be willing to change? Could there be a middle ground such as the one she reached with B'Den this afternoon?

She had a feeling she would find her answers at the dinner she was to attend.

Chapter Eleven

On edge, D'Nar paced inside his office. The evening would show him many things, for state dinners had a way of revealing truths not found in council chambers. Blood, wine, and music could loosen a tightly held tongue.

The door opened and D'Nar turned. His breath locked in his throat. His heart beat madly in his chest as a vision approached. Her red-gold hair flowed in long waves from the top of her head to frame her face. A hint of kohl outlined her eyes, making them stand out like jewels in the sun. A touch of pink highlighted her cheeks and her lips had been darkened to the color of a ripe strawberry, rich and ready for him to taste.

She wore a soft, flowing gown of sea green to match the color of her eyes. The bodice dipped low into the valley of her breasts, making him wish he could travel there. He swallowed hard, fighting his desire for her.

Around her neck, on a thin gold chain, rested a single pearl. Yes, he thought to himself, a pearl was the perfect choice. Whereas Sendara reminded him of a diamond, Ariel was his pearl. Both women were extremely strong in their own ways. Both had been forged to withstand vampyric emotions. But where Sendara was straightforward and her inner emotions were as easily seen as the facets of a diamond, Ariel was softer and more layered, not as easily read.

He bowed. "Your beauty astounds me, my Lady."

He would have kissed her but knew he couldn't, as that would start something that couldn't be finished. Instead he kissed the back of her hand, then turned it over and pressed her palm to his lips. She smelled of moonlight and a summer's evening, making D'Nar forget his duties and the weight of his office for a moment.

"Sendara was most generous."

D'Nar straightened and smiled. "I'm pleased that you like each other."

"The festivities are her work, my Lord. Not mine. I don't know how to plan state functions."

"I didn't expect you would." He linked her arm with his. "Sendara was happy to help."

"In more ways than one," she replied with a smile.

D'Nar raised a brow. There was more to her smile than simple gratitude, he was certain. But now was not the time to pry. "So if I may ask, what kept you this afternoon?"

He watched her face light up with excitement. "B'Den thanked me for saving her son. I mean, truly thanked me. As an equal."

D'Nar was surprised. The vampyress struck him as one who would be hard to win over. "I'm happy for you. If a vampyr matron as proper as B'Den can learn, so can others."

Ariel pulled his arm tight against her body. "The council didn't go well, did it?"

"No," he sighed. "In spite of what I've tried to show them, they've decided this is a struggle for power. They don't want to listen to reason. Only fear. And they've made it very clear they'll use force if necessary."

D'Nar watched Toby approach and bow. The show was about to begin. "All is ready, my Lord."

Then Toby turned to Ariel. "You look very beautiful, my Lady."

"Thank you," she replied, returning the bow.

Toby reversed his direction and began walking down the hallway to the dinner. Banners heralding D'Nar's house and lineage graced the walls. Drapes of linen in black, red, and gold hung from the ceiling.

Several I'man pelts covered the floor, a testament to his family's hunting skills and prowess. Most families were proud to have one.

As they approached the doors, D'Nar said, "Our guests are already seated." He could hear the sounds of their voices.

"Sendara explained."

"Good," he nodded. "I didn't get a chance before, but I'd like to apologize for this afternoon."

"There's no need."

"I'd like to explain, but I think, by the end of the evening, you'll understand."

She frowned. "Don't," he continued. "We must show them we're united. They'll only respect our cause if it's strong."

"I understand," she replied.

He watched her take a deep breath and square her shoulders. He did the same as a thrill of pride ran through him. "Good. And remember, no matter what, we're bound by choice."

Toby halted in front of two solid doors of nanjir wood. He motioned for them to be opened then stepped aside. A single bell tolled and silence reigned. D'Nar lifted Ariel's hand with his. He didn't look at her for everyone in the room watched them. He sensed many emotions from the crowd, from envy and jealousy at his position and his choice of such a beautiful concubine, to sincere warmth and affection.

As a leader, not all his decisions were popular and he'd made enemies. Nor was his lifestyle universally accepted as it proved to those in attendance what was possible when vampyrs and humans lived together with thought and caring. But Ariel was different. She was the inspiration. A hint of a smile played about her lips and she carried herself with a calm that belied the nervousness her touch conveyed. Her carriage spoke of a self-assured dignity they could only guess at. She walked into the Great Hall as if she'd been born into royalty.

The hall had been designed so that everyone within the room would feel equal. To do that, it was circular and the center tables sat well below the outer ones. The highest ranking visitors sat below their less important counterparts, thus at least, giving the sense of equality.

But equality was more than rows of seats. Would both their peoples be able to learn that?

As befitted his rank and status as host, D'Nar's personal guard lined the path to their table in the center of the hall. As he and Ariel passed each pair of guards, the vampyrs snapped to attention and saluted. D'Nar thought he would burst with pride—for his men—but most of all for the woman who walked so regally by his side.

Once they reached the table, their guests applauded. D'Nar bowed in appreciation then swept his hand to include Ariel. The applause grew even louder and he held up his hands for silence.

"My fellow Viceroy's, ladies and gentlemen of our sister cities, brave soldiers and townspeople of I'stara. I bid you welcome."

He paused, waiting for the ensuing roar to quiet. His gaze swept the room. Who would be friend, he wondered? Who would be foe?

"Our visitors come to I'Stara to take part in a Great Council. We have gathered together to make important decisions. Most of you know that change is the only constant in the universe. We must decide how we will deal with the changes that confront us. But not this evening. Not tonight. Tonight, I ask that everyone set their burdens aside, let go of their duties, their cares, and enjoy the hospitality for which I'Stara is famous. Let the festivities begin."

A thunderous shout of approval rang through the hall. As if on cue, platters of meats, cheeses, breads, and fruits were carried to the tables for the human guests. Tall goblets of wine spiced with herbs and blood were brought for the vampyrs.

Before sitting, D'Nar introduced Ariel to the Viceroy of T'Embra, G'Rakor. The vampyr was shorter than D'Nar, more stocky and solidly built. He wasn't exactly ugly, but the man wouldn't win any beauty contests. Perhaps that was why he walked around with a constant scowl. D'Nar didn't know.

"Viceroy G'Rakor? My Lady, Ariel."

G'Rakor gave a grunt of what passed for greeting. D'Nar frowned, but held his tongue. Ariel was wise enough to do the same. She bowed to the vampyr with a graciousness D'Nar knew that only she could give. "My Lord."

G'Rakor drummed his fingers on the table. D'Nar sat and watched Ariel do the same. He wondered at the man's impatience. "Lady."

No bow. No acknowledgement of her position. That didn't sit well on D'Nar's stomach at all. "You don't drink. The wine is not to your liking?"

The vampyr swept his cup to his lips with what D'Nar could see was very little patience. "Bearable. Certainly more acceptable than that waste of time this afternoon."

The meetings had not gone well. In fact, they'd deteriorated into shouting matches and D'Nar had been forced to end them. He looked down and found Ariel's hand covering his. She gave him a light squeeze, reminding him to relax.

"I fear, my Lord," she began, directing her words to the visiting Viceroy, "that I'm confused. If you knew the meeting was going to be a waste of time, why then, did you travel here?"

D'Nar nearly choked on the swallow of wine going down his throat. Ariel had asked the very question that had been in his mind, the one he couldn't voice. G'Rakor's gaze sliced to him first. To see if he'd planned the question? Then the man pinned Ariel with his gaze.

When he couldn't read her thoughts, he scowled. "You play a dangerous game, D'Nar, using this twit to bait me."

He flicked a quick glance at Ariel. He could see her anger simmering in her gaze and prayed she wouldn't lash out. "I'm a fourth generation healer, my Lord," she answered, her tone filled with pride. "I pray you never speak that way should you find yourself in need of our services. You might find that the knife that heals can also tear open the wound."

The man snapped upright in his seat and for a moment, D'Nar feared he would have to intervene. "Do you threaten me, woman?"

"G'Rakor," D'Nar warned in a stern whisper. "We might not agree in council, but I have asked my guests to come here in peace. Sit back and at least try to enjoy yourself."

The man snorted and threw himself back into his chair. He scowled even more, if that was possible, and D'Nar knew being chastised didn't sit well with the vampyr. "Do you ever worry, D'Nar?"

"About what?" he asked, confused by the question.

"That she'll use one of those knives on you? Perhaps, as you sleep?"

D'Nar was about to answer when he was silenced by Ariel's burst of laughter. "Obviously, my Lord, you know nothing of healers then. We take an oath, an oath we would rather die than break. And that is to heal all who need us. All," she stressed again.

"Then why did you threaten me?" G'Rakor asked.

"Threaten, my Lord? Nay. You heard what you wanted to hear. I was merely reminding you that the road to healing could either be more or less painful, depending upon how you wished to travel it."

D'Nar wanted to both beat and then hug Ariel. She'd made G'Rakor aware of his arrogance and his prejudice, while walking a very thin line between socially correct behavior and insolence.

G'Rakor's face turned a mottled red with anger. He knew he'd been bested in the conversation but not how. "You live to serve my needs, human. Never forget that."

D'Nar put a warning hand on her arm, but she shrugged it away. "You're right," she agreed, surprising D'Nar. "I do. I took an oath to do so. Just as I took an oath to serve everyone in this room. I'm no more a threat to you than a cow in a pasture, my Lord."

"On the one hand, you're right," G'Rakor sneered. "You're food. And when I'm done with you, I can throw you out like the slops you feed your pigs." Ariel's gasp cut through him like a knife. "But on the other hand, the cow doesn't think. You do. And that makes you infinitely more dangerous."

Indeed, D'Nar thought, glad the Viceroy understood at least some of the problem that confronted them.

"What is it that frightens you, my Lord?" his concubine asked, her voice barely above a whisper. "The thought of what we can do if pushed? Or the truth of what we are?"

"Truth?" G'Rakor asked. "What truth?"

"That we are your superiors."

"Ariel," D'Nar cried, wondering if the woman wanted to start a war right at his table. "Enough."

G'Rakor had stiffened at the insult. D'Nar watched as the man's gaze turned deadly. "I could snap your neck with my bare hands."

D'Nar growled at the threat as Ariel fired back. "That's your answer to everything, Viceroy. And you're not to blame for it. You were born to be this way. You know only one response to danger and that is to attack, to fight, to use force. You cannot comprehend a middle ground. Until you do," Ariel paused for effect, "you flirt with disaster."

"The only disaster will be your own, woman. I do not accept threats."

"I wasn't threatening you, my Lord. Only attempting to make you understand that brute force won't win."

D'Nar finally realized what Ariel's game was. And he wondered. Had she agreed to live with him to win her point? Her eyes filled with a terrible sadness and tears she would never shed, as she read the truth in his gaze.

"Yes, it will," G'Rakor replied, his tone hard as stone.

"G'Rakor, my friend," D'Nar began even though they barely tolerated each other. "My concubine is young. And perhaps a bit too daring in her new position. I'll make sure she's properly schooled."

He turned to Ariel. "Leave us."

Her gaze begged him to understand. He couldn't. He was vampyr first, lover second. "You would embarrass us both?"

He nodded, steeling himself from the pride he felt. Even now, when she'd lost, she still refused to apologize. Nor would she back down, holding herself tall with that regal assurance that was so much a part of her. She rose from her seat and said, "Very well, my Lord. I bid you both a good evening."

The room grew quiet as she walked up the ramp to the door, then the din started again. Many curious glances came his way along with what he was sure were plenty of whispers.

"Your emotions will get you killed one day," G'Rakor told him.

D'Nar bit back a hard reminder that it was G'Rakor's refusal to accept change that would get them all killed one day. He took a long pull on his wine before answering. Ariel was right to plant seeds. If doubt could reach G'Rakor, surely others would listen.

"My concubine may be young and impetuous. But

she's not stupid."

G'Rakor snorted in disdain. "She showed me what the human's are going to do. If you ask me, that was very stupid."

No, you fool, D'Nar wanted to shout at the man. You've missed the point. Completely. "G'Rakor? What makes an I'man so dangerous?"

The vampyr looked surprised by the question. "I'man's are predators. Carnivores. Hunters. They kill instinctually."

D'Nar shook his head, a deep sadness filling his soul. The vampyr had missed the point again. "No, G'Rakor. What makes an I'man so dangerous is his cunning. He'll take you down when you least expect it."

"What's your point, D'Nar?" the man asked, obviously tired of word games.

D'Nar sighed, already knowing he was fighting a losing battle. "The humans are our I'mans."

****

Ariel paced inside her chamber as she waited for D'Nar. She'd never expected to breach the structure of their society, let alone make her ideas known to one of her fiercest opponents. G'Rakor was vampyr through and through. She'd wondered if he could be swayed at all. She had her answer. And more importantly, so did D'Nar.

"You have a strange way of showing your loyalty, Ariel."

Ariel whirled at the sound of his voice. Her heart somersaulted in her chest. She wanted to run into his arms and hold him, be held in return. But that wasn't possible now. They both knew she'd overstepped several boundaries.

"I thought I was being most loyal," she replied, hoping to repair some of the damage of the evening. "You now know where G'Rakor stands. And I fear most of the other Viceroy's will say the same in varying degrees."

"I already knew that from the Council."

"Did you?" she asked quietly.

His eyes widened as the truth hit home. "You embarrassed me in front of my entire city."

Ariel sighed. Vampyr first, Viceroy second. Lover came somewhere down at the bottom of the list. "I did." She lifted her chin in defiance. "They're your rules, not mine."

She'd caught him off guard, by his expression. "This afternoon we pursued a course of action together. This evening you were thrilled at the progress you'd made to bring about change. Now you seem to have created some kind of fence and made us adversaries. Why? What happened to overcoming our differences together?"

That hurt. "*Our* differences, my Lord? You never defended me to G'Rakor. You took his side. Your side. The side of who you are. You need to live your own words, not just speak them."

His gaze narrowed. "What do you mean?"

"That the rules of society are *your* rules—vampyr rules. Made by those who have the power. You see, I'm not so sure that what I did *was* improper. Except to speak truth to a man who would just as soon discard me like a piece of garbage. To tell him that I live and breathe. That as a living, breathing being I deserve respect."

"Of course you do. I've been trying to get the Council to understand this."

"But you couldn't do that in private, could you? He insulted me as much as I did him."

"To make him a solid enemy serves no purpose. You must work inside the rules we have now. You must act with proper behavior."

"Really? And what is proper, D'Nar? What could generations of vampyr rules mean to humans? Why should we care?"

"Because that's what has to be. Change will come,

but it has to come slowly. You can't expect a vampyr to learn to eat an apple by ramming the entire thing down his throat."

"But it's alright for me to swallow them whole every day, day after day."

She could see the frustration building within him, but if she could just get him to understand. What an ally he would be. "Perhaps we can all learn to become one society again," he answered. "But this cannot happen all at once and certainly not by making each other choke on the opposite point of view."

"You keep telling me change has to take time. And that's true. It does. But you're a vampyr. You come from the position of power. At some point, you must realize that humans have power, too. We can fight back, you know. I'm not saying that we will. But we can. And that had better terrify you," she warned.

"And should terrify you as well because we'll all lose in the end if there's a war."

Yes, she thought, a terrible sadness growing within her. "Think about this long and hard, D'Nar. If there's a war, who has the most to lose? Vampyr or human? That's the real question."

Chapter Twelve

An intense weariness overcame D'Nar. He wasn't exactly sure where the evening had begun to deteriorate, or when. But now, he was standing in the middle of a microcosm of their world. "I must feed. Do you wish me to go elsewhere?"

He watched her blanch. She hadn't expected him to ask. Could there be no softening between them? As much as D'Nar wanted to say yes, he was still a vampyr and his first priority was his life.

She bowed her head. "No."

She walked up and opened her neck to him. He bent down and licked her skin, the taste bittersweet in his mouth. Where once he'd shared all of her, now a piece was missing. An important piece. At first he'd thought it was her pride. And that he could understand; pride was an integral part of his being. But it was more.

She stood still as a statue, her body stiff and unyielding. He knew she wanted him. He would always know. They were bound together.

So, he thought, it's anger. He could understand that as well. He was trapped by the way of their world, which made change all the harder. She was angry that he couldn't simply snap his fingers and be exactly what she wanted him to be.

Yet there was more. He kissed his way up and down her shoulder, a sure-fire way to excite her. She flinched as if he'd hurt her.

D'Nar drew back. He tried to snare her gaze with his, see what was wrong. But she wouldn't look straight at him. Instead, she stared somewhere at the middle of his chest. He grabbed her chin and brought her face to his. She fought him every inch of the way. In the end, he was forced to let go lest he mark her skin.

Confusion slammed into D'Nar. He'd never taken blood from an unwilling participant before. And he didn't know how to make her willing.

Ariel kept her face averted and D'Nar decided to try another avenue. He nuzzled the line of her chin and licked the rim of her ear. He blew softly. He waited for her to shiver. She didn't.

He doubled his efforts. His fingertips floated across the soft crown of her breast. He opened the bodice just as he pictured he would the moment he saw her in this gown. He parted the material and teased her nipple into a tight hard nub. She seemed to steel herself against him.

He wanted to cry out that she was being unfair. He wanted to protest that this wasn't his fault, that he was as much a product of their society as she was. Then he realized. The important piece that was missing was her heart.

In that instant, he became two people. Almost like their races. Vampyr and human. His vampyric side drove him, urged him on, and made him plunge recklessly into the icy waters of her soul. His human side knew better. His human side knew that the more he pushed, the more he would hate himself when he was through. Because she would hate him. Lust was not love and feeding should never be purely animalistic. Remorse was the one emotion he wasn't allowed to indulge in.

Still, he couldn't stop.

He licked his way down her neck to the soft skin of her breast. He bit down on one creamy globe just enough to draw blood and feed. Sanity flew from his mind as his thoughts turned to the river that was her life. And the lust that was for her and her alone.

"Come with me, Ariel," he whispered. "Ride the mountain storm."

Her head swiveled from side to side in answer. "No."

"I must have you."

Sadness radiated off her in waves. "Then you must."

"Damn you, this isn't my fault," he snarled, rearing back to look down at her.

"Yes, it is."

"What do you want from me?" he cried.

"Everything."

The one word he couldn't fight against. He started to challenge her, to force her to make a choice. He'd asked her to let him go to another and she'd refused. He was within his rights to call for Sendara or any other concubine in his house.

But her gaze caught his and he knew how much he'd hurt her if he did. And so they were both trapped. Ariel wanted him to change everything he'd ever known, everything he'd ever believed in. He was asking her to give him time when there was no more time to be had.

Somewhere, there had to be a middle ground. But they wouldn't find it tonight. The blood lust was on him and would not relinquish its hold over him. He leaned over and opened her throat to his mouth.

"Only if you are willing to give everything in return," he whispered. Then he sank his incisors into the flesh of her neck.

****

Sweet river of life, Ariel thought as her insides ignited. She tried to think of herb lists. She tried to recapture the hurt and anger of G'Rakor's prejudice. She failed. Miserably.

A burst of pure pleasure streaked from her breast to her brain as his fingers pulled on her nipple. With each beat of her heart, each suck from his mouth, her

114

life flowed into him. Wrong or right, they were bound by the non-quantifiable. They were bound by blood.

From that blood bond, there could only come great joy or great sadness. He refused to hurt her. No matter their differences, she knew he couldn't be cold or unfeeling.

Instead he made love to her, not as a concubine, but as a wife. With all the equality the word possessed. She'd told him he couldn't live up to his words. Perhaps not in public, but here, behind closed doors, Ariel became his equal.

The dam burst and Ariel couldn't stop the surge of excitement racing through her veins. Her hands laced around the back of his head, pushing his face harder against her flesh. He growled and his arm became a steel band around her back. Closer. Closer. Until finally they met hip to hip, thigh to thigh.

Their bodies writhed in a dance as old as time. Ariel didn't even notice when her dress fell from her body. She let go of his head and raked her nails down his back. He growled again.

And she waited. She waited for his kiss. When she didn't feel his lips against hers, she opened eyes that she hadn't even known were closed. Her blood darkened his lips and, as she drew nearer, she could smell the nutrients that fed him.

"This is what I am, Ariel."

"I know."

His mouth engulfed hers. She tasted him, she tasted herself, and she knew this was what was meant to be. For now, it was everything. They were together.

He released her for a moment, ripped off his clothes, and nuzzled her hair. Her hands slid over the smooth contours of his body, the rock hard muscles of his back, the rounded curve of his thigh, and she marveled at his strength. She bent her head and listened to his heartbeat, knowing she made that possible. Her heart, her life, ran through his veins.

Their power, together, made the fight worthwhile.

Ariel turned her head. Her lips kissed the muscular expanse of his chest. She licked his nipple into a tight pebble then did the same to the other. She worked her way lower and lower until she reached the V of his hip. He jumped as she nipped his skin with her teeth.

A small thatch of hair grew at the base of his manhood and she ran her fingers through the strands, amazed at how soft they were. In every way, he was built the same as a human man, except for his strength and his need for blood.

Her fingers traveled the base of his rampant member and lightly caressed his balls. He growled a third time, knowing she was playing with him. He wasn't a patient man and his fists knotted at his sides as she explored.

Was this her way of reminding him of the true balance of power, she wondered? Perhaps. She certainly reveled in the ability. Each breath across his distended flesh, each well placed lick, each fleeting touch reminded him that she might be on her knees worshiping his body, but that without her, his life was empty.

Ariel licked the tip of his erection and tasted the salty fluid resting there. He jumped and groaned. His hand rested lightly on her head, urging her to do more. She smiled. He needed a lesson in patience first.

Instead of going down on his impatient length, she withdrew and went back to the crease of his hip. She made him spread his legs a little, lightly cupping his balls. His hips flexed, seeking some kind of satisfaction for the poor piece of his flesh she deliberately ignored.

"Ariel," he begged.

She took the entire length of his erection down her throat. His breath caught in surprise. He had what he wanted. Or did he? She knew he didn't dare move. She could feel his orgasm building. And that was not where either of them wanted to share their fulfillment.

He pushed her shoulders back with his hands. An impatient in-drawn breath told her he was through with her game. He swung her into his arms and half-threw, half-fell onto the bed with her, spreading her legs and thrusting inside her soft, wet flesh before she could form her next thought.

He spread tiny kisses all over her face. His arms pushed against the cushions with each of her hands clasped in his. Every inch of his body covered hers. His heart beat on top of hers, two halves of a whole—the earth and sky, always joined, always needing each other.

"Ride the mountain storm with me," he whispered in her ear.

Helpless to refuse, her hips met every thrust. Intense pleasure radiated from her core through her entire body. Lightening cracked. Thunder rumbled. She cried out as he shifted and the entire length of his cock rubbed against her nub. He thrust harder. Faster. The storm came upon them as storms always do, with an unexpected ferocity.

Ariel reached the mountaintop a moment before D'Nar. She screamed as her orgasm burst through her entire body. His cries echoed hers a moment later.

And no matter what their differences, what they'd just shared proved they could forgive each other almost anything.

****

When Ariel awoke, D'Nar was gone. She wondered if there would ever be a time of balance between their two races. Then she smiled as the thought of everyone settling their differences in the bedroom crossed her mind. It would be fun to try.

Ariel paused a moment before rising. D'Nar was a wealthy man, yet he didn't flaunt his wealth. The walls of his bedroom were made of stucco tinted a light cream color. The colors of his house had been woven into a large rug in front of his bed. The linens were cream, red, and black, masculine enough for him but soft enough for her. She would have to see if she could brighten the room a bit more, she thought with a smile.

Lifting up out of the bed, Ariel's stomach lurched. The room swam. She fell back against the pillow and took several deep breaths. She frowned. There was nothing more ironic to her than a healer getting sick.

She tried again. She moved slowly this time and waited in a sitting position until the room steadied. Then she realized she hadn't eaten since yesterday's morning meal. Angry with herself, she called out.

"K'ara. Thank you," she said as the young woman entered the bedchamber.

"My Lady. Are you all right? You're as white as a ghost."

"Yes," she replied with a smile. "Just being foolish. I didn't eat last night and my Lord..." The young woman didn't need to hear any of the details.

"I understand, my Lady," K'ara replied. "Some fruit, I think. Then meat and cheese. And tea."

Ariel nodded, although the thought of food didn't excite her as it should. "Yes. Thank you."

As she waited, she wondered at the fatigue she felt. She should be more lightheaded and less lethargic. But as the door opened, her stomach growled, so she accepted that as the answer.

She got the surprise of her life when she saw Sendara enter carrying her tray.

"Are you well, Ariel?"

The question held many more inside. She read genuine concern in Sendara's gaze and her heart swelled. She was lucky to call this woman friend. "You heard what happened."

Sendara set the tray down on a small table next to the bed and then nodded. "News travels fast, gossip even faster. Was he terribly angry?"

"Yes and no."

Sendara frowned. "You risk a great deal. D'Nar isn't one to be played with."

"I'm not playing."

"I know." Sendara motioned for her to remain in the bed and Ariel nodded. "And I applaud your courage. Not many would stand up to G'Rakor. But you must also know how dangerous this is. For all of us. Right now our lives are balanced on the fine edge of a knife. Violence won't solve anything."

"You know that and I know that. G'Rakor doesn't. Violence seems to be an intricate part of how a vampyr reacts; it seems to be their answer to problems they can't solve. They need to see that violence can't be the answer to this problem," Ariel insisted.

Sendara sighed, sat, and motioned for Ariel to eat. "I don't know, Ariel. I just don't know."

Then the elder woman poured them both a cup of tea. The liquid was warm and soothing and settled her stomach instantly. "K'ara told me you didn't feel well this morning. Although I know D'Nar is not a brute, I wanted to make sure you were unharmed."

She grimaced. "I'm a healer, Sendara. I've seen what happens when vampyr passion gets out of control. But I thank you for your concern. As you said, D'Nar is not a brute."

Ariel bit into a juicy piece of fruit. Sweetness ran down her throat. She finished one then devoured another. And another. Then she polished off several pieces of rare beef and a solid chunk of cheese.

She looked up to find Sendara staring at her in horror. Embarrassed, she muttered, "Forgive me, Lady. I haven't eaten since yesterday. I was famished."

Sendara didn't reply. She rose and quickly made sure the doors to the room were closed and no one was nearby. "What's wrong, Sendara?" Ariel asked, totally bewildered by her friend's behavior.

"Does D'Nar know?" the woman burst out, fear

radiating from her gaze.

"Know what? What are you talking about?"

Sendara shook her head, her countenance changing from fear to disbelief. "You're a healer and you don't know?"

Confused, Ariel replied, "Know what?"

"When was the last time you went through your monthly cycle?"

Ariel stopped dead as a hollow pit of dread drilled deep inside her stomach. She hadn't counted. She hadn't had to count. D'Nar was the only man she'd been with and—

No, what Sendara suggested was impossible.

Ariel started laughing. "Sendara, you of all people should know that what you're suggesting cannot happen. Vampyr and human cannot mix."

Sendara didn't answer and Ariel realized where the woman's thoughts were going.

"Sendara. Don't even think about going there. You know D'Nar. I know you haven't known me a long time, but I would hope you know enough of me not to let the thought enter your mind. I would never betray him. Ever."

"Not even to have a baby."

Ariel shook her head, her tone undeniable. "Not even to have a baby."

"Then you must forgive me. The impossible cannot happen, the possible did not happen. Therefore, I made an incorrect deduction."

But Ariel's mind raced far ahead of Sendara's words. She counted and knew the truth. The impossible could happen. In a glade full of power. Was this the answer to their world? A thrill of hope ran through her heart followed by an intense sear of fear. If someone like Sendara couldn't believe, how would D'Nar?

"Sendara. What I tell you now is the truth. The choice is yours if you want to believe me or not. D'Nar is the only man I have ever been with."

"Then what I thought cannot be possible."

"You don't believe me," she said, more sad than angry with her fellow concubine.

"I love D'Nar with all my heart," Sendara replied, her tone proud yet laced with hurt. "I gave everything I had to him. But I can't fault him for who he is and he was always honest with me. He never truly loved me back."

"You're wrong, Sendara. He does love you."

The elder concubine sighed. "In his own way. Perhaps. But I've never seen him act the way he does with you. I want to be jealous, but I can't. You belong together. Anyone with eyes in their head can see that. Which is why I won't let you betray him. You must get rid of the baby."

Ariel gasped in surprise. Then she stared at Sendara, long and hard. "What I'm about to tell you, you must not share with another living soul. Do you understand?"

Then Ariel explained about the glade and the dream she and D'Nar shared of the Before Time. "Do you really think it's possible?" Sendara asked in a hushed whisper when Ariel finished.

"Yes, I do. There has to be a way back, Sen. A way back to The Before Time. A way to become one race again."

Sendara shook her head at her, a terrible sadness filling her gaze. "He'll never understand, Ariel."

In spite of all she had to lose, her heart soared inside her chest. A baby. A child made from love. A child made from the best of both of them. The beginning of a new and wonderful being. "Yes, he will," she insisted. "He'll have to."

She watched Sendara shiver. "He may have to, but others won't."

"That will take time," Ariel agreed. "More time than a truce, I fear. But it will happen."

"Because you say it shall?" Sendara asked, pity filling her gaze. "I don't know, Ariel. I think of all of us, yours will be the longest, hardest road to travel now."

Ariel lifted her chin. Her hand covered her belly. What she hadn't shared with Sendara was that their world was about to come full circle. She hadn't told her of the letters they'd found in the Great Library. That their race had once been all human and that vampyrs had evolved out of necessity. Or that an even greater menace threatened them all. Could it be that this child she carried was the answer to the silent enemy that now plagued them?

No matter what it was, Ariel's first priority was to make sure they both stayed alive. For as much as the child could be viewed a savior, the baby was also a threat—a threat that would not be taken lightly.

"That may well be, my friend. But it's the road that will save us all. I just hope we can get to it."

"I hope so, too, Ariel. With all my heart, I hope so, too."

Chapter Thirteen

D'Nar held up his hands for silence. Even the faint breeze coming through the open windows seemed to still. He looked at each of the men sitting around the Chamber table. Decisions needed to be made. Without words, he asked each of the Viceroy's if they were up to the task. Search your hearts for the truth, he pleaded in silence.

"My fellow Viceroy's. We are the leaders of this planet. The people, *all* of the people, look to us to protect and defend them. Yet somewhere along the way, we've lost sight of that responsibility. I can't berate any of you, for I, too, fell victim to this lack of vision. However, we can't allow personal feelings to guide us any more than we can let a few isolated instances of violence rule us."

"My Lord?" Viceroy O'Dala asked as he stood. "If I may?"

D'Nar bowed and sat down. "Of course."

"As clearly as one can see things under the circumstances," O'Dala began, bringing a few good-natured smiles from the other Viceroy's because without his glasses, O'Dala was nearly blind, "we have a very pressing problem, an as yet un-named threat that can destroy not only a lone vampyr, but a group. Most distressing. Most distressing." The elder man paused. "This threat should be our first priority."

G'Rakor rose. O'Dala bowed and returned to his seat. "To fight an enemy, you must know your enemy. Whatever the threat is, the humans are behind it. Of that you can be certain."

D'Nar rose. G'Rakor scowled, but by rule was

forced to sit. "What if they aren't?"

O'Dala rose. D'Nar gave way. "How can that be?" he asked.

D'Nar watched the others nod in agreement. He rose, knowing it was important to be careful here but very clear. "Without emotion, let's go over the facts. In order to overpower a vampyr physically, more than one human would have to be involved. Are we agreed on that?"

Even G'Rakor nodded. Good. "You may question any of my men. Perhaps you already have. They'll tell you we found no sign. Of anything. Only of vampyrs. At each place of attack, only vampyr signs."

D'Nar took a deep breath and let the air out slowly. "This is the most puzzling piece, for we are born hunters. We are taught to track from the moment of our first steps. We can smell the scent of any being—animal, human, or vampyr—before we see them. So I ask all of you. How is it possible that one human, even several humans, could overcome three young male vampyrs, tear out the throat of one, and yet leave no sign?"

All right, he had their attention. "Gentlemen. Think on this a moment. Wouldn't they have seen the threat coming? Even drugged? And if that's not enough, how would a human tear out the voice box of a vampyr?"

"What about an I'man?"

Frustrated at the lack of vision the question reflected, D'Nar bit out, "We found no sign. None."

"Then we chase a phantom," G'Rakor snorted with disdain.

Now for the moment of truth. "Perhaps."

The Viceroys looked at him in surprise. "Or perhaps an ancient evil come back to haunt us."

G'Rakor burst out laughing. "You expect us to accept an old wives' tale as an excuse?"

D'Nar shook his head. "Not an old wives' tale and

not an excuse. Only food for thought. What I'm asking is that you all open your eyes and accept that there may be another possibility, another explanation for what is happening that will fit the facts. And for now, I'm not asking any of you to do more than focus on those facts. If you don't do that, then all you're doing is looking for an excuse to start a war."

D'Nar waited, his heart beating hard in his chest. If these men couldn't accept another possibility, then how would they believe the scrolls he and Ariel had found? He dared not show his peers these tomes until they were ready to believe the writing within them.

One by one, he read each Viceroy's countenance. They were evenly divided. "I propose a compromise. We cannot maintain martial law forever. Both races will revolt if we do. Therefore, I suggest that we keep the curfews in place for travel outside the cities, but advise that we lift the restrictions inside and allow life to go on as normally as possible. No one travels outside a city without an armed escort of at least six soldiers. No one travels overnight unless they travel with a trade caravan. All trade caravans must be accompanied by no less than two companies of soldiers."

Everyone at the table nodded in agreement. The traders would grouse at the expense, but safety was paramount. "I also suggest anyone caught outside a city after dark be subject to public arrest and punishment."

Again, everyone agreed. Then G'Rakor rose. D'Nar sat, knowing he'd done what he could for now. "I want the rules of our society enforced if a human threatens a vampyr."

"Are you willing to make that judgement?" O'Dala snapped, his concern so great that he didn't bother to rise from his seat.

G'Rakor nodded with smug satisfaction as he sat. "You threaten to create a breach that will tear our world apart," D'Nar warned, rising and sitting.

"I disagree," G'Rakor replied, not even bothering with protocol. "We've grown lax lately. Word must get out that proper respect will be shown or there will be consequences."

"On an individual basis?"

"Yes."

"With a tribunal of human elders and vampyrs?" D'Nar asked, trying to keep the pleasure of besting his opponent out of his voice.

D'Nar had him there. G'Rakor couldn't refuse. A tribunal was the only fair way to judge. "Very well," the man groused.

Not bad, all things considered. A tribunal, even a sham tribunal, would help. But deep in his heart, D'Nar feared this was simply the beginning of a plan to enslave the humans on their planet.

"I also ask for a group of hunters. The very best from every province. Let them see if they can find any clues to these attacks. They'll also represent a combined effort on our part to see to the safety and well being of all our people."

Each Viceroy nodded his assent. Even G'Rakor. "Then I thank you all for coming to these meetings. May your journeys home be safe and swift."

D'Nar was surprised when G'Rakor didn't leave with the others. He stared at the man a long time before asking, "Yes?"

"Victories may be small, but they are still victories."

"So you think you've won."

The other vampyr shook his head. "There will be order, D'Nar. One way or another."

"Order? Or slavery?"

"I care not what you call it. The humans will know their place or they will die."

D'Nar felt his heart drop to the floor. "So will you."

G'Rakor simply shrugged. "If that's what's

necessary, so be it."

"Can there be no compromise, G'Rakor?" D'Nar asked, already knowing the answer.

"No. Not until order is restored."

"Whose order? Yours or the people's?"

"They are one and the same."

They weren't, but G'Rakor would never understand that. "I pray you don't destroy us all in the process. Be careful what you wish for Viceroy. In the end, you may find it's not what you really wanted." D'Nar bowed. "Good day."

With a heavy heart, he watched the other vampyr quit the room then left as well.

****

Toby paced in the anteroom outside the Council Chamber. Too much time, he thought. They should have come to some kind of decision by now.

When the door finally opened, he jumped. The Viceroys filed past him, several talking amongst themselves. No help there. However, D'Nar remained inside. Then G'Rakor swept by him, a scowl marring the man's dark features. No help there either. Finally, D'Nar emerged, intense weariness on his face.

"The meeting didn't go well, did it?"

He watched D'Nar shake his head. "What happens now is out of my hands, Toby."

Alarmed he asked, "What do you mean? Will they—" Toby couldn't finish.

"The Viceroys want order restored."

"You mean G'Rakor, don't you?"

D'Nar shook his head again. "Not only G'Rakor."

"Were you able to accomplish anything?" Toby asked, his tone hopeful.

"I asked them to open their eyes and consider the facts. But I have no answer for them. Not yet, anyway."

"What will happen now?" A trace of alarm laced his voice.

"As a start, the curfew inside the cities will be lifted. All travel outside will be under armed guard. Any perceived attack by a human against a vampyr will be dealt with on an individual basis."

Toby's heart sank. "And punishment?"

"There must be just cause."

"And a tribunal?"

"I insisted."

Toby started breathing again. "Thank goodness for that."

They left the building and walked down the street. The townspeople they passed, human and vampyr, nodded with genuine affection as they walked by. D'Nar was an exceptional leader.

"We're on the verge of terrible times, Toby. I'm not sure what the future will hold. I'm counting on you to help me keep the peace."

"I'll try."

As they approached the market square, Toby realized a crowd had gathered. Mostly human. And the vampyrs in the area looked nervous and angry. "I fear our first test stands before us," he told D'Nar.

D'Nar threw him a look before making his way through the crowd. "Is there some occasion that has you all gathered here in the middle of the day when there are tasks to be done?"

"We're not slaves," a voice yelled from the crowd. Several voices murmured in agreement.

Toby watched D'Nar take command of the situation immediately. "Did anyone say you were?"

A young man came forward. He swept his arm out over the crowd and pointed. "You all believe it."

Toby admired D'Nar's ability to remain calm and his desire to keep the peace. G'Rakor would have arrested the young man without answering. "We do?" D'Nar asked. "Where did you hear this? Did a vampyr come up to you and say you are my slave?"

"No. But we live to serve."

"And you think we, as vampyrs, live to be served."

Toby recognized the young man who had the courage to speak up. "Jacob, listen to me. D'Nar is a just leader. He fights every day for freedom for all of us. He keeps no servants, pays all of the humans who work for him, and creates an atmosphere of respect and affection within his household. And, I hope, this city. We're fighting to keep it that way."

The young man bowed with a sneer. "Thank you, *my Lord.*"

Toby watched D'Nar's face tighten. "Go back to your homes," D'Nar commanded. "The Viceroys have agreed to lift martial law inside their cities as well as the curfews. Only travel outside the city will be restricted. For *everyone's* safety. Notices are being posted now."

Toby glanced around the square, certain D'Nar had done so as well. Although his announcement had eased some of the tension, most of the people were still angry and all of the vampyrs had their hands close to their swords.

Jacob bowed. "We live to serve."

D'Nar and Jacob faced off in a battle of will. They stared at each other long and hard to see who would back down first. Toby already knew who the winner would be. D'Nar would never retreat.

It didn't take long for Jacob to recognize that as well. He shifted and dropped his gaze first. But the young man lifted his shoulders and his chin, not afraid to stand up for what he believed in.

Toby shifted his gaze to D'Nar. The vampyr was smiling. He gave Jacob a nod of respect. Jacob started as if not believing the gesture then nodded in return.

The crowd, realizing the moment was over, began to disperse. Then a scream of terror rent the air.

****

D'Nar skidded to a halt in an alleyway just a few buildings away from the marketplace. He closed his eyes to the scene before him and spread his arms wide to stop everyone from following. He turned to Toby. The man's skin held a grayish cast and the same horror D'Nar felt filled his features.

"Keep everyone away from here. Have my soldiers stand guard if you must."

"P'Lat. M'Car. With me." He turned to the young man that had caused the unrest in the market square. "Jacob?"

"Yes."

"Let him through as well, Toby. Keep everyone else back."

As they approached, he ordered, "Search for clues. Search for signs. Tell me what you see, hear, smell."

Jacob gasped. The scene wasn't pretty. A woman lay on the ground, broken as if she'd been thrown there by a careless child. They could all smell the blood. Her throat had been torn open. Just like the others'.

"I brought you here so you could see, Jacob. So that you would know. The decisions made by the Council are for the welfare of the people. All of the people. Whatever did this is dangerous and powerful. Now do you understand?"

The young man nodded and swallowed hard. "Go," D'Nar continued. "Tell your friends that we do what we must for a reason."

He watched the young man leave, wondering if it was wise to let him go. Then he turned his attention to his men. They were circling the body on the ground carefully. M'Car started to scan the area around the perimeter, while P'Lat approached the body.

The woman was human and had been quite pretty before her throat had been torn apart. He shuddered at the thought of the death she'd endured.

"My Lord. Look." P'Lat pointed to the body.

D'Nar frowned. All he could see was the devastation. "At what?"

P'Lat hunkered down on his heels next to the body and closed the woman's eyes. Too bad, D'Nar thought, that young Jacob had not seen the respect his soldier gave this woman.

"Doesn't she seem pale to you? Very white?"

D'Nar nodded. "I suppose so. Some concubines are prized for white skin."

"No, Lord. That wasn't what I meant."

"What's your point?"

"The blood in a body falls to the ground after death."

"All right. But I'm not a healer." He turned and called to Toby. "Find my Lady Ariel and bring her here. I have need of her."

Toby seemed surprised by the request, but bowed. "Right away."

M'Car approached. "There are vampyr and human signs all over the alleyway. Many tracks. Most of them are old. Some are new. Some may have been made by the dead woman, but it's very hard to tell. Too many for me to be sure."

"Anything else? Any other kind of sign?"

"No, Lord. None that I can find."

"My Lord," P'Lat called. "Come take a look at this."

P'Lat was still next to the body. He had lifted her shoulder and rolled the body to one side. Then he pulled up the woman's shirt so they could see that the skin of her back was stark white. The same as the rest of her. The only blood left anywhere was the blood on her neck.

"Whatever or whoever did this drained her dry and left her to die."

M'Car knelt down next to P'Lat to take a look. D'Nar joined them, keeping his tone low. "You must both remain silent about this for now. I cannot keep order if people fear for their lives. We just lifted the curfew within the city. This horror will enforce the need for caution, but could also create a panic. Please, be discreet."

D'Nar rose. His soldiers followed. "P'Lat. Get word to S'Nec. Tell him to send two patrols back to the city. Whatever did this may now be targeting I'Stara."

P'Lat saluted, turned on his heel, and left. "M'Car. It will take at least a couple of days for the patrols to return. Organize your men into shifts. Everyone travels in pairs. We'll split the city into sections— North, South, East, and West. Each section must be patrolled day and night. Full armor."

M'Car grinned. "The men will grumble about that."

"Let them. They grow soft. I've been too lenient lately."

M'Car saluted, turned, and left the alley.

D'Nar looked back down at the dead woman. *What enticed you here,* he asked silently? Could there really be such a thing as a shadow demon? *Did you see what took your life?*

How he wished the dead woman could talk.

He whirled away, unable to stand the sight before him any longer. Fear churned inside his belly. Then anger took its place. This was his city. *His* city. A menace outside these walls, that D'Nar could barely accept. But inside? He felt violated. He turned away from the alley entrance and cursed under his breath.

Where the hell was Toby? Where the hell was Ariel?

He needed her. Just to see her face. She lifted him up, kept him steady, and gave him strength. Her smile filled him with hope. Her belief in him made him feel invincible. The simple touch of her hand made him feel whole. He needed her.

D'Nar heard footsteps approach. He listened with a sinking feeling in his stomach. Dread filled his guts as terror threatened to collapse his knees. Only one pair of feet approached.

He whirled and faced Toby, his emotions clear for the man to read. Toby blanched, swallowed, and took a deep breath, letting the air out in a rush. Toby handed him a note with Sendara's writing on it.

"She's gone," he whispered.

Chapter Fourteen

Even though she'd expected no less of an entrance, Sendara started as the doors to her outer chamber were thrown open. She still sat at a small writing table. She hadn't moved since writing the missive to D'Nar.

D'Nar marched toward her. For a moment, she wondered if he would truly lose control. His face had hardened into a tight, tempered mask. But what broke her heart was the question in his gaze. He couldn't understand why.

Sendara couldn't tell him.

"Where is she?" he bit out. "Where is Ariel?"

"I don't know."

His face tightened even further, if that were possible. "What happened?"

"Nothing."

"Did you fight? I know she's made mistakes. But she's young."

"No, D'Nar. We didn't fight." Sen could have reminded him that he'd made mistakes as well, but that reminder wouldn't have been appreciated at the moment.

"Then what happened?" he cried. "Something must have happened."

"I don't know."

"You must know something," he sneered at her.

Taking a deep breath, Sendara met his gaze straight on. She told him a portion of the truth. "I'd been told Ariel wasn't feeling well. I went to your chambers after you left to see to her welfare. She told me you'd been angry with her, that you may have taken a little too much of her blood."

D'Nar winced at the memory. "Did she say anything else?"

"I don't know what you're looking for so I can't answer. We talked about things women talk about."

He was in her face in a heartbeat. She reared back in surprise. His hands gripped her shoulders so tightly they hurt. "I know you, Sen. You did more than just talk about my prowess in the bedroom."

Sendara shook her head with a sad smile, one it seemed, he would never understand. "You poor fool."

She pushed him back, astonished when he let go. He raked his hand through his hair. "Something you said made her flee."

Sen rose and walked to a small side table. She poured herself a cup of water, extremely grateful that her hands didn't shake. The liquid slid down her throat and cooled the ache in her belly. But nothing would ever quench the ache in her heart.

"Something I said? You seem to think I made her feel unwelcome or unwanted. Or that my jealousy pushed her to do something rash."

He raised a brow as if to say 'you didn't?' "You've never been mine to fight for," she told him.

"Then why did she leave?"

Stubborn vampyr. "You don't want an answer to that question because your vanity won't allow it. Did it ever occur to you that she may not want you?"

"No," he fired back. "She left because something happened. What happened, Sen?"

"I don't know," she insisted. "I left her in bed finishing her meal. I went to oversee the clean up from the festivities last night. When I came back to see how she was, I found her gone."

"Weren't you angry that you didn't attend the festivities?"

Although she couldn't tell him everything, she knew that honesty was best. "Of course," she replied.

"You've been set aside for some time now. That has to be a thorn for you."

Sendara laughed. "You haven't been listening, D'Nar. You set me aside a long time ago. Long before you met Ariel."

He whirled to face her. "Tell me the truth," he shouted.

So proud, this vampyr, she thought. "All right. You want the truth?" she shouted back. "Here it is." She took a deep breath, letting the words out in a rush. "You're arrogant, pig-headed, self-centered, and vain. Why anyone would want to love you, I don't know. But people do. And that's made you think that you can simply snap your fingers and get what you want."

She took another deep breath. "Worse, though, you believe the world revolves around you, how *you* feel, what *you* want."

She watched him take her verbal blows without moving a muscle. His lips compressed into a thin line, while his jaw worked. But in his gaze, she read confusion and frustration.

"Help me understand, Sen."

The truth hurt, but she was impressed that he wanted it all. "Just now, you thought like a vampyr. You accused me of being jealous. I can't help that any more than I can help loving you. I know you don't love me back. But I'm human. And being human allows me to do both."

"What do you mean?"

Ah, now I have your attention. Good. "Love and hate at the same time."

He thought about that for a moment. "I don't understand."

She sighed and tried again. "As a man, you think in one direction—you see, you possess, you conquer. As a vampyr, that process is ingrained in your cells. You track, you hunt, you capture. And once you capture, you keep. Look at the I'man skins gracing these floors and walls."

"I am what I am, Sen."

"I know," she replied. "But you can change."

He was listening. Thank goodness for that. "How?"

"Don't try to possess her. She isn't a thing. You can't capture her and keep her like a prize."

She watched him struggle to comprehend. "What you're telling me, then, is that I have to be willing to give her up, to let her walk away from me, if I truly love her."

"Yes."

"Aren't you doing the same for me?"

"Yes." Sendara gave him everything she had inside, hoping it would be enough. "I love you with all my heart. I always will. The truest testament to that love is standing here and letting you go. You belong with Ariel, not with me."

He gave her a sad smile, not one of pity, but one of regret. "There's a menace out there, Sen. I have to find her. There was another attack. Right here in the city."

Sendara gasped. Fear knotted her insides. But she had no right to intervene. "Search your heart, D'Nar. You'll find her."

"I hope so." His whisper came out like a prayer.

Sendara hoped so also. She set the cup down and squared her shoulders. "There's a small house in the eastern section of the city."

"Yours, and anything more you desire."

Except the one thing I want above all else. "Thank you."

"I'm sorry I couldn't love you, Sen."

An apology? From a fierce vampyr warrior? A Viceroy? Perhaps D'Nar was learning after all. "We shared many a night, D'Nar. I have my memories. And new ones to make."

He smiled, remembering too. "Yes."

"When you find her, remember what I said."

"I promise."

Her heart breaking, Sendara walked up to him and opened her neck. "You'll need some. It may be a while before you get any more."

His mouth quirked. "You may be right. My thanks."

He would never betray Ariel, so she knew there would never be anything else between them. "Should you find someone to share your life with, he will be a very lucky man. I wish I could have been what you wanted."

Tears dripped down her cheeks to be noticed later. "No, D'Nar. You've been more than you could ever know."

He bit her skin and the blood pulsed from her neck in bittersweet spurts. There was a scent to him that was like a match to her tinder. The idea that her life was giving him life—that she would always be a part of him—swelled inside her chest. Her nipples grew into tight pebbles. Jolts of desire streaked straight to her core.

Fate, it seemed, had other designs for her. Her hand slid down her belly. She was still as trim and beautiful as the day she caught his eye in the marketplace. His touch still fired her blood like no other.

Her fingers found her core. Sweet heaven, she thought as his lips sucked at her neck. Her thumb circled her clit. Her finger plunged in and out of her moist heat. She climbed the mountain of pleasure with him one last time. With one last sane thought, she captured this moment to be brought out like a treasure in the future. His scent, the way the light danced in his hair, the rock-hard muscles that held her so gently. And Sendara exploded, her juices flowing over her hand, bereft and satiated at the same time.

He stopped drinking and buried his face in her neck for a brief moment. When he pulled back, she caught his gaze and knew he'd never be hers again.

She gave him one swift hug in farewell.

****

D'Nar faced two problems, his heart and his head. His heart urged him to leave immediately. His head ruled otherwise. But time *was* of the essence. Ariel's scent was strong, all around him, painfully reminding him of questions only she could answer.

He strode to his chambers, a man with a purpose. Then he caught sight of her brush lying on a table. A single red-gold strand twined around the bristles. He picked the hair up and held the prize up to the light, marveling at its color. His stomach twisted into a hard knot. Her sign was everywhere.

He believed Sendara—to a point. She might not know why Ariel left, but she did know him. His behavior was no different than any of his kind and that was why he could find no fault with the way he'd acted. But as Sen had pointed out, he had reason to change.

He also knew Ariel was smart enough not to remain in the city. There was no doubt he'd find her if she did.

D'Nar pulled out the oldest of his hunting clothes and put them on. He untied his hair, stepped into a pair of scuffed boots, wrapped a cracked leather belt around his waist, and overlaid the entire outfit with a dark cape and hood. Gone was the princely Viceroy. In his place stood the best hunter in I'Stara. His only concessions to wealth were his knife and sword. Both gleamed with polish and care, so he hid them under his cloak. Besides, if anyone asked, a soldier making his living by knife and sword would keep them in the best condition, as these were the tools of his trade.

He made his way down to the cooking area, waiting until hallways were empty and footsteps couldn't be heard. But now, he faced his first real challenge—how to get hold of a couple of water skins without being seen. He was lucky no vampyrs were around, they'd have smelled his presence a mile away. But humans didn't have that ability. Several women worked flour at a large table, a couple of young men turned spits of meat over a roasting fire.

He remembered sitting in this very kitchen when it was filled with laughter and happiness. Now the workers talked and teased, but he sensed an underlying tension among them, a sad testament to the times they lived in.

He waited until almost no one was in the room, then crossed through the passageway to a smaller storage room. Waterskins hung on the wall on a row of hooks. He took three, then hurried toward the stables. He passed two soldiers, kept his head down, grunted a greeting, and weaved a bit so they would think he'd consumed too much wine. He saluted, sloppily, and they saluted back. He could hear their laughter and one's comment that he'd done the same on many occasions.

To get out of the city, he needed to get to the stables. His horse knew his scent and would smell him if he got too close. But, again, his luck held. A lone animal stood tethered outside the barn, obviously waiting for a rider. Him. He mounted swiftly and rode through the back entryway into the city. There he purchased several sacks of grain and a basket of grass as any other soldier might do, placing them over the horse's rump and tying them into place around his belly.

His next challenge was to leave the city unnoticed. D'Nar hoped to join a caravan leaving the city and slip out with them. He remembered, vaguely, that one was due to leave this day and prayed they would not delay their departure.

As luck would have it, he arrived just in time. He drew his horse next to a group of soldiers and nodded in greeting. Since all caravans were now required to hire guards, his presence wouldn't be questioned. He kept his head down and again used the ruse of too much wine. The other men called out a couple of teasing comments, then left him alone.

Since he had no idea how she'd left the city, he would have to search the walls to find Ariel's exit. But leaving with a caravan presented several obstacles— he wouldn't be able to follow Ariel's scent until he got outside the walls and he wouldn't be able to search those walls as a soldier guarding the caravan. He did have one advantage, though. He didn't think she'd used a gate for that would be the easiest way to get stopped. .

So his first task was not to get caught outside the city breaking his own rules. If he were caught he would, and should, face the same punishment as anyone else. This meant he would have to wait until after dark to search the walls.

Stealth would negate the use of his horse, so he needed to pick a gate and search that one first. The main gate faced South and he'd ordered a full company of his men to guard it. D'Nar was certain she wouldn't use this gate for fear of discovery. Which left the other three directions. North led into a vast desert, which only hunting parties would cross. The trade route to the North led East first through E'Lict, O'Dala's province, then to the North. No, he said to himself. She went West toward the mountains. He was certain of it.

So D'Nar left the city with the caravan, heading for E'Lict. He waited a short while then began to pat his cloak then mutter in disgust. When one of the other guards asked what was the matter, he replied he'd left his favorite knife at the House of A'San, a well-known house of courtesans. He told his compatriots he was going to go back for it and with a hard ride would catch up to them later. They reminded him he wouldn't get paid if he stayed in the city, but they all knew the temptation was great and laughed as he left.

But D'Nar didn't head all the way back to the city. Once he was out of sight of the caravan, he made for the mountains to the West. Then he hid in an outcropping within sight of the city, huddling between two boulders, sheltered from the constant bite of sand and wind. The rounded stone, even though it had been worn smooth by the wind, dug into his back as he tried to rest. Here he was forced to wait until the yellow sun set.

The red sun never would.

Stars topped the night sky before he finally felt safe to move. He gave the horse a handful of grain and left a small mound of grass for him to eat, then sprinted across the open plain in front of the city. Once close, he dropped to his belly and slithered across the sand, just as he would when hunting an I'man. He became one with the sand and no one could see his approach.

He timed his movements for when the guards on the wall were farthest away from him. When they came close, he stilled his heart so they couldn't hear it beat. He took no breath until they turned and walked the other direction. He used his senses to find her sign and caught her scent in the middle of the wall.

He found an ancient gate built within the wall; the hinges were rusted and pitted from time and the elements. It was locked, but he found small footsteps nearby. The sand had been swept smooth in front as if the gate had recently been opened then shut.

D'Nar followed the footsteps as they headed toward the mountains. Bending down close to the ground, he used the light of the red sun to study the impressions made in the sand. Small in length, narrow. A woman's sandal made these marks. The prints were only a couple hours old since they hadn't been torn or shredded by the wind.

He was surprised that Ariel knew about this gate—he was one of the few who did. Then he concentrated, asking himself where she might go. As he leaned his hand against the gate, a picture flashed in his mind.

Urgency filled him. D'Nar had to get back to his horse. She was headed for the glade where they'd first made love.

Chapter Fifteen

Ariel bit her lip, uncertain as to what to do next. All of her thoughts had centered on escaping the city and reaching the glade. Now that she was here, she took a deep breath and waited.

Nothing happened.

Fool, she admonished. Why would you expect anything else?

The silence only fueled her determination.

"A will can be strong, but a fire keeps the body warm," she muttered.

Because of the pool in the glade, plants and trees grew in abundance nearby. A set of boulders on the outskirts of the glade beckoned. They would protect her from the wind and hopefully make an animal attack less likely. So would a fire.

Ariel set up a ring of smaller rocks and gathered thatch and dead leaves as tinder. She struck a spark with her fire stone and blew gently until a small flame flickered, adding twigs and sticks until her fire blazed. She was glad for the warmth and set about gathering larger sticks and wood to keep it burning through the night

Once she had her fire going, Ariel unrolled two blankets. One covered the ground, the other would cover her. She sat down, nearly at the end of her energy, unused to walking all day. Her feet hurt, her muscles were tired, and a fierce pang of hunger reminded her that she hadn't eaten since the mid-day meal. Although twice as hungry, she only ate what she'd rationed. But the water from the pool was available, and she filled the rest of her belly with it.

Funny how tired she felt, yet how alive her mind had become. She'd left because she couldn't test Sendara's loyalty any more than she could D'Nar's. She feared, though, that in the coming days, many would find themselves in that very position.

So easy to be right and yet, at the same time, so hard.

To chose a side meant creating the very rift Ariel wanted to avoid. How, she asked herself? How would they come to terms with telling each other the truth? Could she compromise any more or any less than D'Nar? Ariel shook her head. The real question was, were they willing to try?

Her hand crept over her abdomen to cover her belly. A child. A wondrous gift. An unexplainable gift. Created in love and magic. Here in this very place. She tried to imagine the child, black hair or red-gold? Brown eyes or green? Tall and straight like his father? Would he be a healer like his mother or as great a hunter, as great a leader as his father?

Would he be the answer to their prayers? Ariel fell asleep hoping so. And she dreamed.

Mount C'eres. That is the key to survival.

Ariel heard the words, but she wasn't sure she really heard them.

"Welcome, child."

Confused, she rubbed her eyes. Was she dreaming? She must be dreaming. She could hear but not see the form speaking to her. All she could make out was a shimmering vapor. It was as if she was awake yet asleep at the same time. A waking dream.

"Who are you?" Ariel asked.

"I am one of The Elders. The true Elders. From The Before Time as you call it."

Ariel gasped in wonder. "I never really believed."

"Yes, you did. Otherwise you wouldn't be here. Certainly not in this condition."

"You brought me here, didn't you?" Her fingers

145

splayed wide over her belly. "Did you give me this child?"

"Yes, we made it so."

"Why?"

"Your world is on the brink of destruction."

"Our races are too far apart for them to become one now."

"Perhaps, perhaps not. That will remain to be seen. But no matter what, love holds the answer."

In that moment, Ariel realized what she'd been fighting was mostly herself. "Vampyrs cannot love. They don't know how."

"Then you must teach them."

She laughed. "One at a time?"

She could swear she heard them laugh as well. *"You'll see."*

"And my child?"

This time Ariel was certain she heard a sigh. *"What was done cannot be undone. To survive the terrible effects of our decision, your ancestors had to remain underground for countless generations. Vampyrs are the result. You will never be as we were then. But a blending of your races will eventually lead back to one people born of both."*

"What about the shadow creature? What about war? Your answer will take as many generations to fix as it did to create. We need to repair the damage caused by your decision right now."

This time, she could swear one of them smiled. *"You will, my child. You will."*

****

D'Nar reached the glade closer to the sound of two than one, judging by the star set in the sky. He followed the scent of her fire and found Ariel sound asleep, sandwiched between two boulders. She had a slight smile on her face. He jumped down from his horse, relief flooding his body and making it sag against the saddle. Then he allowed himself to be angry.

D'Nar ripped the bridle off his horse and tethered the animal in the grass. Safe and sound and asleep, he groused, while he was tired, filthy, and wondering how he was going to explain his absence if they were caught. Not to mention getting caught by other things, like a shadow creature.

Damn the woman. How did she manage to get under his skin? He stomped back over to her fire and bent down, intent upon waking her. Before he could touch Ariel, he found a dagger at his throat. If he'd been less angry with her, he'd have appreciated her ability to defend herself. Then he thought of the woman in the marketplace.

"Easy sweet."

"D'Nar?" She sounded sleepy and confused, reminding him of the morning he'd awakened her under far different circumstances.

He wrapped his hand around hers and made her lower the knife. Then he checked his throat for blood. "At least you sleep prepared."

She frowned, apparently still not quite awake, and rose to a sitting position before leaning her back against the rock.

"I'm accustomed to traveling on my own."

"I keep forgetting that you came to me an independent woman. The women I'm used to don't travel without an entourage."

Of course, he acknowledged to himself, that was one of the problems. She was human, but carried herself more like a vampyr. And he wasn't sure how to react to that.

"What are you doing here?" she asked, frowning and crossing her arms in front of her chest as if she wasn't exactly sure what to read into his presence.

"I have several answers to that question. Which one would you like to start with?"

"Sarcasm won't solve anything."

But it makes a man feel a whole lot better. "Agreed."

He stepped closer to her and she shrank against the wall. She seemed almost wary of him, something he'd never seen from her before. "How did you find me?"

Aside from being scared out of my mind for you? "Foolish question. I'm the best hunter in I'Stara." *And you're in for a serious beating when I get you home.*

"Why did you leave?" he asked, countering with a question of his own.

"Sendara didn't tell you?"

He shook his head. "She told me she didn't know. She wouldn't change her story. Which makes you a very lucky woman. Sen is a loyal friend."

D'Nar hunkered down closer to the fire and warmed his hands. Best to keep them where they could both see them, otherwise he might be tempted to forget about waiting until they got home.

"But I think she knew all along," he continued. "So I'll ask again. Why did you leave?"

His gaze raked up and down her body. God, Ariel was so beautiful. The firelight roared in her hair, dazzling the eye. Her heart-shaped face had become so familiar to him. She tantalized, constantly toying with the limit of his patience. But her true beauty, the piece that drew him like a moth to the flame, came from within.

"Something inside me told me to come here."

He frowned. "I understand the symbolism. This is where we first made love. And perhaps you felt this was where we could re-kindle that spark between us without outside pressures tearing us apart. But you have no idea what you've done. The Council decided to publicly punish anyone caught outside the city after dark."

She looked contrite as she apologized. "I'm sorry."

"But I haven't even touched the real issue," he bit

148

out, fear feeding his anger. "We found another body inside the city. This time it was a woman, a courtesan, a human courtesan. Whatever this thing is, it doesn't discriminate with its victims. Only this time, the carnage was worse."

She seemed to sense the pain and anger and frustration roiling in him because she didn't lash back. She simply asked, her tone sad, "Worse than having your throat torn out?"

He nodded as she shivered. "She was drained dry." Seeing the tiny 'o' her mouth made gave him no pleasure. "So as you can see, I have many reasons for being here, not the least of which, is to give you the beating you so richly deserve."

"You can't."

D'Nar's anger skidded to an abrupt halt. "Excuse me?"

"I said, you can't."

Oh, this was good. Really good. How she was going to talk her way out of this? "And who, pray tell, is going to stop me?"

Although her gaze never left him, she didn't seem frightened. She should. "I am."

"And exactly how are you going to do that?"

She straightened her back and lifted her chin, showing him that regal inner fortitude he admired so much.

"By telling you I'm pregnant."

****

Ariel found her fingers wrapped around the hilt of the knife. Would she have to use it? His face registered only shock at the moment.

There was an unknown factor when dealing with a vampyr. Even though they treated humans as animals, in actuality they were much closer to animals than a human could ever be. Some, like G'Rakor, disdained the veneer of civility. Others, like D'Nar, embraced it. But what made vampyrs what they were, was that unknown factor. Pushed to the limit, a vampyr would kill without hesitation.

It was that thrill of imminent danger that had fueled her fantasies as a young girl. Faced with that danger now, she had no idea how to handle it.

Had she pushed D'Nar beyond his limits?

He lunged at her, gripped her by her upper arms, and hauled her into a standing position before she could take her next breath.

"By whom?" he snarled.

Ariel breathed an inner sigh of relief. Although she'd carry bruises for days, she was going to be all right. "D'Nar. Let go. You're hurting me."

He looked down at his hands as if he had no idea how they'd gotten there. Then he let go as if burned. "We've been together nearly every moment of every day, except when I was in Council. Where did you find the time?" he sneered.

Ariel rubbed her arms to ease the pain. Her knees buckled and she half-slid, half-fell back into a sitting position. D'Nar started to reach out to break her fall then caught himself.

"I didn't."

He raked his hand through his hair in disbelief, pushing the strands off his face. "I know the act can be performed without desire. At least tell me there was no pleasure in it for you."

She shook her head. He closed his eyes as if she'd stuck a dagger in his heart.

Ariel had absolutely no idea how to tell him the truth. Then she faced the daunting task of making him believe her. But she refused to lie.

"The child was conceived in love."

His body jumped as if she'd delivered a physical blow. "Was there someone you cared about before we met?"

"No."

He opened his eyes and shook his head. His gaze

held a world of hurt inside. "Don't lie to me, Ariel. Not now," he bit out.

So their relationship had come down to vampyric pride. Well she had pride, too. "I have never lied to you, D'Nar. I never will. I'm not lying to you now. Can you try to believe that?"

His expression turned to one of astonishment. "Our whole relationship has just become a lie and you can ask that of me?"

Proud, stubborn, vampyr. God, he was magnificent. But she was going to ask exactly that of him and a whole lot more.

"I haven't been with another man, D'Nar," she insisted.

He barked out a bitter laugh. "Then perhaps you expect me to believe another woman, say Sendara, for example, made you pregnant."

"There's no need to be crude," she shot back.

"There's every need," he exploded. "I want the truth and I want it now."

"No, you don't," she shouted back. "Because if you did, you'd open mind and your heart and you'd listen."

He ground his teeth together in frustration. "I'm going to ask one last time. Do you understand? One last time. Who's the father?"

"You are."

Chapter Sixteen

He started laughing and once he started, D'Nar couldn't stop. He laughed so hard his body began to shake. He fell to the ground, slapping the earth with his hand. He laughed so hard, tears came to his eyes.

D'Nar would never let her know why he cried.

He sobered slowly, wiping his eyes. Emptiness formed a hollow pit in his stomach. "I don't know what to say. Really, I don't."

Ariel's gaze never left his face. She watched his reactions intently. She had to know how much this hurt him. "D'Nar—"

"No, I'm dead," he paused, taking a breath and her eyes widened. "Seriously. I have no idea what to say. You see, that has to be the most original answer to this kind of betrayal that any woman has ever uttered."

"I'm telling you the truth," she insisted. She leaned forward as if her body could force her words into him.

He shook his head. A black hole seemed to be expanding inside him. He peeked over the edge of the pit and drew back, terrified of the loneliness there. "Ariel, you're a healer. You of all people know that a blending between our races is impossible."

"It's not."

He rolled his eyes. "If you'd come to me and told me you wanted a child, I admit, I would have been hurt. Terribly hurt. When you made your decision to be bound to me, I thought you realized the commitment that bond entailed. But I would like to believe that I would have understood in time. I hope. For a man can never really understand a woman's need to nurture. But to run away? To lie like this?"

"I didn't run away, D'Nar," she explained. "I came here because I had to, I was compelled to. I dreamed again. Of The Elders. Mount C'eres holds the key."

"The Elders? You expect me to believe that? This is your excuse?" A knife of white hot pain stabbed through his heart. "We shared a night of fantasy, of lovemaking so sweet it can never be repeated. But that's all it was, Ariel. Simply fantasy."

Shocked disbelief filled her features. "But what about the scrolls?"

He raked back his hair with both hands. "I'm not denying The Elders existed. Or that our planet is what it is because of what they did."

"At least you believe that," she interrupted, her tone dripping disdain.

"Yes, yes I do. Written words cannot be denied. Neither can countless centans of fact. Vampyrs and humans have never produced a child. Ever."

"Until now."

He stared at her. "Stubborn fool."

"Am I?" she asked. "Why can't there be a blending of the races? Why can't we be the ones?"

"Because it is impossible!" he exploded.

"No, it isn't!" Ariel fired back.

"End this charade now," he commanded.

"I can't. It's the truth."

"The truth is," he barked back, "that you wanted a child. Now you have one."

"Our child."

"Never," he hissed, pride clawing up through the emptiness. "I will never accept a human child."

"He won't be human. He'll be half-vampyr."

"Damn you, woman, will you stop? I won't hurt you. I promise. But lying, it's pointless."

"I'm not lying."

D'Nar wanted to throttle her. "Saying a thing won't make it so, Ariel. No matter how much you want it." Then a realization struck him. Of course. That had to be it. What else would explain her behavior?

"Your mind is confused. You've obviously wanted this to happen so much between us that you've lost sight of reality. I'm flattered."

He watched as her face flushed red with anger. "Flattered? Why you egotistical bastard. The next thing you know, you'll have me smoking Tarba and playing the k'ettes in a guarded room. I-am-not-playing-mind-games. I-am-not-crazy."

She enunciated each word for emphasis, but D'Nar was tired of listening. He'd had enough. She was his concubine, he was responsible for her. And more importantly, he was responsible for her behavior.

"In the morning," he began, his tone tightly controlled, "we will return to the city. You will accept public punishment for being outside the city after curfew. I will accept public humiliation for allowing my concubine to run away."

She gasped, but didn't answer, so he continued. "I understand your heart, Ariel. But there were proper ways to do this. We have rules that must be followed."

"Rules?" she threw back at him. "Yes, of course. Allow the woman to have her baby. Keep her happy. Send her away for a time so her shame is hidden. Let the baby live with relatives, but nearby, so the great, almighty vampyr can have the best of both worlds."

"The rules of society cannot be broken. They keep order. That's the proper way to handle this situation and has been for a very long time."

She shook her head at him, her gaze sad. "And you wonder why humans want to revolt."

"When the child is born," he told her, ignoring her remark and her bitterness, "I'll decide whether or not to allow you to return to my household. In the meantime, I'll see to your welfare."

"All neat and tidy and pushed under the rug," she accused.

"As society dictates."

"Your society," she spit out.

"Yes, mine," he replied, finding no comfort in it.

Ariel shook her head. "I never thought this day would come, D'Nar. I always believed you were different. But you aren't. You're just like them. But you know something? You're worse. Because you make people believe in something you aren't. You put on a show, a veneer, that you want equality for everyone. But there's only one place that true equality resides."

"Where's that?"

"In your heart."

****

Ariel dozed for a time, listening as D'Nar moved about the camp. Then she heard him unroll a blanket and spread it upon the ground. She waited for what seemed like forever until she was certain he was asleep. Then she forced herself to move very slowly so as not to make a sound. D'Nar might be exhausted, but he would wake if she made a mistake. She'd made her bed on one side of the fire, he on the other, crying silent tears as she tossed and turned. His attitude had torn her heart to shreds and even the glade couldn't comfort her.

Why, she wondered. *Why are you making this so difficult?*

She couldn't come close to an answer. But she had to hold on to her faith. The Elders knew what they were doing. They had to. Besides, this wasn't about Ariel anymore. Or D'Nar. No, this was about the child she carried in her womb and the future of their world. This was about demolishing the very attitude D'Nar had spewed at her in all his vampyric arrogance.

Ariel lifted her pack ever so carefully and turned to look at him one last time. He seemed so innocent in repose. His hair fell about his face in chaotic perfection, framed by one arm wrapped above his head and the other across his chest. He was so beautiful.

Yet a sword gleamed in the firelight next to him, hammering home with startling clarity exactly who and what this man was.

As disappointed as she was in him, she couldn't blame him for his attitude. The hardest challenge she was going to face was trying to change an attitude without changing the man inside.

She wasn't sure it could ever be done.

Yet how magnificent the possibility was.

The Elders said that Mount C'eres was the key. The mountain had saved their race, sheltered them while the cataclysm broke apart a sun and destroyed an enemy. Why? So they could be reborn.

Could The Elders have foreseen what would happen? Could they have known that living inside the mountain for so many generations would cause two races to be born? Ariel didn't think so any more than she thought they would have wanted the schism to occur.

But a question nagged at her. Living inside a mountain *had* caused them to split apart and there *was* a schism between them. So what made The Elders correct now, she wondered? She watched D'Nar sleep and her heart melted. Did D'Nar have any less right to exist as a vampyr than she as a human?

She sighed, her hand caressing her abdomen. Did her baby have any less right to exist now than either one of them?

The answers were all no. Inside, Ariel knew The Elders were responsible for what had happened physically, not socially. Prejudice and bigotry were their sins alone to atone for.

She could only hope the lesson wasn't so painful that they ended up killing each other first.

That goes for you too, she told the prone body lying on the ground.

She stared at him a long time, trying to engrave his countenance into her soul. Then she realized he already resided there.

I love you, D'Nar. For better or for worse, through all the trials the heavens can throw at us, I love you. Someday, perhaps...

Ariel shook her head and crept out of their encampment. She went to the pool, filled two waterskins, and drank until she could drink no more. She wasn't sure how easy it would be to find water again. The knowledge that it existed at the moment were the twin rivulets making their way down her cheeks.

****

D'Nar awoke to a pain in his back and a sense that something was very wrong. He opened his eyes, thinking he'd dozed for a short while. He expected to see the darkness of the night sky mixed with the glow of the red sun. Instead, he found the yellow orb above the horizon, mocking his expectations.

He lifted his head and reached behind him to remove the rock he was lying on. Then it hit him. Ariel was gone.

Damn the woman.

He bolted upright, ready to run to his horse when sanity prevailed. But he had to wonder. Was she fey? Didn't she understand the danger she was in?

He drew in a deep breath and tasted the air. Her scent lingered, but by the remnants of the fire, he knew she'd left long before dawn. She might have a large head start, but he'd have no trouble catching up to her on horseback.

And then what?

D'Nar walked over to the pool. He filled a skin then doused the embers of the fire. Using his boot, he scattered the ashes and mixed them with dirt. Then he doused the mixture again. Once he was certain the fire was out, he returned to the pool, refilled his skin, and cut as much grass as the basket would hold.

Did she do this on purpose?

D'Nar wasn't sure what irked him more, her stubborn refusal to see the danger she was in or her blatant disobedience. He mounted his horse knowing the sour knot in his stomach was from both.

Her footprints led toward the mountains. He followed at a normal pace, almost certain of her direction, but dared not go faster in case he lost her trail. Once he caught up with her, he vowed, she—

He pounded the pommel of his saddle in frustration. Damn it, he was the Viceroy of his city, responsible for its entire population, and he couldn't even control one woman, his very own concubine.

He couldn't imagine what would happen when the people found out.

Ariel was his responsibility in every sense of the word. If they managed to survive this insane farce, he would be required to mete out punishment. Then he would be forced to relinquish his leadership of I'Stara.

A man who cannot control his house cannot control a city.

Taking a deep breath, D'Nar forced himself to stay calm. He kept his focus on the trail. His first priority was still their safety, for he wasn't arrogant enough to believe he was in any less danger than Ariel. And that was what confused him the most. She'd seen the damage the shadow creature had wrought, yet her actions defied the reality of their situation.

He shook his head, bending down to scan the ground. There. He sighed with relief. He'd found her footprints again.

Ariel was a healer. She hadn't even blanched at the sight of C'Cin's throat. She'd barked out orders to his men with so much authority, they didn't question her directions but jumped to do her bidding.

Ariel was one of the sanest people he knew. Why was she talking about dreams and physical impossibilities?

He had to admit that she couldn't have picked a

better one.

D'Nar pulled his horse to a halt. He looked up to the horizon. Mount C'eres loomed large in the distance. He shivered. His memories of the place were not fond ones.

Young and full of the fire of his vampyric blood, D'Nar had looked forward to his first hunt. He'd counted the days in anticipation until eventually he was sitting on a horse right before the mountains. His heart beat high in his throat, but he held himself straight and tall in the saddle.

He had wanted to make his father proud of him.

At first he'd stayed with the men, following signs as he'd been taught. But then he noticed that the tracks led in a different direction. He was so intent on tracking the animal that he forgot just how cunning it was. The I'man had doubled back on him. The hunter became the hunted.

Terror clawed its way through his belly as he faced the animal. He swallowed hard, but dared not call out. He drew his knife and faced down his enemy, staring into bottomless black eyes. Funny, but in that moment, he almost felt a kinship with his adversary. The I'man only wanted to live free.

They circled each other several times before the animal sprang. They fought for what seemed like forever, but was probably only moments. Then, the animal lifted its head as if it were listening. It reared back and, for a reason he would never understand, bolted away. D'Nar told himself it was because his father was searching for him. But the truth was that he had no idea how much time passed before he was found. All he remembered was that he felt no pain from his father's embrace against his wounds, only remorse at the terror in his gaze.

The hunting party never found the I'man that attacked him. Nor had he seen the animal since in the many times he'd come to the mountains to hunt. But he had a feeling it still lived.

Just another reason to find Ariel and bring her home.

He shivered again. Her trail led between two smaller peaks and up toward C'eres. Soon he would have to walk his horse because the way ahead looked as if it would become too steep to ride. From what he could see in the far distance, there seemed a place where she would stop—a small gouge in the mountain that offered a large ledge and shelter from the wind. She would be able to light a fire there. When he caught up with her, they would have this out between them once and for all. Then he would drag her home, even if it meant tying her to the saddle. But not until he punished her. As she had punished him.

Chapter Seventeen

Tired and hungry, Ariel stopped to rest a moment. She sat down on a boulder, took off her boots, and rubbed her feet. She drank no more than a mouthful of water, not knowing where she would find more.

While putting her boots back on, Ariel wondered if she'd truly lost her mind. She'd placed not only her own welfare, but also that of her child in the hands of a dream. She didn't want to doubt, but there was so much at stake.

What if she was wrong? What if there were no Elders? What if this was simply her mind trying to project her deepest desires?

She knew D'Nar would follow. So that put not one, not two, but all three of them at risk.

For a fantasy?

No. She had to have faith. With every step into the unknown, her belief would be tested. Then it hit her. She'd only thought of the child in her womb as the answer to the bitterness stealing the life from their planet.

But she suddenly realized that she'd just become the mother to a new race.

A fierce determination swelled inside her chest. She rose refreshed. Her goal was to reach and climb Mount C'eres. The Elders would guide her from there.

The city of I'Stara sat in a desert valley, sheltered by the mountains on one side but subject to the hot winds of the desert on the other. This made the climate of the city hot and arid. But in the mountains and higher elevations, the wind crossed snow-capped peaks. The higher she climbed, the colder it would become.

At first, the climb seemed easy. The paths were clear and the footing was still sand and dirt. But this changed eventually, for now the rocks seemed to sprout from one another. The way narrowed and the path finally disappeared altogether.

Ariel glanced at the sky. The red sun stood ever present. The yellow sun had crested and begun its journey back toward the horizon. She needed to search for a place to shelter for the night. In the distance, she caught sight of a ledge with a natural hollow in the rock. A perfect place to camp for the night.

Once she reached the ledge, Ariel started a small fire using the dried grass and twigs she'd brought with her. That, too, presented a problem. She'd only been able to carry enough wood for one fire. She wouldn't be able to start another tomorrow.

Have faith. The Elders aren't about to let you freeze to death.

She sat down and unwrapped a portion of her food, drank a little water, and wiped her face with a dampened cloth. Feeling much more refreshed and, yes, more human, Ariel sat back against the rock wall and waited for D'Nar to find her.

He entered her camp a short while later. D'Nar didn't say anything, simply went about unsaddling and caring for his horse. He looked tired and, for the first time since she'd known him, unkempt. Checking her fire with a nod, he pulled out a round brown lump which he placed on top of her burning wood. It caught fire immediately, sending up acrid smoke that stung her eyes. But once it began to burn, the smoke cleared, and the fire gave out a good deal of warmth.

D'Nar took his water, gave some to his horse, spread grass on the ground for the animal, then refreshed his hands and face. He pulled a blanket from his gear and dragged it next to hers. Ariel arched a brow at him, but he ignored her.

"Give me your hand," he said, pulling out a piece of twine from his pack.

Not sure what he was doing or why, she said, "No."

Strangely enough, her refusal didn't seem to bother him at all. Indeed, he stared at her, his gaze completely blank.

What have I done?

Without emotion, he walked up to her, hauled her up to a standing position, set her down in front of him, then tied one end of the rope around her wrist and the other around his.

She pulled out her knife to cut the bond. He grabbed her wrist, squeezed, and she stared at him in defiance. He squeezed harder. She winced but refused to let go.

Ariel lifted her chin and set her shoulders. She would be damned if she would give in to him. He simply stared back, his gaze neutral and unfeeling. But he continued to apply pressure to her wrist. She grimaced in pain. He didn't seem to care. Her emotions bounced off him as if he'd become part of the rock they were standing upon.

Her fingers began to go numb. She bit her lip to keep from crying out. Not an ounce of remorse crossed his face.

Finally, the knife fell from her hand.

He let go, picked up the weapon, and pulled her toward his horse. She fought him every inch, digging in her heels and forcing him to drag her every step of the way. He put the knife in a pack attached to his saddle, then yanked her back over to their blankets.

"Now there will be no more running away."

"That's what you think," she sneered back at him.

He smiled without a trace of warmth. Ariel shivered. "Open your neck."

"I will not," she declared.

How dare he! She was not a cow at his beck and

call.

He swept her up into his arms and pushed her down onto the blankets. Contact with the hard ground, as well the surprise, knocked the wind out of her for a moment. But his words startled her most of all as he followed her to the ground.

"You've been complaining about being used as food. Now you'll get the chance to know exactly how that feels."

With that, he sank his incisors into her neck.

****

Caging the beast that raged inside was easy compared to locking away the agony in his heart. As soon as he tasted her blood, he knew the truth of the baby. Ariel was pregnant.

But what truth, D'Nar asked himself? Who was the father?

The question became a stake that kept driving through his chest. With each spurt of her blood, each touch of her skin, with the very scent of her driving him insane, he asked that question.

His was tortured with every vicious detail as he imagined Ariel entwined with her human lover. The beast inside him raged to be freed. He was going to wash away every thought of another man possessing her.

He tore his mouth away. He didn't seal the wound in her neck, but let the smell of her blood feed the beast. He ground his mouth down upon hers, trying to assuage his inner anger. "This is what I am," he growled as she pushed at his shoulders to get free. "This is what you craved when you dreamed of being with a vampyr in your virginal bed."

She tried to hit him. But her actions weren't a denial of anything but the truth. "You can't compare lovemaking with a human to this. This is what your heart beats for."

He bent down and engulfed her mouth with his.

His tongue searched for hers. He knew he had her when they began to mate. "This is what fuels you inside, the danger, the wonder," he gasped as desire streaked through his veins. "You wonder, 'Will he lose control? Will he take me as I want to be taken?'"

He pulled down her leggings, spread her legs, freed himself from his own pants, and thrust into her. Her pussy was so hot inside, so slick, and so ready for him.

"You've wanted this all your life, Ariel. You want the edge, you want the pain and the pleasure, and you want the extreme. You want a vampyr filling your body with his seed, making your insides heave at the sensation. You want to explode in desire."

He pushed into her with an erection like steel; her core felt like a furnace. "Tell me."

Her head twisted from side to side. "No," she moaned.

"You want all of me and more. Don't you? Admit it."

"I—" Her legs wrapped around his waist and her arms around his neck, pushing him to drink more. "Yes, yes," she cried. "Take my blood. Take all of me."

As soon as he bit into her again, she screamed in orgasm. But that was just the first one of many. A moment later she bucked and heaved and screamed again.

He continued to thrust, to pound into her. "Now you understand. No restraint. The beast rages free inside both of us." His body shook with sensation. He kept reaching for the peak, the pinnacle of desire.

He spread her legs, opening her core to him and thrusting into her with a mindless mass of need. He lost sight of whether he was hurting her or not. Her pleas drove him on, pushed him to the limit.

Then the world stopped turning.

A split second later her guttural cry of completion matched his own. He didn't just come, his entire body exploded in sensation. D'Nar poured his seed into her, his orgasm pounding as fiercely as the pounding of his own heartbeat. He drew in a ragged breath and fell on top of her, coming back to earth slowly. Then he rolled away, knowing what just happened would hurt him more than it would ever hurt her.

****

With major explosions, not just aftershocks, still racing through her core and his seed dripping down her leg, Ariel could no more deny he was right than she could stop her next breath. But she never thought he would use her desire for him against her.

Their passion was a testament to his belief that she'd betrayed him.

Her hand wiped at her throat. He hadn't sealed her neck, but her own body had. Still, remnants of his meal smeared across her fingers.

"You keep trying to convince me you're an animal, D'Nar. That you react without thought, that your need for blood somehow debases you in my eyes. And as an animal, I respond to you with an animal instinct of my own."

He didn't respond, didn't even look at her. She pulled his chin toward her, chagrined by the lack of feeling in his countenance. Then she caught it. That tiny hint of remorse in his gaze.

Breathing a sigh of relief, she sat up. Her hand tugged on his to do the same. Then she leaned up against the rock wall. Pride seared through her as the rest of his seed dripped from between her legs. She belonged to him, heart and soul.

Now she faced the daunting task of getting him to understand that.

She turned her head to face him and he seemed to have no control as he did the same. "We've been through the logic and the facts of what you believe has happened and what you think I believe has happened. The end result of which is the child I carry."

She picked up his hand, but he yanked it away. His action hurt, though she hadn't expected him to do anything less.

"But what you don't know is what lies within my heart."

He frowned as if to say he wasn't listening. It didn't matter. He was going to hear the truth.

"You were right, you know. I do crave the danger and excitement of loving a vampyr. I always have. I suppressed my desire because I had a job to do and because the people needed my skills. But you can't suppress what's inside of you forever. It comes out whether you want it to or not."

He snorted in disdain. But Ariel didn't care at this point. She was going to get through that thick head of his if it killed her.

It just might.

"But I'm not the only one with desires. You didn't crave one of your kind the way you crave a human. And do you know why? It's because you can't dominate a vampyress the way you can a human. You'll mate with your own kind, but can never be sure if they want to make love to you or stick a knife in your back. So you turn to us. Helpless human females. But we're not so helpless after all. Are we?"

He didn't answer. He didn't have to. He knew she was right.

"You were attracted to Sendara because she could outthink you, because her logic either matched your own or surpassed it, because her grasp of the intricacies of politics helped you out think your opponents."

Although his face showed no change in his demeanor, she was certain she had his attention.

"But I couldn't figure out why you wanted me. I'm not as smart as Sen; I'm not as beautiful as half the concubines in your home. Now I understand. I'm not frightened of you, D'Nar. The unknown factor, the one that makes most women uncertain or wary of you, makes me desire you even more. And that turns you on. I'm a healer and I represent, in a symbolic way, the opposite of everything you are. And that turns you on even more."

She watched his face very carefully. Although her words were hard to accept, he seemed to be accepting them. Now for the last hurdle.

"You know, though, just as I know, this isn't about sex. It's about love. We just had the most incredible sex. The night in the glade, we made love. You have a choice now, D'Nar. You can either love me or hate me. But this is one fence you can't straddle."

Understand this please, she begged silently. She picked up his hand once more. "I love you. All of you. Your vampyr side and yes, your human side. But I want both. I want incredible sex made with love. I want the strong, animal vampyr with the human tenderness. I want the man who cares with the passion of the beast inside. I want a mate."

She looked down at the hand she was holding and gave the back of it a kiss that came from the depths of her being. "I love you. Now it's your choice to either love me back or let me go."

****

Her words haunted him all night.

He tossed and turned knowing that each tug upon the rope kept her awake. A part of him wanted her to suffer as he was suffering. Then his pride would rush through his veins and he would toy with the idea of letting her go. All he had to do was release her from his care.

Break the bond, a tiny voice inside his head whispered.

He was the only one who could.

With Sendara, the bond died over time, aged into a mutual fondness. She still loved him, of that he was certain, but not to the extent that she couldn't love another. Her heart was still her own.

But with Ariel, the bond had become steel bands weaving their way through his heart. He feared that if he tried to let her go now, he'd bleed to death. Or tear out so many pieces that he'd never repair the damage.

Besides, she loved him.

Lovemaking or sex? Wasn't that the question she'd asked?

He fell asleep knowing the answer. He woke up to find Ariel gone.

D'Nar bolted upright and scanned the area. How? How had she slipped out of the binding? He'd tied it tight enough that she couldn't wriggle her hand free. And he'd taken her knife.

Were they forever doomed to play this game? Hunt, find, capture, flee?

Something strange was at work here. His body thrummed with awareness of her, her scent lingered in the air. He should never have slept so deeply. Her movements, a sound, a breath even, would have awakened him.

D'Nar rubbed his face with his hands. And he wondered. Was her escape any more impossible than her insistence that the child belonged to him?

He rose and wiped a damp cloth all over his face. He rinsed his mouth with a sip of water. He fed the horse some grain, loath to say goodbye, but where he was headed a horse would be useless.

Ariel was climbing high through the passes and up to Mount C'eres.

She'd said, no insisted, that this was where she had to go. She was compelled to follow a dream. Now she was going to get them killed trying to fulfill that promise.

D'Nar released the horse, slapped its rump, and watched it bolt back down toward the glade. The animal would rest and feed there until someone caught it or it decided to go home.

It occurred to him as he re-packed his gear that their life together had distilled down to a test of wills. Her stubborn pride versus his. His sense of right and wrong against hers. And, as strange as it may seem, the more they clashed, the more entwined they became.

Without realization, they were forging together to become steel.

He wasn't sure how or why. He wasn't sure if it even mattered anymore. He had a responsibility to her that matched his dedication to his people. And if that wasn't reason enough, there was one more reason, even more challenging and damning than all the others.

He was in love with her.

Chapter Eighteen

Ariel feared many things: D'Nar's anger when he caught up with her, the alarming rate at which her rations dwindled, the heat of the sun during the day, the cold of the wind during the night, the chance meeting with an animal she might not be able to defend against. But they all paled in comparison to her need for water.

As careful as she was, her never-ending thirst tore at her. Her body had begun to change to accommodate the baby's needs. No matter what she did, the craving never ceased to haunt her.

Was this how it felt? Was this what D'Nar suffered every waking moment of every day? A need that gnawed at the very soul?

How did he stand it? Where did he find the strength of will not to give in? She would hear the slosh of the precious fluid in the skin at her waist and hot juice would fill her mouth in answer. Then she would spend the next hour or two trying to forget what she heard.

Ariel marveled at a vampyr's fortitude. She knew hunger. She'd been in situations where she'd been forced to go hungry. But nothing like this.

Would the baby feel this terrible need too? Tears filled her eyes. She didn't want her child to suffer. But the baby would, she sighed, for it would be part of two worlds not just one. And Ariel knew all too well what kind of prejudice that would spawn.

A steely determination filled her soul. She scrabbled, clawed, and scraped her way up the mountain. She broke nails, cut her fingers, and even gashed the palm of one of her hands. Her legs ached with the strain of climbing over boulders. Her arms trembled from pulling herself up and over all kinds of obstacles.

Yet she never stopped, never hesitated, always continued to work her way toward her goal.

If she had a legacy to impart to her child, this would be it. To never give up hope and to never give up. Period.

The day was not bright and the sun was hard to find among the clouds in the sky. Ariel scanned the area for a place to stop. When she didn't see anything nearby, she continued to climb. Besides, she was nearing the summit anyway. She might as well see what lay ahead.

With a last pull, she swung her legs over the edge of the peak. A breathtaking panorama spread out before her. She'd climbed so high that some of the clouds wrapped around peaks below her. In the distance, the desert stretched as far as the horizon. In the center, she could see the lights of I'Stara and a pang of homesickness hit her hard.

But her way lay in the opposite direction. Mount C'eres. Huge, magnificent, and deadly. A place of hope and uncertainty.

Her destiny. Her baby's destiny. D'Nar's destiny if he chose.

From her high vantage point, Ariel could see that to get to the mountain she would now have to climb down so that she could climb up again. But not too far away, she spied another natural hollow in a rock wall. A perfect place to shelter for the night.

And wait for her vampyr to catch up.

****

D'Nar wasn't sure if he felt like laughing or crying. The scene before him seemed almost comical. Ariel was sound asleep. She'd used a waterskin as a pillow and lay curled up on her side like a child. No fire had been lit, indeed it seemed as if she'd been so exhausted, she'd simply dropped.

Ariel wasn't the only one to carry wood and tinder although the urga, the mountain of dead beetles that graced the desert floor, would burn hotter and longer. The insects were pests inside the city, but their carcasses saved lives during the hunt. Especially now.

Once he had the fire burning brightly, he added a chunk of urga and sat back against the mountain wall. At least she'd found decent shelter. The wind blew and he pulled his cloak tight. Then he looked down at her. If he was this tired, he couldn't imagine how exhausted she felt.

What fortitude the woman had.

He shifted closer to her and used his body to block the wind. He dozed for a while, knowing he would need to wake her soon to feed. The physical exertion of climbing had given him a terrible thirst. And he smiled. There might be some payback, perhaps a spanking for slipping her bonds and continuing this farce.

But resting wouldn't hurt. As long as he kept one eye open for danger.

D'Nar came to as his chin hit his chest. Startled, he made to move then stopped, his senses on full alert. He took a deep breath and tasted the air. Danger screamed at him as the scent of I'man filled his nostrils. He didn't dare move. He sent up a silent prayer that Ariel didn't either.

Otherwise, they were both dead.

He opened one eye a fraction then the other. A majestic animal paced in front of him, its tawny pelt glistening in spite of the darkening twilight. It didn't seem to know what to make of the situation—this meal was simply too easy to eat. It wanted to attack, that was clear. But it wore many winters on its coat judging by the scars. Prudence and caution had gotten it this far; the animal wasn't about to rush into anything.

Yet.

D'Nar calculated quickly. His best defense was to attack now while it paced with indecision. If he could wrestle the beast and wound the creature, he'd even the odds quite a bit.

"D'Nar?"

Damn. The I'man started. It turned toward Ariel. He rolled to his feet, ripped out his knife, and sprang at the I'man all in one movement, landing on the creature's back. He got in two solid blows to the animal's side before the creature shook him off.

It growled in anger. D'Nar rolled to his feet and faced the I'man. They circled, sizing each other up. Out of the corner of his eye, he caught Ariel rise in sleepy confusion. She gasped as she realized what was going on. He sent up a silent prayer that she wouldn't move.

But that gasp caught the creature's attention. The distraction gave D'Nar an opening to attack again. He shifted so that his body was between the animal and Ariel. He charged head on. The animal roared in anger. But with its mouth open, D'Nar was able to press his arm horizontally into the animal's mouth, much as he would slide a bridle into a horse, to keep the I'man from biting him. He was certain his arm would break, even though it pressed against skin and muscle, but it kept those deadly teeth from his neck. With his other arm, he stabbed several times. Once he hit something hard, probably bone.

The beast roared in pain, but D'Nar was the hunter now—a vampyr, a beast capable of defeating a beast. He tackled the animal, twisting it to the ground. He opened its neck and sank his incisors into the I'man's flesh, reveling in the taste of its blood. The creature snarled and rolled from side to side trying to throw D'Nar off of him. D'Nar lost his grip on its neck, but hung on to its body and continued to use his knife. The fresh blood gave him strength and the continuous knife wounds weakened his adversary.

Desperate to get free, the I'man scrambled to its feet and charged the mountain wall. He rammed D'Nar against the rock. D'Nar grunted as the wind got knocked out of him. He let go of the animal and fell to the ground. The I'man sank its teeth into his body, lifting and shaking him in a fit of rage. As he flew through the air and hit the ground, an eerie realization came to him. This was the same I'man that had tried to kill him once before.

But D'Nar was no longer a child. He landed knowing he wouldn't give up his life without a fight, a damned good fight.

Pain screamed through his side and chest. He was certain that his ribs were broken, along with the puncture wounds from the I'man's bite. But he still breathed and, as long as he could breathe, he could fight.

The animal pounced, its jaws wide open to latch onto his neck. D'Nar stared straight into its eyes. He could feel hot, fetid breath, almost like its teeth had already pierced his skin. He could sense the animal thought it was about to make a kill.

With all his might, he stabbed the knife upward and caught the I'man on the soft skin just below its jaw and pushed the knife through its throat.

The animal couldn't scream or cry out. He'd pierced its vocal chords. A terrible rattle issued from the creature as blood filled its throat and lungs. The I'man fell on him, blood gushing everywhere, writhing in pain and slowly strangling to death. The animal's weight began to crush him, so he rolled and pushed until he could crawl out from beneath the carcass, gasping for breath.

But the job wasn't complete yet. The I'man still lived.

D'Nar lifted himself to his knees. Ariel cried out and ran to him, her hands searching his face and body. He pushed her away and motioned for her to bring her cup and a bowl.

The animal stared at him, the light in its magnificent eyes fading.

"Thank you," he whispered, then cut the main artery to its brain.

Blood spurted from the hole. He placed his hand over the gushing geyser and forced the blood into the cup and the bowl. He drank as much as he could then handed what remained back to Ariel with shaking hands.

He looked at her, smiled, and then the world went black.

****

Ariel screamed. She watched D'Nar collapse and fear threatened to consume her. Fear? She hadn't known the meaning of the word until now.

So broken. His body was a mass of cuts and bruises. Blood spattered everywhere.

She didn't want to move him, but he needed the protection of the wall and the fire. Fire? She shook her head. She'd hear about that when he awoke.

If he awoke.

As gently as she could, she washed his face and hands with a damp cloth. Without the I'man's blood all over him, Ariel was able to assess her patient more clearly. She pressed against his side and he moaned. He had a broken rib, possibly two. He had puncture wounds on his side, one of which may have gone through a lung. She would know later if he began to wheeze and gasp as he breathed.

The fresh blood, even though from an animal, had helped him immensely. He'd known how broken he was so he'd consumed as much as he could. Vampyrs never ceased to amaze her. They were able to seal most wounds almost immediately. But they couldn't repair flesh as fast, so he might still be bleeding internally. And bone was still bone. Broken ones still needed time to knit together.

She examined his arms. The one that had been in the I'man's mouth was bruised and torn, but not broken. That was good. No wounds on his legs, no other broken bones that she could find. That was very good.

Ariel now faced another problem. D'Nar was resting and as comfortable as he was going to get for the moment, but she had a dead animal on her hands and the smell of blood was going to attract other animals if she didn't take care of it.

She drained what she could from the animal's neck and set the blood aside to give to D'Nar later. Using his knife, she began to skin the animal. She cut large sections off first then cut them into smaller pieces. Then she took as much flesh as she could get at easily, cut that into pieces, and wrapped the meat in the skin. While she worked, she roasted a large section of the I'man's thigh on a rock beside the fire. Once she'd taken all the meat and skin and blood she could use, she dragged the carcass to the edge of the ledge far down the trail. Although considerably lighter with the meat gone, the animal was still very heavy. She could only move the carcass a foot or so at a time. And she was very glad that she didn't have to go far. Outside the lee of the rock, there was a deep drop. She peered over the edge into a deep crevice.

D'Nar would be angry with her for wasting the I'man, but there were only two of them and he didn't eat. Besides, she had no need of a trophy to mark the occasion. She pushed and rolled the animal until it toppled over the edge.

When she returned to camp, the smell of the roasting meat forced her to stop as she appreciated the tempting aroma. She pulled the meat off the rock and onto a plate to cool. She tore at it, burning her fingers a little, but she was very hungry. With the meat to supplement her rations, she would have enough food to live on for quite a while.

Once she was sated, Ariel took one of her blankets over to D'Nar. She rolled the blanket and placed it next to him, then rolled him onto his side and pushed the blanket underneath his back. Then she let him roll down again. By doing the same to his other side, she was able to put the blanket underneath his body.

Now came the hard part. D'Nar was a fully-grown male vampyr. But she pulled on the blanket and tugged and pulled again as she had with the I'man, until she was able to drag his body closer to the fire. Gasping for breath, she sat down and took a few sips of precious water. He seemed comfortable enough and his breathing was normal. But she was concerned with infection and feared he might run a fever as he healed.

If he did, their lack of water was going to become a real problem.

But for now, they were both alive. And for that, she was very grateful.

****

You never said the dream would be this hard.

We never said it wouldn't.

You can't let him die.

That's up to him now.

Why? Why are you doing this?

You haven't guessed yet?

This trek. You wanted to see if I—no, we—would survive.

Yes.

The terrible thirst. You wanted me to feel what D'Nar feels.

Yes.

We are the mother and father of a new race. We need to be strong.

Stronger.

Will there be others?

That's for them to decide.

Will you make them go through the same test?

A race must be able to survive.

We will be hated, our children and their children reviled.

You will also be revered. So will they.

Will we ever learn to live together? To survive, we must.

The Elders didn't answer. They didn't need to.

Mount C'eres holds the key.

We are waiting for you.

Chapter Nineteen

Ariel never really slept. She dozed, waking every time D'Nar moved. By the middle of the night, his temperature was rising. Several hours later, his fever raged. At first he mumbled, thrashing about as if in the throes of a bad dream. She tried to calm him, sometimes by talking to him, sometimes by covering his body with her own.

She needed water. Her thirst was constant but bearable. But because of the fever, D'Nar was consuming their water at an alarming rate. By mixing several herbs from her pouch and pulverizing them, she was able to dissolve them in some water and get them inside D'Nar. With a vampyr, she couldn't heal injuries from the outside, so she had to heal them from within.

Now Ariel faced a hard decision. Stay with D'Nar or search for water. She couldn't believe that The Elders would test them to the brink of death. There had to be water somewhere nearby. So she filled one last skin with all of the water that was left and gathered the remaining skins.

With the herbs in his system, D'Nar seemed more peaceful.

"D'Nar." She nudged his shoulder. "D'Nar."

He opened his eyes. "Ariel."

"How do you feel?"

He grimaced. "I'll live."

She most certainly hoped so. "I must find water. You're running a fever. It'll spike again."

He gripped her hand, squeezing hard. "You must let the fever kill—"

Let the fever kill him? Never. The infection? Absolutely. "I know."

He didn't hear her. He'd already passed out again. Ariel buried her face in his hands and whispered a prayer to The Elders. "Please don't let him die."

To make her way back to camp without getting lost, Ariel found a flint rock. Harder than most other rocks, the flint allowed her to mark her passage on stones as she walked. And walked. And scrambled. And climbed.

Then her senses took over. Amazed, Ariel followed her sense of smell until she came to a small pool created by the rocks. It seemed to be fed by an underground spring for she could find no sign of its beginning.

With a whoop of joy, she plunged her face into the succulent fluid and drank. Then she filled all of their skins. And she drank some more. She took out a piece of meat and chewed happily. They were going to be all right now.

Prudence advised that she rest a moment before making the return journey to their camp. What she wouldn't give for a hot bath. And clean clothes. She hadn't thought to bring extra. But she *could* do something about the bath and quickly stripped and scrubbed herself clean. The heat of the yellow sun helped dry her. Then she shook as much dust from her clothes as she could and dressed again.

Ariel hurried back to D'Nar with as much speed as she could muster, considering she was carrying several waterskins. But fear for D'Nar's safety gave her extra strength. In his present condition, D'Nar could not defend himself. And though she'd removed the carcass of the dead I'man, any animal might pick up the scent of its blood.

Breathing a huge sigh of relief when she returned to their encampment and found him sound asleep, Ariel tended the fire by adding a chunk of the fuel

D'Nar had brought with him. Ariel had never considered herself more than a healer yet here she was, building fires, placing meat on a stone to cook for herself, and performing tasks usually reserved for hunters like D'Nar. Of course, her vampyr made a very bad patient. When she took what was left of the herb mixture and tried to feed it to him, D'Nar pushed her hand away.

"You must take the medicine," Ariel insisted.

D'Nar became agitated so she left him alone.

His body was telling her, it seemed, that it didn't need her services.

Of course, that didn't sit well with her, but choices were scarce at the moment. She would, if necessary, force it down his throat. But for now, his comfort was her first priority.

Her vampyr. Her D'Nar. Stubborn, proud, courageous. How Ariel loved this amazing man.

In spite of being wounded to the very soul, D'Nar had saved her life. "You love me," she whispered. "I know you do." Even a little. And a little would be enough.

Try to believe. My love will make you strong, strong enough to see the truth. We have been chosen. A new life awaits us.

If only you will believe.

****

At first, D'Nar believed he was burning in the fires of the earth. Then he shook with cold, encased in mountain snow. A voice came to him every now and then, a soothing voice, telling him to rest, to be at peace.

And for a time he would. He would dream of a glade with green grass and a pool of sweet water. Then his dreams would scatter as fragments of pictures ran through his mind. Strange, yet wonderful pictures. Were they the past? The future? He didn't know.

A comforting warmth snuggled against his back.

He sighed, falling into a deep cushion of darkness and dreamed of the glade again.

Two people performed the dance of the ages. Hip to hip, thigh to thigh, entwined in a lover's embrace. He felt the power of the glade surge through his veins and became one with the couple on the ground, awash in the pleasure of their desire, feeling the ecstasy of their lovemaking and the wonder of fulfillment.

D'Nar became voyeur and participant. The dream was more than just the two of them making love. The dream gave him the chance to become part of her. As female mated with male, she drank in his seed. A part of her body joined with that seed.

A new life was created.

D'Nar opened his eyes to find Ariel staring down at him. Her liquid gaze enveloped him in warmth and love. Her face bore the ravages of hardship and fear. For him?

Her fingertips searched his face as if she couldn't believe he was real. Or alive. Or both.

He felt the hard surface of the ground against his back and knew the soreness of his wounds as he moved. Flashes of the fight with the I'man filtered back into his brain. All tempered by the truth. The truth of a dream that wasn't a dream. The truth he'd known all along, yet refused to believe.

His hand reached up and wrapped around the back of her neck. He urged her to bend down so he could kiss her. Their tongues mated and melded. Her lips tasted sweeter than any wine he'd ever consumed. When he let go, his hand slid down to cover her heart. His own beat in time with hers. They were two and yet one.

"You never cease to amaze me."

She smiled. "*You* never cease to amaze *me*."

"Your capacity to love seems endless."

"Because it is."

"Why me, Ariel?" he asked in wonder.

"I could ask the same of you."

She could. "I'm sorry."

"For what?" she cried. "You saved my life."

He smiled. "For being pig-headed, stubborn, arrogant. Shall I go on?"

She giggled. "Oh, please do."

"Unh, unh, unh," he answered, waggling a finger at her. "That would give you a swelled head."

She caught his hand and kissed his fingertips. "Thank goodness you're alive."

The horror of the last few days remained etched on her features. D'Nar wished he could make the pain go away. He couldn't.

"Ariel, I—" He paused, trying to find the right words to say. "I love you. I've always loved you. I fell in love with you that first day we met in the marketplace. You weren't afraid of me. But there was more. You were proud of who you were. As proud of being human as I was of being vampyr. I didn't think anyone could match that pride. You exceeded it."

He swallowed. She motioned to see if he wanted some water. When he nodded, she lifted his head to help him drink. "When two prides like that clash, there are bound to be sparks and wounds. But you never backed down. You never gave up an ounce of who you were even when compromise was the only true solution."

She motioned to see if he wanted more water and he shook his head. "Your strength amazed me," he continued. "I became jealous of it. For again, it exceeded mine."

"No, D'Nar. Never. Look at what you've suffered because of me."

"Suffered?" he exclaimed. He kissed the back of her hand. "Of all the words to describe what you mean to me and what you've given to me, that is the last I would choose."

He rubbed his cheek against her skin. "No, *lived* is

the word I would use. As I never thought I could. You are a force of nature, Ariel. You are my other half. Together we are complete. I am the red sun. You are the yellow. Together we make one."

"That one lives inside my womb, D'Nar."

He squeezed her hand. "I know. I suppose I knew all along. But true reality is sometimes harder to accept than one that is perceived. I clung to what I thought had to be right. And damn near got us both killed in the process."

She shook her head, her eyes filling with tears. "No, you didn't. The Elders were testing us. We had to prove to them that we were strong. We had to prove to them that the bond between us was stronger than steel. We are the creators of a new race."

A deep sadness filled him only to be replaced by stern resolve. "We will be hated and feared. The G'Rakor's of the world will want to destroy us."

"All the more reason to make sure we were one, don't you think?"

"Yes, although I'm not happy about it."

She smiled down at him. "Then don't think about them. Think about me. How do you feel?"

He grinned. "Well enough that if you're careful—"

She seemed taken aback at first. "Are you sure?"

"I promise to lie here and not move a muscle."

She arched a brow at him. "Oh, really?"

"Well—" They both laughed.

"You have at least one if not two broken ribs."

He pouted at her. At least he tried to. "If you love me, you'll—"

She raised her hand to cuff him before realizing what she was about to do. "Not fair."

His mouth quirked, that little smile that could melt her heart. "I know."

Her mouth came down on his, gently but with a ferocity that took his breath away. "I love you."

"I love you, too."

****

Ariel leaned on her elbow to look down at him. Her heart pounded inside her chest. They'd suffered so much. They were going to suffer more. But at least now, they would face life together.

She smoothed back the hair from his face as his gaze melted before her eyes. Love rushed out, threatening to drown them both.

Her palm cupped his cheek. He turned his head to kiss it. Her fingertips smoothed a crease in his forehead in a vain attempt to remove the worry and the care she found there.

He caught her wrist with his hand and shook his head. He was telling her, without words, what was important at the moment. And what would be important in the future.

She threaded her fingers through his beard. He gave her a rueful grin. She'd never seen him with one, but decided she liked it. Her eyes darkened as she imagined how it would feel against the inside of her thighs. He must have thought the same thing for his mouth quirked with the hint of a smile. The one that went straight to her heart.

She bent down and spread tiny kisses all over his face. When she reached the heat of his mouth, her tongue explored. As they fenced, streaks of pure pleasure shot through her veins. She wondered why then thought better of it. Some things in life simply needed to be accepted.

She traced the outline of his lips with her tongue. He shivered. His chin lifted as he tried to capture her mouth with his. But this was her show and she was going to make love to him the way she wanted.

He wouldn't complain.

She nuzzled her cheek against his then rimmed the shell of his ear with her tongue. She blew softly. He gasped. She smiled and worked her way down his neck.

She'd washed away as much blood and dirt as she could. Funny how the smell still lingered along with D'Nar's masculine scent. It reminded her of how powerful he was, how strong, and the combination acted like an aphrodisiac by going straight to her head.

A fierce need to mate gripped her. She kissed and sucked and even bit him. She played with the skin of his neck between her teeth.

So this is how it feels.

He moaned in pleasure. Her hand splayed across his chest over his heart. As she leaned over him, she could feel the organ race beneath her palm.

She spread the folds of his shirt. His hard powerful muscles reminded her of the mountains she'd climbed. They could be hard, tortuous, and unforgiving or they could be warm and welcoming. The choice was hers. And always had been.

She opened her own shirt. His one good hand reached up to cup her breast. She threw back her head and reveled in the pleasure of his touch. Her nipples tightened into tiny pebbles. They thrust out begging for more. He gave it to her.

Bending over, Ariel placed a globe at his mouth. He suckled and lathed her breast, drinking in her nectar.

D'Nar's touch had always elicited untold sensation and pleasure. But her body had changed. Now there were no words to describe the sparks shooting through her insides, except to say that they ended in her core, heating her to seismic proportions.

She went wild on him.

Ariel tore off her shirt. She rose and stripped off the rest of her clothes. Her hands ran up and down her body. She snared his gaze with hers, watching it darken as she pushed her breasts together and pulled on her nipples.

"Come here," he begged.

She intended to. But first, his clothes had to go.

She unlaced his pants and urged him to lift his hips. As he did, she pulled them off him. His erection stood straight up from the thatch of his black hair. But she wasn't ready to go there yet.

She couldn't sit on his chest, but she could turn the other way.

He growled as the aroma of her core reached him. Her heart raced as she placed herself over his mouth, juices dripped from her. His tongue lapped at them. Her legs quivered as she lowered herself down to his lips.

He groaned. His tongue became his shaft, piercing her core. Intense waves of pleasure rolled through her body. His tongue traced the periphery, licking everywhere except where she wanted. Ariel withstood the torture for only a moment before she lifted slightly and gave him access to her nub.

One lick. Two. The third pushed her over the edge.

She screamed as her orgasm pulsed through her body. Her juices flooded his mouth. He drank and drank, as he would her blood in a few minutes. But first, she needed to return the favor.

Moving down his body, Ariel swirled her tongue over his belly. His muscles tightened and his shaft twitched. She swirled around the base of his cock, taking special care to tease his balls, then worked her way up. He was steel covered in velvet.

She licked the drop of pre-cum from the tip. He tasted salty and sweet at the same time. His musky scent made her crave him more and her core turned to lava once again.

His breath caught as she went down on him. His hips pumped even though he tried to stay still. He grew even larger inside her mouth, if that were possible. Still, she continued to lick and to suck. She wanted him to want her, to be frantic for her. So she lapped at his balls and used her fist to pump his engorged cock.

She showed no mercy.

"Ariel," he cried.

Maybe he was ready now. She let go and rose, flipping around to face him. She spread her legs and straddled his hips. Her daring side took over and she opened her folds with her fingers and began to play with her clit.

His gaze darkened with a fierce intensity. A hunger tightened his features to the breaking point and his incisors grew. He wanted to plunge inside of her all right, so far inside that he would never come out. She pushed her fingers in and out of her core and his tongue licked his lips in anticipation of that very act. She forced him to the edge of his control and made him want to come so badly that she was certain he would.

Before he lost control, she took his erection in her hand, placed it at the center of her core, and plunged down his shaft.

Sweet, sweet, heaven.

He filled her up. Every inch of her. She'd never felt so much of him before. She'd never been so aware of him before.

With his control nonexistent, D'Nar bucked and heaved beneath her. He thrust upward with all his might, reaching for their pleasure.

Ariel joined him, lifting her hips and riding him hard. Neither lasted more than a few moments. But before she reached the pinnacle, before she rode out the mountain storm, she opened her neck to him.

He reached up and bit the soft flesh as she whispered in his ear. "I love you."

Chapter Twenty

"Ariel?"

"Hmm?" she answered, still half asleep.

"We can't stay here." He didn't need to taste the air to know.

"Why not?"

"A storm is coming."

She lifted her head from his shoulder. "Are you sure?"

He nodded. It was encoded in his genes to know. "Yes."

"How long before it reaches us?" she asked. She hadn't moved, but already he could feel her pulling away, her mind far ahead of her body. A part of him didn't want to let her go.

"I don't know. Several hours I would think."

She rose and he resisted the urge to pull her down on top of him. "Then we'd better break camp. Unless you think it unwise."

He shook his head. "No. The wall is a good windbreak, but not enough shelter for a storm."

"We may not find better," she cautioned.

He rose and pulled her hard against him. One savage kiss later, he let go. "I'm not familiar with this section of the mountains. You still insist upon going to Mount C'eres?"

She nodded. "Yes."

"Then the closer we get to the mountain, the more I should recognize."

"You're the hunter," she quipped.

A shaft of pain tore through him. "And I almost got you killed."

"Don't," she told him. She caught his head with her hands and forced him to look straight into her eyes. "Don't doubt yourself, D'Nar. I won't. Ever. We no longer have that luxury."

He hesitated, not wanting to say the words, but knowing he had to. "We could go back to the city."

"Never."

"Then you're stuck with me," he replied with a small smile.

She looped her arms around his waist, careful of his side, and beamed at him. "Yes, I am."

Kissing the top of her head, D'Nar urged her to get moving. "We must try to hurry. I want to fill the water skins at the spring before we leave the area. Shelter we can find. Water, I'm not so sure of. So you must drink as much as you can."

She opened her neck to him. "And you?"

He declined. "I'm fine for now. Later."

She threw him a look that said he'd feed later or else and he saluted. "Yes, ma'am."

With a hearty laugh, he watched Ariel pack their things, while he took care of the fire and the ashes. "You know, you keep protesting you don't know how to hunt."

She looked up at him with a frown. "I don't."

"Yet you picked a safe spot and made a good camp, you found water. You did a good job."

She bowed. "Thank you."

He bowed back. Then he reached out to take her hand. "Are you ready?" She nodded. "Then we go to Mount C'eres."

He led her out of the hollow in the rock and up to the spring, making sure she drank until she couldn't swallow another drop. Since there was no clear-cut trail to follow, he picked his own, sometimes on judgment, mostly on instinct. Twice they had to backtrack because the trail led to an insurmountable rock wall. With a broken rib and without a solid length of rope, he couldn't attempt a climb. But eventually, D'Nar began to feel that some of the landscape was becoming slightly familiar.

By the time they'd reached the spring, the sky had grown overcast. Now, each time he looked up, he watched the clouds darken. The wind grew stronger, swirling around them as they walked. His hair whipped across his eyes and he pulled the strands back with a grimace. Then he felt her hands at his nape. She was tying the errant locks back with a length of twine from her pack.

He kissed her once hard on the mouth and then let go. "Thank you."

She smiled back at him. "This way," she said, pointing to what looked like a dead end.

He shook his head. "The path is clearer to the left."

"Trust me," she pleaded. "Please. I cannot explain now. But we must go right, not left."

D'Nar wasn't about to argue. The storm was nearly upon them. He grabbed her hand and started to run. She followed as best she could and he was forced to slow down. Soon his side began to burn with fire. He found it hard to take a deep breath. But he kept them going, kept them moving, just ahead of the storm.

She tugged on his arm. The wind howled in his ears. He shook his head, signaling that he didn't understand. She pointed. He followed her direction. Straight toward a dead end.

He shook his head no. She didn't waste time, but pulled him with her, urging him to follow. But to where?

A sizzling crack of lightening rent the air, followed by another one even closer. It struck so close he could smell the burn of ozone filling his nostrils. His heart pounded. They had to get out of the open. Now.

"Hurry," he shouted.

She didn't need to hear the word to know they

were in trouble.

He pushed at her back, urging her ahead of him. They scrambled over rocks, no longer picking their way around them. The wind forced them to bend over into a crouch for protection from the dust and stones that flew at them. Then he heard Ariel cry out as a rock caught her in the arm.

"Hurry," he cried.

He looked up into the eye of the fast-approaching storm. Ominous black clouds swirled inside a ring of gray. Lightening strikes hit the ground, thundering in his ears. One, two, now three at a time.

This was no ordinary storm.

Ariel continued to run as fast as she could and D'Nar followed. Huge drops of rain, at any other time a delight to the senses, caused nothing but fear to blanch his heart.

D'Nar looked up again. Ariel was leading them the wrong way. She'd taken them straight into another dead end.

"Ariel," he cried, grabbing her arm. "No. We must go back. Look."

She shook her head. She was leading them on pure instinct now, but that instinct was going to get them both killed.

She tore her arm from his grasp. She ran toward the sheer rock wall. And she didn't stop.

Alarmed that she was going to hurt herself, D'Nar sprinted after her. She'd taken off at full speed along a path that led deeper and deeper into a crevasse. As the mountain walls rose higher and higher, the gorge became narrower and narrower.

The rock would protect them, he thought, seeing her reasoning at last. But if a bolt of lightening struck inside the gorge, they were both dead.

With his heart in his throat, D'Nar watched in amazement as Ariel, rather than slowing down, sped up as she reached the end of the gorge. The wall loomed large in front of him. He skidded to a stop, but she kept on going. His mind told him she was going to hurt herself.

Then she simply disappeared.

****

The silence, after the pounding blows of the storm, deafened her.

Ariel had expected some resistance to the wall. Without any, her momentum carried her forward and she fell headfirst onto a hard stone floor. She grunted as the wind was knocked out of her lungs.

Sitting up slowly, Ariel rubbed an abused elbow. Suddenly she realized D'Nar had followed, albeit much more cautiously. He caught sight of her disheveled figure on the floor and the fear left his gaze.

"That'll teach you not to run full speed into a solid wall of rock," he quipped.

"Thanks," she groused.

The hint of humor dancing around in his gaze fled as he hauled her up against his body with his good arm. "Don't you ever frighten me that way again. You almost got us killed back there."

His mouth swooped down upon hers. Ariel thought about arguing with him. But what was the sense? They were both safe. And that was all that mattered.

Then it hit her. They were in a room built out of solid rock and it was bright as day. Made even brighter as the storm darkened the sky outside as black as pitch.

D'Nar must have sensed her amazement for he didn't so much stop kissing her as his mouth fell open on top of hers.

"What is this place?" he breathed, with a bewildered look on his face.

"I don't know."

He frowned. "I don't understand. You drove us here. Why?"

"The Elders." She looked around her in awe. The

194

stone was as smooth as the finish on D'Nar's sword and nearly as shiny. Whatever gave the room light bounced off the walls in a delicate dance. Their voices sounded much louder in the room than outside and she found herself whispering.

"But how did you know the wall would—" She heard him pause in wonder. "—break."

"The Elders told me."

"The Elders are a fantasy, my love. A dream."

She shook her head. Then a voice sounded in the room. The same voice she'd heard telling her the way to the mountain.

"No dream, my son."

D'Nar spun around to the sound, his sword drawn by the time he circled the room.

"Put your sword away," Ariel cried. "Please, D'Nar. This is an Elder."

She watched him turn in a slow circle, his gaze searching the room. "Show yourself," he commanded. His hand flexed on the hilt of his sword. Her mate itched for a fight. Terrified he might do something foolish, she grabbed onto his arm. His muscles vibrated with the need to react. Only an iron will kept him from attacking.

"D'Nar," she begged. "Please trust me. They won't harm us."

"They won't?" he scoffed. He shrugged off her hand and braced his legs, ready to do battle. "So far they've done nothing but."

She gasped. "No, my love," she countered. "They—"

"Hold, child. We can answer for ourselves."

A strained silence grew within the room. Ariel could hear her heart beat in her ears. She didn't understand D'Nar's anger. These were the people who were going to save them, right the wrongs of the past.

"Put the sword down, vampyr. Your weapon is useless here."

195

D'Nar's face tightened in defiance. "But yours wasn't, was it?"

She could have sworn she heard the room sigh in answer. *"You wound well enough without the steel."*

A cry caught in her throat as the sword flew out of D'Nar's hand and clattered against a wall.

"Please don't harm him. He doesn't understand."

D'Nar laughed in answer. "I understand, Ariel. More than they think." His countenance showed his disappointment and disapproval.

"We did what we had to do."

Ariel felt their anguish seep deep inside her. Countless years of remorse. So much sorrow. Why couldn't D'Nar feel it?

"You should have let us die."

"Ah, vampyr. If only it had been that simple. We would have perished as we were meant to."

"You went outside the bounds of natural law."

"We did."

"Why?"

"Because there is evil and then there is evil for evil's sake. The Inistrari were a plague. We were only one of many universes they wished to destroy."

"You should have let them do exactly that."

"Perhaps. But before you judge, understand this. They didn't simply want us to die, they wanted us to suffer. They wanted to use our people as food and make them perform the slaughter."

Ariel gasped. She remembered the beings from her dream. She remembered the pure unadulterated sound of their laughter. She couldn't conceive of the horror they must have known.

"But their true banquet became despair. They wanted to suck the life from our very souls."

D'Nar didn't answer. He stood stock-still. Then Ariel realized what they were doing.

"No," she cried. "Don't do this to him. If you give him the agony of the past, he'll carry it forever. What happened to you was for you to bear, not us. We will have our own sorrows to shoulder."

Pain etched lines into his face that would never go away. Tiny threads of silver grew through his hair at each temple, a permanent mark of his distress. She'd caught only glimpses of the destruction and devastation, she couldn't imagine the pictures they were giving to D'Nar.

"No, please," she begged.

"He must see child. He must learn for himself. He must know the reality of the menace he faces."

Ariel wanted to cry. But she didn't. Instead, she spread tiny kisses all over his face. "D'Nar," she whispered.

His arms wrapped around her like steel bands. "Ariel," he breathed as he came back to her. Her hands tried to wipe away the pain. They never would.

Grief filled his countenance. "Forgive me," he said as he bowed to the room.

"Somewhere through the years, the truth got lost," D'Nar continued. "What our world faces now is child's play compared to the danger our ancestors were in."

She watched her mate shudder. "Still. We would have been better off dead."

"That was not for us to decide. Look at the magnificent struggle your ancestors survived over the years. Can you honestly say you owe them anything less?"

"No," D'Nar answered, his tone quiet.

But Ariel had her own questions to ask. "Is this our reward, then? We did what you wanted. I carry a child of both races, conceived in love. I carry a child who will now be outcast by both races. Is this our reward? Is this his reward? For simply being?"

Before The Elders could answer, D'Nar did. "In a way, my love, yes."

"I don't understand," she frowned.

"Someone or something has given our nemesis life

again. The evil that once was lives again."

"Oh, no," she breathed. She shook her head, her stomach dropping to her knees. "Don't tell me you split a sun for naught."

"No. The plague will never regain its full strength. But hatred allows evil to continue in many forms. Such as the one that threatens you now."

"And will continue to threaten us," D'Nar added.

"We fear so."

The truth nearly killed her. "The child inside me. His true purpose isn't to join our races and heal the breach. His purpose is to seek out this evil and destroy it."

"Yes."

D'Nar, in spite of understanding, exploded. "Are we nothing but pawns to you then?" She could feel his heart shatter into the same bits hers was breaking into. "Have we no right to live and exist on our own?"

"You tried. Look what happened."

"But we already suffer the consequences," Ariel reminded them.

"And you will suffer more."

"Why?" she railed at them. "Why?"

"Because that which is worthwhile comes at a great price. The race you begin now can end the suffering and the devastation between your peoples as well as destroy the evil that threatens you.

"The choice is yours."

Ariel looked at her mate. "D'Nar?"

He turned to her. "You told me not to doubt myself."

He stood so tall beside her. She'd always believed that he carried himself with dignity, with a depth of character few men shared. He was so strong, strong in his beliefs, in his leadership, in his knowledge of right and wrong.

"We'll be tested to the very limits."

"Yes." He smiled down at her, his smile grim.

"Survival will be our greatest challenge."

"Will we be alone? Just the two of us?"

D'Nar shook his head. His mouth quirked in sardonic amusement. "Somehow I don't think that would be possible. But I don't foresee a large number joining us. Ours will be the hardest road to travel."

Ariel cupped his cheek and her fingers grazed over the hair at his temple. Sadness filled her. He covered her hand with his, pulled her fingers away, and kissed her palm to show her what was important, what would always be the most important, to them.

"You didn't speak of love," she called out to The Elders. "You fight great evil with an even greater love."

She thought she heard laughter.

"You were the ones who finally gave hope to our dream. Never before has there been such a love between a man and a woman of each race."

She accepted their reasoning, but it was D'Nar who asked, "Never before?"

"Very observant, vampyr. Only one other couple in all these ages came close."

"A'Shar and L'Iara," she breathed.

"The time was not right for them. It is right for both of you now. The storm outside these walls has ended, but a new one begins. You must journey home and stop your people before full-scale war breaks out. You must stop the menace that threatens everyone. To that end, we give you the gift of your ancestors. May that gift see you through the trials you will face."

"What gift?" she asked D'Nar.

"I don't know. But I have a feeling we're about to find out."

Chapter Twenty-One

D'Nar needed to celebrate life to wipe away the devastating vision The Elders had given him. Ariel had said that the only way to counteract great evil was with greater love. He agreed.

Although he had no idea where the light came from, Ariel's hair sparkled with its fire. He was a moth to her flame, helpless in the face of her beauty. Most certainly she possessed physical beauty, the likes of which he didn't think he'd ever see again. But there was so much more to her than a simple outer shell.

She was the earth, soft on the outside, round and full with peaks and valleys to explore. She was the rock beneath the softer ground, the rock that surrounded them now, solid, unshakable, protecting them with nothing but her being. No matter how many storms breached her surface, he would always be able to count on her. Even when they fought, even when it seemed they would never reconcile, he always knew she would be his other half.

He stared at her in awe. He'd never realized a woman, a human woman, would complete him. He'd always chosen his concubines with care, searching for the best he could find. Sendara was a prime example. But Sen couldn't hold a candle to his mate.

Ariel carried her beauty inside her. She was the jewel that graced the radiant chamber, outshining the yellow sun itself. She radiated the light of goodness. Was that part of her healing abilities? He supposed so. However, there was more.

Intrinsic beauty comes from strength. It took almost losing her for him to see that. It took a dying race for him to appreciate that strength. He'd always admired vampyr females for being disciplined and smart and tough, both mentally and physically.

They couldn't compare with Ariel.

How many of them would treat a gaping wound without flinching? How many of them would stand up to the likes of G'Rakor and not back down? How many of them would carry out the instructions of The Elders with nothing to guide them but faith?

Could she battle him with a sword? No. But how many times had he defended himself from her tongue? He smiled to himself. That was indeed an appendage stronger than the hardest steel.

Could she hunt? Slay an I'man? No. But how many vampyrs would have kept them both alive on sheer guts, determination, instinct, and ingenuity?

Was she stubborn? His smile grew. Wasn't he?

Would he need her beside him as they ventured forth on this new life? He couldn't imagine delving into it without of her.

****

"D'Nar?"

Her heart melted. He looked as if he wanted to envelope her, hold her, never let go. He opened his arms and she stepped into them.

"Ariel," he breathed. "I've been so wrong. Can you forgive me?"

"There's nothing to forgive."

He pulled her hard against his body. "And yet, there's everything."

"I never wanted you to suffer."

"I had to."

She smiled. "That's because you think with your head and not your heart."

He pushed her shoulders away from his chest and stared deep into her eyes. "My heart is speaking now, so full I fear it will break the confines of my body. I love you, Ariel. For all that you are and all that you will be."

Her own heart swelled in answer. "I love you also, D'Nar. For all that you have been and all that you will be."

She reached up with her fingers and smoothed back the hair from his forehead. Neither of them would ever be the same. But she decided she liked the stronger D'Nar better. In this new world they were about to create, D'Nar could let go of his rules and regulations, his right and proper; he could lay down the mantle of statesman and be who he truly was.

He could also be wild and tender. He didn't have to be what others expected. The thought excited her.

As soon as her thoughts turned toward the two of them, he grinned. But Ariel wanted more. She wanted A'Shar and L'Iara.

As soon as her thoughts turned to their ancestors, he smiled. His gaze darkened, filled with love. He melted.

His hands cupped her cheeks and his lips grazed her forehead, sending tiny shivers down her spine. He kissed her eyelids, her cheekbones, her nose, as if committing her face to memory by touch rather than by sight. And when he finally found her mouth, he drank her in as if she were the sweetest wine spiced with herbs.

And a hint of blood.

His hands slid around her neck and pushed her hair back. "Your eyes are like the sea of old, so dark, so green, so intense, the color reaches inside of me."

He kissed her. "Then I taste your sweetness and they turn even darker, filled with the earth and the knowledge that you're ready to receive my seed."

Her heart swelled to overflowing. Her insides became all jumbled up and crazy. "Your hair is like fire. Sometimes the strands glow red and gold, sometimes they burst with yellow flame. My hand begs to touch, but fears getting burned."

She shook her head. She would never hurt him.

He parted her blouse and bent his head. Again, his lips roamed free. "Your breasts are round and full. Soon they will fill with the fluid that gives our child life."

He sucked on each one of them and her knees buckled. He pulled and teased, torturing her with desire. Then he bit one gently. Not to drink, but to torment. A streak of pleasure ran straight to her core.

He slipped to his knees and opened her pants, sliding them down over her hips. She stepped out of them as his arms wrapped around her abdomen and he pressed his cheek against her belly.

She looked down. His eyes were closed. In all the days to come, she would never be able to find words to describe the look on his face. Filled with love? To be sure. But there was more. As if he were worshipping the child, as if his feeling transcended time and place—even memory.

Ariel had no idea how she was still standing.

Tears of joy and love dripped down her cheeks. He pressed a kiss against her skin that reached straight into her womb. He tilted his head to look up at her. The tears she shed reflected back in his eyes, reaching straight into her heart and telling her they would never let go.

This time he didn't have to say the words.

He let go a moment to shrug out of his shirt. She watched his muscles ripple as they moved. He was so strong, yet he was being so gentle. Her wish was coming true.

Strangely enough, she didn't feel cold. Indeed, everywhere D'Nar touched left a fiery trail of heat in its wake. He swirled his tongue over one hip then the other as Ariel realized her changing body had become even more sensitive to his touch.

If that were possible.

He nudged her legs apart and Ariel gasped as he

cupped her core with his palm. He slid his hand back and forth, using her wetness to slip his fingers inside her core. She gasped. Sensation seared through her. She grabbed onto his shoulders to steady herself. And she knew this was just the beginning, a precursor to the many times they would make love in this chamber. In her heart, Ariel was certain they would conceive many more children in this place—a place now embedded as deeply in her heart as it was inside the mountain.

His tongue touched her nub. She stiffened, her fingers digging into his muscles. She was ready to explode, but she didn't want to. She wanted a joining between them.

As they were meant to be.

Ariel reached out to hold both sides of his face, forcing him to look up at her. She shook her head. He grinned. His head tilted as if to ask if she was certain. She shook her head again. He shrugged in disappointment, but the gleam in his gaze told her there would be other times when she wouldn't spoil his fun.

He rose to stand before her and her hand closed over his distended flesh. His hand covered hers and she laughed softly. It seemed she wasn't the only one with a problem.

She slid his pants down and he stepped out of them. He threw a blanket down on the floor then lifted her into his arms. Her arms looped around his neck and she looked up. All she could see was love and more love, pouring from his gaze, wrapping a protective cocoon around both of them.

He set her down and slipped to his knees. She followed. She marveled at his strength as he laid her down like she was the most precious item in his world. He settled next to her and bent over to kiss her. Ariel became so lost in that kiss that she didn't realize he'd nudged her legs apart. But her body knew and opened to him like a flower to the touch of the anecea, the flying insect found only in the desert.

She yearned for him to fill her core, so ready for his entry that he didn't so much push as slide inside her body. She wrapped her legs around his waist, her hips meeting each thrust of his with a thrust of her own.

"Ride the mountain storm with me," he whispered.

Her insides turned to liquid. She didn't have a solid bone left in her body. Her entire being centered between her legs. She gave him the physical proof of her love; man and woman joined together. As A'Shar and L'Iara had all those years ago.

Ariel opened her neck for him to drink. His teeth worried at the skin sending sharp stabs of pleasure to her core. She bucked and heaved against him.

"Love me," she pleaded.

"I do," he gasped.

He bit down and Ariel screamed. Her heart pumped, pushing her life into him. Her core convulsed around his shaft. His length rammed into her, heightening the explosiveness of her orgasm. His mouth sucked blood with each beat of her heart as he pounded into her body.

Then he stopped.

His entire body went still as he toppled over the edge. He screamed out his release, a guttural cry that swirled all around them. He pushed and he pumped until he'd filled her with his seed.

****

D'Nar couldn't believe the roar in his ears; then he realized that roar was his own heartbeat. Seismic aftershocks quaked through his body. He gasped for breath, sucking in each precious drop as he had her blood, the sweetest nectar he'd ever tasted.

Ariel drew in deep draughts as well. Her hips wiggled and twisted in a vain attempt to keep feeling. And that's when he realized that, although he'd just experienced one of the most explosive orgasms of his life, he was still fully erect inside her.

She moaned. "D'Nar. Please."

He got the message. And found, to his utter amazement, that he was already half way up the mountain slope himself.

He pulled out and she clutched at him with a moan of protest, not wanting him to leave. But he wanted to give her the pleasure she gave him so he flipped her over onto her knees. He slid back inside her hot, wet heat with ease and caught the magic rhythm once more.

He fit his thighs tight against hers. Skin to skin. She pushed back against him to feel his massive cock even more. Taking her motion as a sign she wanted his cock even deeper, he lifted her shoulders, sat back on his heels, and forced her to sit back on top of him. He couldn't penetrate her any further.

She groaned.

With his hands free, he lifted the milky globes of her breasts with his hands and pulled on her nipples. With each pull, her internal muscles clenched around him, creating an exquisite torture. He licked his fingers and pulled on her nipples even harder.

She growled.

Ah, this was what he wanted. He wanted her hungry. He wanted her fierce. He wanted her—like a vampyr.

She lifted up and sat back down, impaling herself on his staff. Bending his head, he found the pulse in her neck and the fresh marks he'd made. He bit down again, not as hungry this time, but feeding the bond between them.

Her core went nova.

Oh, the sweet heat. No longer satisfied being a spectator, D'Nar became a participant. He took a few last pulls on her neck before pushing her back down on her knees in front of him. His hands gripped her hips and each time he pulled out, his hands held her steady. Then he would thrust with all his might, reveling in the sound of his balls slapping against her skin.

Her nether lips squeezed and sucked in his erection. Her muscles clenched and tightened, a velvet band of steel stoking his fire. He pushed his cock deep inside, let go of her hips, and pulled on her nipples as they hung down from her breasts.

Ariel screamed.

Lava poured over him as he thrust. Then he let go of her breasts to tease her sensitive clit. He was almost there, nearly at the peak. All he needed was her—

Her body hitched and exploded all around him. She came with a ferocity that even he didn't expect. Her orgasm triggered his as he knew it would and he cried out as the world tilted. He shuddered with his own convulsions, racked from head to toe.

As he finally left her writhing body, the gush of his seed followed. He couldn't believe they were still upright. But he sprawled against her back as she rested on her hands and knees.

Although she was paying homage to him, he wished it were the other way around.

There's always next time, he told himself.

She collapsed onto the blanket and he spooned himself next to her. She was still drinking in deep draughts of air. So was he. His hand covered her heart and he could both hear and feel it pound.

"Each time becomes better than the one before," she whispered.

"And will continue to do so," he agreed.

She snuggled her head against his shoulder. "We have to go back, don't we?"

"Yes. But we both need to rest. We won't do our people any good by collapsing in front of them. Ours must remain a united front."

"And back?" she quipped.

D'Nar laughed softly. "Only in private."

"Very well. But if you keep that up, the babe might get the surprise of his life."

He lifted his head in surprise. "You carry a boy? How do you know?"

"The Elders."

A son. Pride swelled his chest. He couldn't have been happier. He gave her a kiss hot enough to melt her to the floor.

"I can only pray he finds his life less difficult than I fear it will be."

D'Nar nodded. "We have to make sure he gets there first."

He could feel alarm race through her and tightened his arms around her. "Remember," he said, trying to reassure. "We've been chosen. They may make the road hard, but they won't make it impossible."

She nodded, snuggling into his body. They both fell asleep. Safe. For the moment.

Chapter Twenty-Two

Before returning to the city, D'Nar wanted to explore. Ariel still lay beside him, sound asleep, so he moved with care as he got up. She woke up anyway, rising onto her elbow. She looked tousled, incredibly beautiful, and terribly tempting.

He bent down for a quick but thorough kiss. "I'm going to look around. I'm curious about this place. The Elder's brought you—"

"Us," she corrected.

"Us, here for a reason."

She started to rise. "I'll come with you."

He shook his head. "No," pushing her back down. "We have a long journey ahead of us. You need to rest." When Ariel didn't argue with him, he knew how exhausted she really was.

He dressed quickly. By the time he was done, she'd fallen asleep again. He smiled down at her. "Sleep well, my love," he whispered.

D'Nar crossed the chamber and picked up his sword. He checked the blade to make sure it was undamaged then slid the steel into its sheath. He'd probably have no need of it. The survivors of their world lived in the cities and had for many centans.

D'Nar studied the chamber as if seeing it for the first time. The walls were made of dark rock, polished so much that they shined. On both sides of each wall, he found hollowed out areas. Within each holder, he found the source of the light. Amazing stones. True fire stones. Not ones that made sparks for their fires, but ones that carried those sparks within.

Each stone radiated light, yet when he picked one

up and pulled it away from the holder, it dimmed. Fascinating.

Obviously, the rocks worked in harmony. Light and dark. Together they were strong. Apart?

The metaphor wasn't lost on him. He put the fire stone back.

He continued through an archway into another, similar chamber. Again, fire stones set into the rock gave the room light and a small amount of heat. But the exit from this room seemed to be a tunnel of some sort. At the entrance to the tunnel, he found an old torch. The cloth had rotted, but the staff was made of metal. He tore a piece of cloth from the bottom of his shirt and wrapped it around the pole. He struck a spark on an edge and managed to get it to burn. The fire wouldn't last long but it would be enough to light the way.

As he stepped into the tunnel, he found a torch holder in the rock. The one torch lit the tunnel well enough for him to see. But as he walked, he realized it wasn't the torch that lit the other end of the tunnel.

D'Nar expected the air to get colder. He was walking into the center of a mountain. Yet as he approached the other end, the air became warmer. He ducked his head to leave the tunnel and stepped out onto a rock ledge. The ledge opened into the most amazing cavern he'd ever seen, and would never truly be able to describe.

Levels had been carved into the solid face of the rock wall as far up and as far down as the eye could see. Each level seemed to have openings like the one he stood in. He could only surmise that they emptied into chambers like the ones he and Ariel had fallen into.

The walls of the cavern were made of the same highly polished rock as the chambers. But lower down, the cavern radiated fire. The cavern seemed to be made, as far as he could tell, out of the same fire stones as the ones he'd found in the chambers. Combined, the light dazzled the eye, brighter than looking straight into the yellow sun. And together, the firestones gave out incredible warmth. Hot, but not too hot to support life.

A small gasp caused him to whirl. "D'Nar."

"Amazing, isn't it?" he asked, lifting his arm and inviting her to snuggle next to him.

"This is how our ancestors survived," she breathed.

He nodded and pulled her close against him. Pressing his cheek against her hair, he breathed in her unique scent. There was beauty in the panorama surrounding him, but true beauty rested safe in his arms. "Yes."

"And why our races evolved the way they did."

"Not enough food to sustain all life," he agreed. "But another source readily available if one cared to look."

"I'm sure they didn't. But they had no choice."

He smiled without humor. "I wish there had been another way."

"So do I."

"The Elders have given us a true second chance."

"True?" she asked, looking up at him with a frown.

"They've recreated the past. So we can really make amends."

"What do you mean?"

His hand splayed over her belly. Wonder filled his being. *His son.* "Perhaps living here as they did for all those years will complete the circle of what was and what was meant to be. Perhaps The Elders understand that the separation of the races isn't the natural progress of evolution, but the joining of our races isn't just an answer, it's a necessity."

He kissed the top of her head and rubbed his cheek against her hair. "Perhaps," she agreed.

"Come. We must go. How do you feel?"

"Much better," she replied with a grin.

"I have a feeling we will live in all worlds. But this will be our home, our real home, from now on."

He watched her nod in agreement. "Small victories, D'Nar. We dare not ask for more. But just remember."

"What?"

"Small victories add up."

He smiled, taking her hand to kiss the palm. She placed that palm against his cheek, her gaze full of the love they shared. As she did, a word came to him. And the more he thought about it, the more he liked it.

"K'Mera."

Ariel turned to look up at him. "What?"

A gift of The Elders, he asked himself? Probably. "K'Mera," he repeated.

She smiled. "Two become one." Her smile grew bigger. "They live in harmony."

"Together."

Her face filled with wonder, lit up with joy. "I like that. I like that a lot."

He hugged her hard and turned to leave. "So do I."

Once they reached the chamber again, D'Nar smiled. "I'm going to miss this place."

Her gaze darkened, matching his. She smiled back. "We'll return."

He could see the doorway now, as plain as day. Another gift from The Elders.

"D'Nar?" He looked back at her. A fire stone had been placed in front of the door, about the size of his fist. "A keepsake?" she asked.

"I don't know. But we'd better take it with us."

In his heart, though, D'Nar had a very bad feeling that they would find a use for the stone when they returned to the city. And that didn't sit well with him at all.

****

After the cool, crisp air of the mountains, Ariel

found the heat and dust of the desert choking her. She longed to go back, but they had a task to fulfill and a city to save.

As they approached the South Gate, her heart sped up in her chest. She watched the stone of the walls surrounding the city loom before her with trepidation. They weren't above the law and she would accept whatever judgment the people chose. But she couldn't shake the terrible sense of foreboding. D'Nar must have felt the same way because he motioned to her to put up her hood.

She nodded and did as he asked. His hand tightened on hers, not in fear, but in hope. He wanted to enter the city without recognition so he could search out the source of the evil that threatened their people.

As they stepped up to the main gate, Ariel noticed the somber mood of the people and the sullen stances of the vampyr guards. Again, D'Nar's hand tightened on hers, this time in warning. A quick glance reinforced his desire that she say nothing and follow his lead. She squeezed back to let him know she understood.

"Halt."

Two guards approached. One, sensing another vampyr, nodded in respect. But they stood in front of Ariel. She felt D'Nar tense, but when he didn't remove his hood, she realized he was testing his men.

In a rough, gravelly voice he asked, "What's wrong? Why do you stop us?"

The guards eyed her mate with suspicion. "Is this your property?"

"She's a woman. Treat her with respect."

The first guard, the younger one, seemed to agree. But the second guard spread his feet ready for battle. "State your business inside the city."

"Since when does the hospitality of I'Stara not extend to her guests?"

The guard held his ground beneath her mate's

stare. "There's a menace that threatens the city, sir. We have orders to question all visitors, especially humans."

D'Nar laughed though Ariel heard no humor in the sound. "So a human woman, one whose bones I can crush with my bare hands, is now a menace to a vampyr?"

"No, sir," the first guard tried to explain. "But—"

"No excuses, O'Tan," D'Nar hissed.

"My, my, Lord," the young guard stammered, recognizing D'Nar. "You're alive."

"Indeed," D'Nar remarked dryly. "Who gave this order?"

"Master Toby—"

When the young man would have said more, D'Nar raised a hand to cut him off. "Does Master Toby run the city now?" D'Nar exploded in a harsh whisper. Ariel was truly impressed. He was keeping their identities as secret as he could even while his blood boiled with anger.

The young guard made to bow. D'Nar put a hand on his shoulder to stop him. With a quick shake of his head, he dismissed the formality. The young guard's gaze filled with curiosity, but to his credit, he said only, "My Lord. Command me. Please."

"I have been tracking the shadow of evil. It has led me back to the city. So now I must enter the city in secret. As a hunter. Do you understand?"

The young man nodded. "And you?" he asked the other guard. That vampyr swallowed hard and nodded also.

"Good. Now, I need some answers. Has Commander S'Nec returned to the city? He and his troops should have been here by now."

Both men shook their heads no. Ariel could tell the news didn't sit well with D'Nar at all. "What would you have us do, Lord?"

"Be ready. Stand tall. And remember that you

214

protect *all* the citizens who enter and leave this city."

The men made to salute and D'Nar warned them again with a quick shake of his head. As they spread their legs, ready to battle if necessary, Ariel watched their pride and purpose return to them. Just his presence, she mused. And a simple lesson in right and wrong.

"O'Tan. You must find S'Nec. He and his troops must come back to the city immediately."

The young vampyr made to salute then shook his head and whirled away, obviously eager to make amends.

"And you," he told the other guard. "You must remember. All. Inside the city and out."

The guard nodded and let them pass through the gate. They entered as travelers, their disguise intact for the moment. The first thing Ariel noticed was the strange quiet that filled the streets. There were fewer people out and about. But those that did pass gave no sign of greeting, no smile of friendship. They kept their gazes elsewhere.

"Do you feel the tension?" D'Nar asked.

She shivered. Something was very wrong. It was as if a pall had fallen over the people, slowly choking the life out of them. "Yes."

"I don't like this, Ariel."

"Fear runs rampant like the dust in a storm. It's everywhere."

She watched her mate try to hold onto his anger. His mouth tightened into a thin line. "Now, even more, I feel we were right to enter the city in secret."

They turned a corner and began walking toward the marketplace. Ariel expected to see more people here, especially near the main square. But again, the streets were nearly empty.

A shout filled the air, followed by another. Two young vampyr's were chasing a human male of middle age. As they turned onto the street ahead of Ariel and

D'Nar, they cornered the man up against the wall of a building. One pulled out a feeding stiletto.

A rumble began deep inside D'Nar's chest ending in a piercing command. "*Rista!*"

The youths whirled to see who protested. When they watched D'Nar draw a sword, they fled.

Ariel ran to the man to catch him as he slumped against the wall. She pulled out a cloth and wet the fabric, wiping the perspiration from his brow. The man was having trouble breathing so she waited as he tried to reclaim his breath. She recognized him as a mason who'd worked on many buildings in the area.

"Are you hurt?"

The man shook his head. "My thanks." He drew in a few more deep breaths. "To both of you."

"You're shaking. Are you certain you're all right?" she asked. "I'm a healer."

She heard D'Nar sheath his sword. He was strung tighter than an archer's bow.

The man tried to straighten. "Don't," she told him, realizing he didn't know who she was because her hood covered her face. "Rest a moment," She pulled the fabric back.

"Lady?"

She smiled. "I was wondering if you would recognize me, Adam."

The man paled as he lifted his head and realized whom she was with. "My Lord," he breathed.

As Adam struggled to rise, he tried to bow. Ariel watched D'Nar put a hand upon the man's shoulder. He shook his head. "No, my friend. Don't. There's no need."

"But—" The poor man looked terribly confused.

"Tell us," D'Nar continued. "What caused those young men to attack you?"

"I don't know, my Lord. I swear. I did nothing. I was simply walking down the street."

Ariel frowned. She couldn't believe things could

break down so quickly between their people. "Did you know them?"

"No, Lady. And I didn't invite them to feed. Honest."

"Hush," she soothed. "We believe you." She studied the man to make sure he was recovering. "Can you walk now?"

"Yes, my Lady. I think so." She helped steady him as he moved.

"Adam." Ariel could hear D'Nar's effort to keep his voice even. "Where are all the people? The marketplace should be filled at this hour."

"Frightened, my Lord. Attacks like this are happening all over the city. I didn't want to come out either, but I needed to buy food. For my family."

A knife sliced through Ariel's heart. D'Nar turned toward her and she saw the same hurt mirrored in his gaze. They both knew the remnant of evil caused these attacks and would continue to do so. She tried to tell D'Nar without words that it was despair that the evil sought. He nodded in understanding.

"My friend," D'Nar began. "I need you to be brave. Can you do that for me?"

Adam straightened his shoulders. "Yes, my Lord."

"Good." D'Nar reached out a reassuring hand. "I need you to find the vampyr T'Meric. He lives in the northern section of the city on the street of the flying horses."

"I know the family, Lord. I'm a mason. I repaired their home once."

D'Nar smiled. "Bring him to my home. In secret, if this is possible. Tell him it is a matter of life and death and don't let him say no. Do you understand?"

Adam bowed. "Right away, Lord."

"My thanks," her mate replied.

Adam smiled. "Blessings on both of you."

Ariel watched the man hurry off, her insides a roiling mass of contradictions. "Oh, D'Nar," she breathed. "What has happened? Has the world gone mad?"

She could feel his emotions in turmoil as well. "Beyond mad, I fear."

"What do we do? Our place lies with the mountain now."

She watched his shoulders slump. "I don't know. I can bring the city back to order. Just the knowledge of my presence will do that, it seems. But what happens when I leave again? The people, all the people, have to want freedom and harmony for themselves."

Ariel ached for her mate. "You can't live their lives for them, D'Nar."

"Has it all been for naught, then?" he whispered.

"No," she told him in a fierce whisper. "Never. Look at what's happening to us, my love."

"I know. The same despair that the evil wants to feed upon."

"Exactly. Remember what The Elders said? This evil doesn't just want chaos. It feeds on hopelessness. If we become discouraged, we give it the fuel it craves."

He reached out and pulled her hard against his body. "Don't ever leave my side," he begged. "I don't know what I'd do without you. You are my world, Ariel. My heart." He smiled down at her then gave her a kiss the world could see. "Come. We have work to do."

Ariel beamed up at him, her lips still tingling from his kiss. "That's the spirit." She let go of him and they started back down the street. "But I'm a bit confused. Why T'Meric? He's been the instigator in much of this, hasn't he?"

She watched D'Nar smile. "Exactly, my love. Exactly."

Chapter Twenty-Three

D'Nar watched Sendara pack her belongings with mixed emotions. On the one hand, his heart ached for her. She was leaving all that she'd known for quite some time. But on the other, this was Sen's chance for a new life. And though she loved him, he hoped she would find someone to love her back. He wanted her to find happiness. As he had.

Once all the serving girls had left the room, he motioned to Ariel to come out. He made another motion to lock the doors and Ariel nodded.

"Sen."

She whirled, paled, then cried out. "Hush, my friend," Ariel cautioned.

"Thank the two suns," Sendara exclaimed. "You're both alive. I must get Toby. We need to alert—"

D'Nar moved swiftly and caught Sen's arm. He covered her mouth. "No, Sen. We come to you in secret." He let go very carefully.

"But I don't understand." Confusion swirled in her dark black gaze.

"First, you must trust me. Trust us."

She nodded. "Of course."

"We need your help, Sendara," Ariel continued. "The city's in grave peril."

"What?" she gasped. "What do you mean?" For a moment, Sen looked torn. Then she brightened. "You're both alive. I can't believe it."

D'Nar threw back his hood. He wrapped his arms around his concubine and gave her a quick hug. Then he stepped back and Ariel did the same. "I like the beard," Sen teased.

Ariel laughed softly. "So do I."

He caught a flash of pain as Sen looked up at him, but then she hid her feelings. He watched her turn to Ariel with nothing but love in her gaze. "I'm so glad you're together."

"I took a bit of convincing," he admitted.

Sen looked alarmed then relaxed. "You've accepted the baby?"

This was going to be interesting. "Sen. The child is mine."

His concubine looked taken aback for a moment. Few vampyrs ever gave their concubines' children their family name. "You love each other that much." The words came out in wonder, more of a statement than a question.

"Yes, but the child is really mine."

"So you believe Ariel's story? About a place with power beyond what we know?"

He nodded. "Yes. The Elders exist. The child is mine."

"That's impossible."

D'Nar watched as Ariel smiled and clasped Sendara's hand with hers. "Nothing is impossible if you open your heart, Sendara."

"You ask a great deal of me."

"I know," Ariel replied. "But I know your love for D'Nar is so great that it will allow you to accept what we say."

"A part of me will always feel that he belongs to me."

Ariel grew sad. "I know. And I wish there could have been another way."

"You were meant for each other."

His mate nodded. "The child in my belly is half human, half vampyr."

Sen looked at both of them as if they'd lost their minds. "But that's not important now," D'Nar continued. "Tell us. What's been happening here? A man was attacked right in front of us."

Sendara related the troubles of the city to them, confirming what they'd seen and felt. "I've asked Adam to bring T'Meric here," D'Nar told Sendara. "If anyone can control the young vampyrs in the city, he can."

"But I don't understand. Why don't you simply tell Toby—" Her voice trailed off as the truth hit her. "You don't trust him, do you?"

D'Nar shook his head. "No."

"He's been frantic with worry, sending patrols out looking for you."

Hmm. That was interesting. "Sen, we saw no patrols searching for us. We saw no sign of them outside the walls of the city."

He watched as comprehension dawned. "Oh, no."

Just then, banging on one of the doors startled them. D'Nar threw up his hood and motioned for Ariel to do the same and return to their hiding places. He indicated to Sen to open the door. "My Lady. My Lady."

Sen put on a good act as she unlocked the door. "What is it?" she asked, obviously annoyed at being disturbed.

A young serving girl called Terra burst through the doorway. "There was a riot. In the square. Three humans have been killed. One vampyr. Master Toby has declared—"

The young girl's face paled as D'Nar stepped out into the room. "Ariel. Lock the door."

"My Lord." The girl bowed and as she rose, her face paled. "They said you were dead."

A hot coil of anger burned inside his guts. But that would be dealt with later. "Not dead," he told them all. "Not dead by a long shot."

He turned to Sen. "Now do you understand?"

She nodded. "What would you have me do, D'Nar?"

"Is the house in the eastern section yours yet?"

"Yes. I've been gathering my things to move there."

"First, you'll have no need of it anymore. It will be ours now. Terra, you are a witness. Sendara, by my rights as a vampyr and the owner of this property, I give you this house, full title, and all in it in return for the house you just purchased. Do you accept?"

Sendara gasped. "Yes." D'Nar looked over to find Ariel trying hard to hide a smile.

"The house in the eastern section. What street is it on?"

"The street of the blue water."

D'Nar nodded in appreciation. Not too ostentatious, but very comfortable. "Receive T'Meric when he arrives. Then if Toby asks why he was here, you can tell him the truth. That you were trying to gather information informally. To help."

Sen nodded. "That will work."

"Send T'Meric to the house of the blue water, but don't tell him why. In case he's questioned."

"On my way to find Ariel, I sent P'Lat to find S'Nec. I've sent O'Tan as well."

He turned to the startled serving girl. "Terra?"

"Yes, my Lord?" she strangled out.

"You will come with us and see to my Lady."

The young girl looked to Sen first. Good. She would be loyal. Sen nodded and the girl relaxed.

"At the sound of eight, meet us at the house," he told Sendara. "No one will question why you're going there."

"Terra, go fetch some of my Lady's clothes and bring them with you. Hurry. But be careful. No one must see you do this, do you understand?

The girl nodded and hurried off.

"Can you have food sent for Ariel?"

"Consider it already done," Sendara replied. "Now tell me. What's going on? Why don't you trust Toby?"

D'Nar related a very short version of their days in the mountains. When he was done, the look on Sen's face remained skeptical, but much more accepting that it had been.

"The baby is really D'Nar's?" she asked Ariel.

Ariel beamed with love. "Yes."

"And you both really believe The Elders exist and that this evil, as you call it, is what's causing our troubles?"

"Yes," they replied in unison.

"And Toby?"

D'Nar answered. "I'm not sure about anyone right now, except you. The less people who know I'm back, the better. For all of us. I don't trust anyone. Period. When Terra returns, she's coming with us where we can keep an eye on her. I'll return her to your care later."

"Very well."

"Have you heard any news from any of the other cities?" Ariel asked.

Good question. Sendara, however, shook her head no. "Nothing. And that frightens me."

But it made sense to him. Divide and conquer. One city at a time. "But not me, Sen. Nor Ariel. We understand its purpose. But we all have to be brave. We'll get through this together."

His concubine nodded. "I understand."

"At the sound of eight?"

"At the sound of eight."

****

"Are you sure this is the right path to follow? I'm afraid T'Meric won't understand. Look at Sen. Even she's not sure," Ariel told D'Nar as they hurried toward the house Sendara had purchased.

D'Nar didn't answer right away. "He has a fire inside him. And a fearlessness. He may be brash and young, but his argument has always been strong. And from his point of view, correct."

Ariel grinned. "Remind you of anyone we know?"

Her mate smiled back at her. "Am I that easy to read?" he asked in mock disgust.

223

"Only to me, my love. Only to me."

The house was small but elegant with two stories, which was a rarity in the city. As they entered, Ariel found the lower level consisted of a greeting room, a kitchen, and a public room. Three sleeping rooms and a huge bath made up the upper level.

"Sen has excellent taste," D'Nar remarked, throwing back his hood.

"Now that you've given away our home," she teased. He threw her a look as she also removed her hood and cloak. "This will be perfect when we travel to the city."

"We will?" D'Nar asked, an astonished look on his face.

"Of course. We'll live in many homes as we journey to other cities."

A look of comprehension dawned on his face. "Ahh. And gather those who wish to join us," he finished for her.

Ariel nodded. D'Nar pulled her to him, placing his knuckle under her chin and lifting her face to his. He gazed down at her with the same feelings that melted her heart and never ceased to amaze her. She melted at the mere touch of his lips.

She was certain he would have deepened his kiss, but a knock on the door broke them apart. He grinned down at her. "Would you answer that for me, please? I need a moment."

Ariel smiled up at him. "Certainly," she said, choking back her laughter. But she couldn't and ended up answering the door as she chuckled which seemed to confuse T'Meric who stood in the doorway.

"Come in, T'Meric," she told the young vampyr.

"*You* sent for me?" he asked, disbelief written in his gaze.

"Yes," D'Nar replied, throwing a look at her, telling her to stop.

"I wasn't going to answer the summons. But now

I'm glad that I did. And seeing you in the flesh—" The young vampyr sniffed delicately. "Smelling you in the flesh."

Ariel guffawed and clutched her sides in merriment. "We've been traveling," D'Nar replied stiffly, rubbing a rueful hand over his beard.

T'Meric simply smiled. "I'm grateful for your safe return, my Lord." By his tone, Ariel could tell he was sincere not just being polite.

"Come, sit." D'Nar took off his cloak and handed the garment to her. The question in his gaze asked if they had any amenities for their guest. Still holding back her laughter, she nodded to tell him she would check.

In the kitchen, she found some wine and herbs and some meats and cheeses and bread for herself. Suddenly, Ariel found she was starving and looked down at her belly. Someone else, it seemed, was hungry, too.

She placed the wine and food on a tray and returned to the greeting room. D'Nar jumped up to help her with the heavy load. Once settled, she put wine goblets in front of the men and made a plate for herself. She ate in silence as D'Nar spoke.

"What I'm about to tell you cannot leave this room, T'Meric. I must have your word on that."

"All right," T'Meric agreed, his gaze filled with curiosity. But Ariel also sensed his hesitancy. The young man wanted desperately to know what was going on, but tempered his desire with caution. D'Nar, it seemed *had* made a good choice in trusting this young vampyr.

As D'Nar related their tale, Ariel ate. They were still talking, but she found she was getting sleepy so she took the remains of her dinner into the kitchen. There she found that Terra had been busy. More spiced wine sat in casks in the storage area. The larder had been filled. And Ariel found herself with an unexpected addition to their family, Terra's sister, Mirena.

"She won't be any trouble, my Lady. I promise. I asked the Lady Sendara if I could serve you. When she accepted, I told Mirena I was leaving and she begged to come with me."

Both girls pleaded for permission without saying a word. "Our journeys will take us to every city on this planet."

"I have always wanted to travel," Mirena answered.

"Our life will be hard and much of it will lie in the mountains, not on perfumed beds with satin covers."

"I have never become a concubine for that very reason, my Lady," Terra answered. Mirena nodded in agreement. "I would be bored with silks and floral arrangements."

"Can you gut and skin an animal?"

"We worked in the kitchens of another's home," Mirena told her.

Ariel gave in. She would need help. Especially when her time to birth her son came near. "All right, you can stay for now."

The girls hugged with joy. "Run a bath for my Lord. Then see to your rest until tomorrow."

Ariel returned to the greeting room to hear T'Meric say, "My Lord, I have no doubt that you believe all of this to be true but—"

She watched her mate smile. "Remain skeptical, my young friend. I would, too, if I walked in your shoes. But keep an open mind. The evil that attacks us is real."

T'Meric nodded. "There have been several more deaths since you left. Panic is spreading. That's the reason—"

T'Meric didn't go on and alarm filled D'Nar's countenance. "What?"

"Master Toby made it seem as if you disappeared

because this thing that attacks us had taken you, probably killed you."

"And not because I was hunting it."

He couldn't know, Ariel said to herself. But if Toby wanted to foment rebellion, what better way to create fear than for the strongest hunter in the city to succumb to their enemy.

"The seeds of despair and defeat," she told D'Nar.

Chapter Twenty-Four

D'Nar bit his lip to contain the anger boiling up inside him. But when he looked over at Ariel, he knew real pain had yet to come. Toby had been a father to him when his own died. He'd loved him outside the bounds of Lord and servant. He'd entrusted his secret thoughts to this man. Only to be betrayed.

"Why?" he whispered, bewilderment lacing the torment in his voice.

His mate reached out to hold his hand, squeezing tight. Had they been alone, she would have embraced him. "Power, my Lord. And the belief that humans should live as equals. Injustice is as powerful a motivator as love."

"Powerful enough to betray one who was like a son?"

She nodded and he turned to T'Meric, hardening his heart. "Learn from this, young one. For unless you agree that all people live as one, this kind of hurt and betrayal will continue until no one is left."

D'Nar held T'Meric's gaze for what seemed a lifetime. T'Meric finally broke the contact. "I was wrong, my Lord. Forgive me. What we do and how we live our lives will come back to haunt us—all of us, it seems."

D'Nar sighed as his inner agony tore at him. He'd only tried to live the right way. He'd never really believed it, not until a spitfire with hair the color of the sun had shown him how wrong he was.

"You have to believe it in here," he told the young man as he pointed to his heart.

He would have said more, but the door to the

house burst open with a huge crash. Sendara was pushed into the room. She stumbled and fell to the floor. A growl issued from D'Nar's throat, but before he could draw his sword, one was pointed at his mate. Sen lifted herself from the floor with dignity and glared at the soldier who threw her there.

"What's the meaning of this?"

"Your sword. Now," Toby replied, entering the house behind two guards.

D'Nar growled again, but knew he had no choice but to comply. He unbuckled his belt and handed it to one of the guards. "Leave the women alone."

Toby smiled at him, the mask finally gone from his face. D'Nar could feel the man's hatred come at him in waves. "The great Viceroy. How I've waited for this moment. To watch you grovel, watch you fawn at my feet. As I have had to do with you all these years."

"Traitor," he hissed, bitter bile rising in his throat.

"Never," Toby answered. "A true patriot, willing to give up my life if necessary to free my people. Something you'll get a taste of now."

"You are the dust of the desert, Toby. Nothing more," he answered, dismissing the man from his heart. He turned to the soldiers in the room. "Who do you follow? Human or vampyr?"

"They follow me."

G'Rakor. So that was the game. He pinned Toby with his gaze. "You poor fool. Don't you realize you've made your bed with a serpent?"

G'Rakor entered the room with a glow of smug satisfaction. "Well met, D'Nar."

"I would say the same, but I'm not in the mood for being polite."

His response earned him a blow to the midsection by one of the guards. But the aftermath of pain was worth it. Ariel cried out, but he begged her with his gaze to be strong.

T'Meric rolled to his feet. He began to laugh. "You

adults seem to make such a complicated mess out of things that are so simple."

"Not so fast, young one," G'Rakor warned.

T'Meric gave the Viceroy a bored look. "Do you have a reason to keep me here?"

"Your association with a traitor."

So that was how things were going to play out. The pieces of the puzzle fell into place inside his head. Toby was going to blame the attacks on D'Nar and take control of the city with G'Rakor's help. But Toby had to know G'Rakor would betray him. Unless he had a secret of some kind, a hold on G'Rakor that would keep him in line.

"Traitor? Really? How interesting." T'Meric sounded bored with the entire scene unfolding before him. "Some human came to me and told me D'Nar was still alive and wanted to see me. Of course, I didn't believe him. But I was curious."

"That curiosity can get a young man killed," G'Rakor warned.

"My father wouldn't like that." T'Meric smiled at G'Rakor. A purely vampyric smile. So G'Rakor would know whose side he was on.

G'Rakor stepped aside to let T'Meric leave. Toby protested. "You're making a mistake. That young one is trouble."

"We'll deal with him later. For now, we have the one we want."

"Yes, we do," Toby answered with barely contained glee.

"Bring the women. He won't try to escape if we have them."

D'Nar caught Ariel's gaze with his. *Have faith. Remember The Elders.* Then he looked over at Sendara. Her fiery gaze filled with anger. *Patience.*

Though his guts screamed at him to fight, he knew he didn't dare. They tied his hands with leather bindings and marched him out into the street. Few were around to witness his captivity.

"Tomorrow," Toby told him. "In front of every man, woman, and child in the city. By the time I'm finished, they'll stone you to death themselves."

Be careful what you wish for, traitor. Be careful what you wish for.

****

Ariel watched Sendara pace, wanting to do the same. Instead, she leaned her back against the cold stone wall. A light bed of straw covered the floor and goodness knew what else. A bucket graced the corner for their bodily needs.

She shivered. "You can't wear out stone, Sen. Come and sit. Conserve your energy."

Sendara shook her head. "That little bastard," she swore, her voice tight and bitter. "If I get my hands on him—"

Ariel smiled. Sen had been repeating that threat since the door shut. "Have faith. The Elders won't let us die. They've got too much invested in us."

Sen stopped pacing and kneeled down. Leave it to Sendara to realize someone was probably spying on them.

Ariel rose, as did her friend. As they hugged, Ariel whispered, "By now P'Lat has found S'Nec. So has O'Tan. They won't let anything happen to D'Nar."

Sen nodded as they let go of each other. Ariel made a motion with her hand that she was going to explore their cell. When Sen finally understood her intent, she helped. The building was old and unused, for D'Nar managed to settle most disputes in chambers rather than with force.

As she studied the walls, Ariel put her hand in her pocket and her fingers closed around her fire stone. A plan began to form. She motioned to Sen to come close.

"We need to get out of here." Sendara simply threw her a look. "I'm going to start a fire."

Alarm raced through Sen's features. "And kill us

both?" she exclaimed in a fierce whisper.

"They won't let us come to any harm. We're too important. In the smoke and confusion, one of us can slip away."

"Me?"

"Find T'Meric."

Sen nodded in understanding. They would need the help of the people of the city, many of whom wouldn't believe D'Nar to be a traitor.

Ariel put a pile of the straw in the middle of the room, making sure to use some of the pieces from the corners that were damp. She struck a spark to a couple of pieces then threw them into the pile.

"Hey," one of the guards yelled when he smelled something burning. "What do you think you're doing?"

"We're cold," Sen sneered.

Ariel would have laughed if she could. But she focused instead on making sure the guards ran past her first. As they did, she pushed one in the back. He lost his balance and nearly fell to his knees. As the other guard looked at his compatriot, Sen reached out and grabbed the keys out of his hand.

They ran out the door and slammed it shut. Sen fumbled with the lock, but they were just able to close it when both vampyrs hit their shoulders against the wood. Ariel smiled at Sendara. She reached out and hugged her. "Good luck."

Ariel turned and began running down the hallway. Sen followed. They skidded to a halt at the corner. Ariel peered around and saw a guard to her left, but the way was clear to the right. She pointed that Sen should go that way.

"Be careful, my friend," she whispered.

Once Sen was out of sight, Ariel moved as quietly down the hallway as she could. Where there were guards, there had to be prisoners, she reasoned. When these guards finally smelled smoke, they ran to the fire, leaving the hallway clear. She checked every cell until she found him.

"D'Nar," she whispered.

He sprang to his feet, alarm warring with joy in his face. "Ariel."

His hands wrapped around the bars. Her fingers wrapped around his hands. "How did you—what are you doing here?"

He inhaled. "Did you start a fire?"

"Sen's escaped, I think. I'm the decoy. We don't have long until they realize where I am." Ariel pressed her forehead against their hands. Then she kissed his fingers.

"I love you."

His gaze melted her insides. "I love you, also."

Time seemed to stand still. Then D'Nar whispered, "They're coming back."

"Have faith."

"And you."

When they found her, her guards were not happy. Ariel didn't recognize any of these men. They probably belonged to G'Rakor. Since she'd never been mistreated by a vampyr before, she was surprised by their cruelty. But she didn't cry out when one of them slapped her and another ground his filthy mouth on hers.

"*Rista!*"

How ironic that she was actually glad to see the man. Toby motioned for her to go back into her cell. "You try my patience, woman."

Ariel felt her cheek swell and her eye begin to close so she figured her grin came out a bit lopsided.

"We'll find Sendara. Mark my words, we'll find her."

Ariel shrugged. "It doesn't matter. You have both of us."

"Yes, yes I do."

So, he didn't know about the baby. Relief sang through her. "Why, Toby? If you do this, no one will win. A mind can't be changed by force. You know that. You change a mind with an idea."

"I got tired of waiting."

His hand reached out to touch her face. Anger burned in his gaze. "Those vampyrs think brute force can control an entire race. But I've outsmarted them."

"How?"

He gave her a smug smile. "You'll see."

Ariel shivered. Whatever he'd done, she had a very bad feeling about it. "I have a request."

Toby raised a brow. "Indeed."

"Let me spend my last night with my chosen mate."

"Why should I? You've caused me enough trouble as it is."

"Because D'Nar is starving right now and needs to feed. Or do you plan to present him half dead to the public tomorrow?"

She watched the man rub his chin in thought. "Do I have your word there'll be no more tricks?"

"You have my word."

****

D'Nar heard footsteps approach. He wondered if Toby had returned to torment him some more. He rose, confused when he realized they were going to open the door.

"Stand back."

He complied just as they threw his mate into the cell and slammed the door shut. "Ariel," he breathed, not comprehending her presence. Then her arms were around him and he knew he wasn't dreaming.

He held onto her, deciding he'd never let go. He rubbed his cheek against the silk of her hair and felt her heart beat beneath his. He sent up a silent thank you to The Elders.

"D'Nar. D'Nar," she kept whispering into his chest.

"Oh, my love," he whispered back as he finally let go. With shaking hands, he pushed back the hair from her face. Then he saw the bruise on her cheek. Anger swelled inside him.

"No, D'Nar." Her warning warred with his need for revenge. Then he swooped down for a kiss that erased all the pain. When he finally raised his head, the anger was gone. But the dream was not. Ariel was alive and that was all that mattered.

"What are you doing here?" he asked, wonder filling his being.

"I convinced Toby to let me feed you." She lifted up on her toes and whispered, "He probably wants to spy on us."

D'Nar agreed, but this was too easy. There was more. He was certain of it.

"You must be starving."

He was. She opened her neck to him and hot juice filled his mouth. But before he fed, he kissed her again, with all the love in his heart. Then he nipped his way down her neck. He could hear her breath quicken, feel her blood pulse through her veins beneath his fingertips. He would never make love to her under these conditions, but she never failed to reach inside him.

Her blood called to him. The river of her life rushed just beneath his lips. His incisors grew. As they pierced her flesh, she jumped, not in pain but with intense feeling. Her rich metallic sustenance was now his.

Each beat of her heart pumped life into him. He drank with deep draughts. Of course, his body rose and her hand slipped inside his pants to give him ease.

He growled softly and continued to drink. He'd gone too long without feeding. Her blood sang through his veins. Fresh energy roared through his body. He wanted more.

His hips flexed. Her fingers cupped his balls, rolling them gently. This time, though, he didn't want gentle. He pulled her hand back where he needed it to be, wrapped around his massive cock. She pumped her fist up and down, and he continued to inhale her blood. Darkness came over him. The blood called to that darkness. He couldn't help himself. He kept drinking.

When Ariel began to struggle beneath his lips, his erection swelled. Blood and ecstasy. He wanted it all.

D'Nar.

He reared back, realizing what was happening, and ripped his teeth from her neck. Her blood soared through his veins as an intense orgasm shuddered through his body. Once the aftershocks subsided, he realized what had happened. He laid her down on the stone floor and shame coursed through him.

He could have drained her.

A terrible laughter mocked him. "You see how easy it is now, don't you, D'Nar?"

G'Rakor. The harbinger of evil. "I was hoping you'd kill her and save me the trouble."

He didn't answer. He simply held onto his mate as tears filled his eyes. "I'm so sorry, my love. So, so sorry."

Chapter Twenty-Five

"D'Nar?"

Her head rested in his lap.

"I nearly drained you." His words were filled with remorse.

"But you didn't."

His fingertips grazed her cheek as if he couldn't believe how close he'd come to losing her. "The Elder's stopped me."

"Not just The Elders," Ariel insisted. "My love. Our love."

She watched him close his eyes in agony and let his head fall back against the stone. "I lost control."

"How human of you."

His head lifted immediately and his eyes snapped open. He stared at her with such self-loathing she wondered how he withstood the emotion.

"How can you be so forgiving? How can you not blame me? I tried to kill you."

She sighed. "Because I love you. Now stop being so dramatic."

"I'm not being dramatic. You don't understand. I wanted—"

She cut him off. "Neither the man nor the vampyr would do such a thing. The real you wouldn't hurt us—either of us."

She watched him grimace. "The baby," he breathed as if just remembering her condition. His grip tightened on her hand. "A darkness filled me. I gave in to it."

"D'Nar, listen to me," she told him. "To destroy an enemy, you have to understand it. Now you do."

"Why don't you hate me?"

"Because then I'd have to hate myself."

He was silent a long time. "We have to end this."

"Yes."

"No matter what."

"Of course."

"You and the baby have to survive."

"We all will."

Her mate lifted her into his arms. He gave her the sweetest kiss imaginable. Then, before she could move or cry out, he bit her neck again.

"Sleep, my love. Sleep."

As he laid her on the floor, he tied the pouch with the fire stone around her waist. He prayed The Elders would keep her safe.

****

They came for him the next morning. He steeled himself as the door opened. He didn't say anything at first, simply stared at the men entering his cell.

"She's dead."

"No," Toby cried, rushing to Ariel's body.

G'Rakor stepped into the cell, surveyed the scene, and smiled.

"You fool," Toby hissed. "He wasn't supposed to kill her." He checked the body, his face growing livid when he couldn't find a pulse.

D'Nar simply stared at them as if they were all meaningless. Toby spied his blank look. "Get him out of here," the man commanded, his disgust plain for all to see. "Bathe him and make him look presentable. I want the people to watch a hero fall, not a vagabond."

"What should we do with her body?" one of the guards asked.

"Leave her here until later. She's not going anywhere, is she?"

True to his word, Toby had him bathed and dressed. All the while, D'Nar moved as if he were a puppet. He felt dead inside. As dead as his mate.

At the sound of ten, they marched D'Nar through the streets to the Great Hall. Flanked by soldiers, the people of the city followed. Word spread of his return and arrest. By the time they reached their destination, the guards had to clear a path through the throng so they could climb the steps.

Once they reached the top, Toby put up his hands for quiet.

"Great people of I'Stara. This is a sad day. A terrible and sad day. But a necessary day. For we have found the one who has been killing our people."

A collective gasp ran through the crowd, followed by murmurs of disbelief. Many, D'Nar noted, simply looked confused. Obviously they were having trouble equating the man and the crimes he was being accused of.

"Has it ever occurred to any of you why no one could find any sign of an attack by humans? Because the perpetrator of these heinous crimes wasn't human. He was a vampyr."

Toby had their attention now and, as he spoke, D'Nar could see he was enjoying himself. He watched the man draw himself up and wait, drawing out the moment.

"How could a single vampyr slay three. It's unheard of."

"As unheard of as a group of humans?" Toby snapped back. Then realizing he'd made an error the man continued, "There's much in this world we don't understand. I didn't understand it myself. But I went to the Great Library. And I read."

About how to unleash evil into our world, D'Nar thought sadly.

"Long ago, a great evil tried to destroy E'randor. They were called the Inistrari. Our ancestors split their sun with an explosion that destroyed these terrible people. The price they paid was to split one sun into two and one race into two.

"But a remnant of that evil remained, hidden deep inside Mount C'eres. Your Viceroy, the man you thought was your leader, the man you looked up to for protection, the man you trusted," Toby paused for effect again. "This man unleashed the evil that now threatens us all."

A lone voice in the background started to laugh. T'Meric worked his way through the crowd, clapping his hands. The people parted, allowing the young vampyr to reach the steps and watched as he climbed them.

He stopped about halfway up and turned. "Do you really expect these good people, these intelligent," T'Meric stressed the word, "people to believe this, this fairy tale?"

"Your Viceroy, the man you seem so willing to protect, was more than willing to let the human population of this city become his scapegoats and let them pay for his crimes, was he not?"

T'Meric shook his head. "I heard D'Nar was trying to do just the opposite in Council."

G'Rakor stepped forward. "I was there. You weren't. D'Nar wanted to use force to enslave all the humans."

Of course, it was his word against G'Rakor's and D'Nar knew who was going to win that battle. But he wanted to see what the people believed. Most of them wore angry expressions and a low rumble ran through the crowd.

"I am a Viceroy. As such, I may accuse another Viceroy. I charge D'Nar with murder. What say you all?"

A deadly silence ensued.

The silence might be deadly, but it was still silence. Seeing his opportunity slip away, Toby cried, "He even killed his own concubine, the Lady Ariel."

The silence grew even deadlier.

"Sorry to disappoint you, Master Toby. But I'm far

from dead."

Toby whirled and looked as if he were seeing a ghost.

"What's going on here?" someone in the crowd yelled.

"Is this some kind of game?" yelled another.

"The stupidest kind," G'Rakor roared. Only the sound didn't come from G'Rakor. It was lower and much more menacing.

As everyone in the crowd gasped, tendrils of black smoke rose from every part of G'Rakor's body. Evil incarnate snaked out toward the crowd.

"Hold," Toby cried. "I command you. You must listen and obey."

The entity laughed, a sound so terrible that many covered their ears. Several women screamed and a child began to cry.

D'Nar watched T'Meric draw his sword. So did the guards. But D'Nar knew swords were useless by themselves.

"Hold, I say." Toby screeched.

Evil tentacles snaked out from G'Rakor's body, wrapping themselves around Toby's body. "I command you. I brought you into the world. You must obey me."

The thing before them simply laughed until the ground shook with the sound. "Fool. Did you really think you could control us?"

Terror galvanized D'Nar into action. "Sword," he yelled. A soldier threw him one. He cut his bindings and ran to face the evil before him.

The monster had lifted Toby from the ground and held him suspended. Then the smoke weaved its way through Toby's body and slipped inside his cells, breaking them apart. Toby screamed in agony as blood poured through his skin.

Use the fire stone.

D'Nar wasn't about to question The Elders this time. While the evil had its attention on Toby, D'Nar caught Ariel's gaze. "The fire stone," he cried.

She lifted it out of the pouch at her waist and ran to him. The creature turned, sensing something. It dropped Toby and whirled to face them. D'Nar thrust and parried, but every time he sliced off a tentacle, it simply grew back.

"For The Elders," he heard Ariel cry. She ran at the beast holding the fire stone aloft. The light of a thousand suns blinded them all. But D'Nar didn't need to see to know exactly where to kill the beast. He thrust his sword with all his might, right into where its heart should have been.

The evil beast screamed in agony. Its tentacles flailed. D'Nar turned to protect Ariel, but found T'Meric had beaten him to it. The young vampyr slashed out just as one of the tendrils tried to invade his mate.

D'Nar ducked, withdrew his sword and with one swipe, cut off G'Rakor's head. Some day, he would have to tell Ariel how good that felt.

A terrible scream rent the air. The fire stone began to absorb all of the black smoke that contained the evil of the Inistrari. And as the smoke cleared, a great roar of approval rose from the people.

D'Nar motioned for the guards to cover both bodies. Then he reached out and hauled Ariel into his arms. He kissed her, not caring who watched. "You scared me half to death, woman. I'm going to beat you for that one."

"Promises, promises," she grinned back at him.

D'Nar released his mate and helped T'Meric to his feet. They clasped hands as brothers. "Thank you."

T'Meric shrugged. "You're welcome."

They let go and a great hunting horn sounded. "S'Nec," D'Nar groused.

T'Meric grinned. "Better late than never."

D'Nar supposed so. He waited until his troops joined the people in the square. Then he turned his sword point down and leaned on the hilt.

"Brothers and sisters of I'Stara. What Toby told you was true. Except, of course, that he was the one who conjured the great evil, not I. And he has paid a great price for his foolishness. But we will now pay an even greater price, for he has opened a door I cannot close.

"I went to Mount C'eres in search of answers. I think I found them."

He took a deep breath and continued. "The evil that threatened us here today will never truly die until we replace fear and mistrust with love. My wife, yes, my wife, Ariel, carries a child created in love. He will be half human and half vampyr. He is K'Mera, one being made from two. Until we learn to live in harmony with each other, the evil Toby has unleashed will flourish and grow.

"Please. I beg of you. Stop feeding this terror. Learn to live together. Be at peace with one another. Only you, the people, all of the people, can truly defeat this enemy.

"Until then, my wife and I go to the mountains to live. Those of you who wish to join us may follow. Our life in the mountains will be harsh, but we will be free—free to live as The Elders meant us to live. Together. As one."

D'Nar bowed to his people and walked slowly down the steps. He motioned to T'Meric to join him. "I give you the city of I'Stara, T'Meric. Serve her well."

"My Lord?" the young man stammered.

"I will send word to the city leaders. And S'Nec will follow my orders. He won't be happy about it, but he'll follow them."

"But I don't understand. Why?"

"Because the city needs youth, T'Meric. Someone young to lead them. Someone with new ideas. And you need to temper your youth with the knowledge that what you do affects everyone around you."

"But, my Lord," T'Meric protested. "The city leaders won't allow it."

D'Nar smiled. "Take Sendara with you. Make her your concubine. She has the best political mind I know. She'll help you persuade them. And she's—" D'Nar grinned. "You'll see."

The young man looked about to protest again when D'Nar added, "No questions, T'Meric. Go and do what you were meant to do."

D'Nar looked up and found Ariel gazing at him with so much love he could barely stand it. He raised her hand to his lips then clasped it between both of his hands. He led her down the steps and onto the street.

One by one, those compelled to join them followed. A picture of the future came to D'Nar. Each couple would spend the night in the glade. Their children, half human and half vampyr, would be conceived there. K'Mera would be born there.

"I'm sorry I had to put you to sleep. If it's any consolation, The Elders didn't like my objections to their plan. But they reinforced, ever so gently, that making our enemy believe you were asleep would thwart Toby's plan."

"We're all safe and alive, so I'll forgive you. This time. But what I don't understand is how you knew the fire stone was the key."

"I didn't. Not at first. I just had a feeling I should take it. The Elders told me to tie it to your waist. But, being The Elders, they still didn't tell me why until the very end."

"D'Nar," she cautioned. "They can hear."

That was something they were going to have to live with. "You could have been killed," he breathed with all the pent up anguish he'd felt in his voice.

"So could you."

He heard her sigh and smiled. "I might just have to have a talk with them," she continued. "When we get to the mountain."

D'Nar threw back his head and roared. He felt the same way. "That's a conversation I'd like to be a part of."

He stopped walking and drew Ariel into his embrace. "I love you, Ariel. Through all that has happened and all that will. I love you."

Tears filled her eyes. "I can't imagine what the future holds for us, but as long as we're together, we can do anything. I love you, also, D'Nar."

With hands clasped, they kept walking. And with those words, D'Nar and Ariel set off to create a new future for their world. Together.

Erika Sands

About the Author

Erika Sand's idea of a perfect hero is tall, dark, handsome, and dashing, yet mysterious and edgy; a cross between Frank Langella's Zorro and his Dracula with a little of his Sphinx thrown in for good measure. Her heroines will never give up or give in so sparks fly until her characters finally reach their happy ending. The fun of erotica is creating characters that navigate the knife-edge of control and then fall, only to realize that they wouldn't have it any other way. And along the way, if they sizzle, well, some like it hot and some like it hotter.

Also available

Captive Fantasy

by

L. Rosario

Seraphina Scala has just confessed she's never had an orgasm and now her friend has the perfect solution—a night spent at Captive Fantasy, a club that guarantees to fulfill every deep, dark, secret desire. Sera would rather admit she's a vampire than join her friend at such a place, but she doesn't, and she finds herself surrounded by ravenous women and drop-dead gorgeous men. One in particular steals her attention...

Valentino was literally created to make fantasies come true. He's used to the eager women who flood into Captive Fantasy every night to take what he offers, but when he meets the shy Sera, he knows he has his work cut out for him. Something about her strikes a chord deep inside, and he soon realizes he wants more than just a breathy thank you for a "job" well done.

Valentino awakens a side of Sera she's kept locked away for nearly three centuries, and now she must confront her past, her present and her future. Doing so won't be so bad with Valentino by her side, but will he want her once he realizes what she really is? Or will his secret be the one thing they cannot overcome?

Chapter One

"I have a solution to your problem."

Seraphina Scala looked down from her perch high atop the library's shelving ladder and found her friend and coworker, Becca, staring up at her. "What problem?"

Becca rolled her eyes and glanced around before answering. "Your *problem*." She moved closer to the base of the ladder. "You know? The one you told me about the other day."

Oh, Sera knew, and she had regretted that little conversation from the moment it ended. So much for hoping Becca had forgotten about it. Climbing down from the ladder, she met her friend face to face. "I did not tell you about that in order for you to discover a solution."

"Nevertheless, here." Becca shoved what looked to be two tickets toward Sera. "They're for tonight."

Sera took the tickets, read the name emblazoned across the front, then gaped at Becca. "You've got to be kidding?"

Becca shook her head, causing her wild red curls to bounce around her cheeks. "Nope, no joke. We'll bug out of here early and get there before midnight."

Sera shoved the tickets back. "No, we won't." She turned away and grabbed another stack of books. Becca huffed and then jumped between her and the ladder.

"Why so set against it? Don't you want to have an orgasm?"

Sera nearly dropped the books. "Keep your voice down," she hissed.

Never mind that the library was closed, and they were the only two still here. For two years they had shared the "graveyard shift" as Becca called it. They came in a half hour before the big old library closed and worked through the night to get it ready for the next day. Sera loved the quiet peace of the vacant library. Becca tolerated it, but she took classes during the day, so she didn't have a choice.

"You are too uptight for your own good, Sera, that's why you've never had an—"

"Enough! I get it, Becca, so stop saying it."

Becca giggled behind her hand and stepped aside to allow Sera to climb the ladder. Her voice followed her the whole way up. "We're going tonight, whether you want to or not, and Jen is going to meet us there."

"You'll have to hog tie me and drag me there against my will."

Becca clucked her tongue in disgust. "Finish putting those away and then meet me in the computer room. I'll show you tons of reasons why you will not have to be forced to go to Captive Fantasy." With that, Becca walked away on the tiny tips of her ridiculously high heels.

Sera shook her head. No matter what the website offered, she wouldn't agree to go. Captive Fantasy—although touted as the greatest experience a woman could have in San Francisco—was nothing more than a glorified strip club. She really doubted sitting in a room full of drooling women while a guy gyrated in front of her was going to solve her *problem*. It was a problem she'd had for over 300 years, after all, and things like that didn't get fixed in one night.

But Becca didn't know that because Sera had been hiding an even bigger secret than the fact that she'd never had an orgasm during sex.

She'd been hiding the fact that she was a vampire.

****

Becca was already tapping away at the computer

when Sera strolled into the room. She beamed and waved toward the screen. "Come here and take a look. I dare you not to see something that gets your blood flowing faster."

Sera rolled her eyes and moved to stand behind Becca's chair. The computer screen flashed a red scrolling banner with the words Captive Fantasy written on it. Becca clicked on one of the twinkling stars at the top of the page, marked "the men," and another page opened. Tiny thumbnail pictures began to fill the screen, and Becca glanced up and over her shoulder. "Do you prefer light haired guys or dark?"

"Does it matter?"

Becca sighed and turned back to the computer. "We'll say blond, since you're so dark." She clicked on the third row of thumbnails, prompting another page to show the headshots larger. At least a dozen beautiful men stared out from the screen. "See anyone you like?"

Sera wanted to say no and walk away, but she knew how Becca was once she had a bone between her teeth. Squinting at the screen, Sera focused on one guy with bright blue eyes and a slightly crooked nose. "He's cute." She tapped the screen with her nail, and Becca immediately clicked the picture.

"Stefano," Becca read once the guy's face filled more than half the monitor. "Says here, he's good with his hands," she snickered and glanced back. "If I click on the star, we can see him naked."

Sera reeled back from the chair. "Oh my God, Becca, this is ridiculous." She blushed, despite how difficult it was for a vampire to do so.

Becca took it upon herself to click on the star, and in seconds Stefano was displayed in all his glory. No woman, dead or otherwise, could have possibly *not* looked. "Well, I'll be," Becca breathed and leaned closer to the screen.

Sera's blush intensified. If this kept up she'd need

a little snack.

"I have never seen a man built like that." Becca moved the cursor and clicked another star. Stefano, in another provocative pose, appeared before their eyes. "Admit he's hot, Sera."

"He's hot," Sera said robotically. Of course the guy was hot. He was paid to be hot. That didn't mean watching him strip would make her come.

Becca backed out of Stefano's pictorial and aimed for another blond. "Raphael."

If possible, Raphael was hotter than Stefano. Of course Becca clicked the necessary star to see him naked and Sera gasped. "That can't be real."

Becca glared over her shoulder. "According to Jennifer, these guys are very real and much more impressive in person."

"We'll see about that."

Becca's eyes blazed with triumph. "Does that mean you agree to go?"

Nothing like walking right into a trap. Sera pulled her gaze from Raphael and reached around Becca to take control of the mouse. "Let's see what else there is."

Becca giggled, and they spent the next hour clicking on various thumbnails. Eventually, they each had a favorite. For Becca, it was Raphael. For Sera, it was a dark haired guy named Valentino. Becca shut down the computer. "Let's hope they're both working tonight."

"Let's hope Mr. Henry doesn't figure out how we were using the computer." That would be beyond mortifying.

"He never comes in here," Becca assured her. "Let's get the rest of the shelving done, so we can bug out early enough to go home and change."

Sera glanced down at her practical black slacks and white blouse. "What does a girl wear to a place like Captive Fantasy?"

"Something sexy." Becca left the room without looking back.

Sera had been afraid that would be the answer. She didn't do sexy.

****

Jennifer was waiting for them in front of the club. She was dressed in tiny cuffed shorts, a halter top, and a pair of killer stilettos; all in black. With her long blonde hair, big brown eyes and wide smile, she looked exactly like Jessica Simpson. Damn her. She frowned at Sera. "You've got to be kidding. Jeans?" She then looked at Becca, who was dressed in a sparkly, emerald-green, mini dress. "You let her wear jeans?"

Becca shrugged. "It was all she had, trust me."

Sera saw nothing wrong with her outfit. The dark wash jeans were tight and low cut, she'd allowed Becca to convince her to leave several of the buttons undone on her black blouse, and her black lace bra peeked out as a result. Surely she didn't look *that* bad? Her boots even had heels. "I promise to go with you the next time you guys make a run to sluts are us, okay?"

Jennifer was not amused. She spun around and headed for the door.

Becca shot Sera a dark look. "Must you irritate her?"

"Must she belittle me?"

"It's her way."

"Well I don't like it," Sera admitted.

Jennifer glanced back with an impatient look as she reached the door. "Coming?"

Becca grabbed Sera's hand and dragged her toward the entrance. "Try to have a good time, okay?"

Sera began to nod, then froze as she came face to face with fantasy land. The club was not at all what she had expected. There were no large round tables, no bar, and no stage. Where did the guys dance then?

Women, all dressed in the same vain as Jennifer and Becca, milled around with drinks in their hands.

Their mixed voices caused a low drone of noise that actually hurt Sera's sensitive ears. This was why she avoided clubs. The sounds and smells were just too much for a vampire, not to mention all the heartbeats.

As a rule, she didn't drink from humans, but at one time, she had. It was too easy to remember the feel of flesh pinched between her teeth and warm blood dripping down her throat. The need to escape this place increased by the second.

Becca tugged her hand and she had no choice but to move deeper into the club. The sharp smell of incense clogged her senses and made her flinch. Piled on top of the droning voices, she could hear liquid dripping and wood scraping against wood. Other sounds reached her as well, but she refused to identify them. The thought that there might be rattling chains somewhere left her more than a tad uneasy.

"They are with me," Jennifer said to the doorman.

Sera pulled her gaze from the unusual environs and focused on the large man holding his hand out for their tickets. At first glance she thought he was naked, but then she noticed the flesh toned pouch cupping his genitalia. Good God! She yanked her eyes away, and Becca laughed softly at her side.

"Do you recognize him?" she whispered in Sera's ear.

Sera refused to take another look, so she shook her head.

"It's Stefano."

A quick peek out the corner of her eye confirmed Becca's observation. He had his longish blond hair pulled back in a low ponytail and it changed the angles of his face just enough to make him slightly unrecognizable. He felt her gaze and looked at her with his bright blue eyes. Sera ducked her head and the sound of low masculine laughter poured over her.

"Enjoy your night, ladies," Stefano said.

"Oh, we will," Jennifer piped back.

Sera wasn't so sure that all three of them would. She hadn't even made it past the door and already she felt horribly uncomfortable. Maybe she'd slip away once Jen and Becca were distracted by the performers. She looked around the club, but didn't see any. Hmm. Her senses were definitely picking up the unmistakable musk of man, so she knew they were here somewhere. Maybe they filed out together in a parade of sorts? Maybe the show just hadn't started yet?

"I'm going to get a drink," Jen announced, then headed away without waiting to see if Becca or Sera might follow. They didn't.

"So what do we do now?"

Becca scanned the club and gave a little shrug. "I don't know."

Just then, the buzz of conversation shifted. The strong flavor of anticipation hung in the air, and Becca and Sera looked around to see what had caused the commotion. A guy, dressed in a black tuxedo, strolled into the center of the milling women and lifted a microphone to his lips. He was gorgeous enough to be the first performer, and Sera realized she was holding her breath.

Would the tuxedo come off a piece at a time? Would he take the clip out of his long black hair and let it drift down over his bare shoulders? Would he find her hungry gaze among the crowd and dance his way in her direction? She blushed as the last thought formed.

"Welcome to Captive Fantasy, ladies," the man announced. A smattering of clapping followed, and he waited for silence. "I do hope you've all had ample time to glance through your brochures."

Sera met Becca's gaze and mouthed, "What brochure?"

Becca shrugged then slid her glance behind Sera. She motioned with her head, and Sera turned to find

Stefano at her back. He held out two shiny brochures. "You forgot these." He winked and slipped away.

Sera looked at the brochure and saw all the same headshots that had been on the website. Good lord, it was like a catalogue.

"Do we just choose and point, do you figure?"

She didn't know, so she let Becca's question go unanswered. The man with the microphone pulled their attention back to the center of the club.

"If it is your first visit tonight, I suggest you take the time to allow the gentlemen to get to know you, before making your selections. For those of you who have been here before, you know where to go and what to do." He lowered the microphone and gave a little bow.

Sera looked away from the women splitting up into tiny groups. "This place is creepy."

Becca shrugged. "Let's stick around long enough to see the guys, okay?"

"Where did Jennifer go?" Sera didn't see anything that resembled a bar, but obviously the drinks had come from somewhere.

"She comes here all the time, so she must know where to go and what to do."

"I'm right here," Jennifer said behind them. She smiled at their startled expressions and held up her little glass. "I told you I was getting a drink."

"Where?" Sera demanded. "There isn't any bar."

"Are you going to question everything that happens tonight, Sera?" Jen's tone made it clear how annoying the prospect was.

Sera bit her tongue and looked away.

"Let's go over here, Becca, and leave the spoil sport to her own devices."

To Sera's horror, Becca allowed Jen to lead her away. Fine, if they didn't want to be with her, she'd leave. She turned back toward the door, only to have her way blocked by a solid male body. She stumbled to a halt, stared at the open collar of his dark brown shirt, then lifted her gaze slowly to his face. Her heart, which most definitely never raced, sped up and flipped over as she recognized Valentino from his pictures on the website. He had been handsome online, in a poster boy sort of way, but in the flesh he was staggering.

"You aren't leaving are you?"

Sera searched for her voice and forced it out past the lump in her throat. "Um…"

Valentino smiled, showing a set of dimples and a mouth full of perfect white teeth. "I'll take that as a no." He reached for her and slipped his fingers around her elbow. "Can I get you a drink?"

"Shouldn't you be working?"

His smile grew, and he jerked his head to toss a few sable locks out of his eyes. His hair had a natural wave to it that was really sexy, and his eyes were deep chocolaty brown. "I have a few minutes before I need to clock in, and I thought I should spend them convincing the sexiest woman in the place to stay a little longer."

Sera tried to stay immune to the heavy dose of charm but failed. She blushed and licked her lips. "Considering the reaction my friends had to the outfit I'm wearing, I know I am far from the sexiest woman here."

Valentino arched a brow and began to lead her back toward the club proper. "Let me be the judge of that, all right?" He led her past the milling women, and Sera realized there really was a bar. It was tucked into a shadowy corner and unnoticeable until you almost slammed into it. Valentino stretched his free hand across the polished surface and slapped a little bell. Then he glanced over at her. "What do you drink?"

Blood. Not that she dared to say that out loud. "Um…water?"

His eyes widened, as did his smile. "All right, water it is." The bartender appeared, and Sera tried not to stare as Valentino ordered an ice cold water and a beer. The tall, muscular, nearly naked man nodded his head and walked away.

"You seem overdressed." Sera longed to die the moment the words slipped out, but wait, that wasn't an option. She felt Valentino's gaze on her profile, but refused to return it. His fingers squeezed her elbow, and his soft chuckle crept under her skin.

"We're allowed to wear clothes when we're not working, but if you'd like, I can get into uniform for you."

Maybe the floor would open up and suck her into the pits of hell? She stared at the ceiling, and Valentino chuckled again.

"Here's your water." He pressed the glass against her arm, chilling her through the thin sleeve of her blouse.

Sera avoided his gaze as she took the glass. He released her elbow to take his beer from the bartender. "Thanks, Mike."

"Mike?" Sera echoed. The name sounded too normal for this place.

Valentino sipped his beer and nodded. "Yep. Actually his name is Michelangelo, but he prefers Mike."

"And do you prefer Val?"

He looked impressed. "You know my name."

Sera carried her drink to her lips to hide her embarrassment. She sipped the water, really wishing it was something else. Valentino's blood, to be exact. The thought rocked her. She didn't do humans. It was a code she lived by, and it wasn't one she planned on breaking. The little bags of blood waiting in her fridge were good enough, and she'd snap one open the moment she got home. Her strange little craving was probably just a result of not drinking enough before Becca picked her up.

"Does that mean you've been on the site, 'cause I

know I've never seen you here before."

Sera pushed away the thought of blood. "I was on the website, yes."

"See anything you like?"

He was teasing her, and she knew it, but still she felt compelled to answer. "Maybe." It wasn't like her to play coy, but if ever the time seemed right, it was now.

"I see," Valentino mumbled then took another swig of beer. "Only seems fair to tell me your name."

Surely there was no harm. "Sera."

"Just Sera?"

Sera nodded. "Yeah, just Sera."

"Okay. Sera. Have I convinced you to stay a while longer?"

She laughed, surprising both of them. "A glass of cold water is supposed to convince me to stay?"

Valentino set the beer bottle down and turned to lean a hip against the bar. He crossed his arms and steadied his gaze on her face. "What if I told you I could make all your deepest, darkest fantasies come true?"

Sera suppressed a shiver and looked anywhere but into chocolate depths of Valentino's eyes. "You sound like a commercial I've heard on the radio."

He chuckled. "But it's true."

Sera risked a glance at his face. "I'm not the kind of girl to harbor deep dark fantasies."

He looked her over then shook his head. "I don't believe that. You strike me as someone with a great deal of depth."

The observation unnerved her. After another sip of water, she placed her glass on the bar. "I think I'll go now." His arm snaked around her waist to stop her from moving away. In that instant his scent nearly overwhelmed her. It was a mixture of rain and dewy grass. Odd, but pleasant. It took a lot of willpower not to lean into the solid wall of his body.

"I didn't mean to offend you. I'm sorry." He looked

so sincere, she instantly nodded. His gaze softened and he reached up to feather his fingertips over her lips.

Sera jerked at the contact and pulled against the arm at her waist. She was strong enough to break free, just one of the perks of being a vampire, but something stopped her from doing so. She stared into Valentino's eyes and stilled as he made another pass over her mouth.

"Why are you here, Sera?"

She licked her lips and tasted the flavor of his skin. "My friends forced me to come."

"But you'd rather be at home, I take it?" He sounded offended.

"Maybe."

"I want you to stay. I want to perform for you."

Her stomach did a little flip. The visual of this guy peeling his clothes off for her, and her alone, did mighty strange things to her insides. "Um..."

He smiled and tightened his arm to snuggle her flush against his chest. His body was all hard muscle, and it felt really nice through her jeans and blouse. It would feel even better if they were both naked.

Good God! Where had that come from?

"Is that a yes?" he teased.

"Um..."

"I say it is." He touched her lips again then set her away from his body. "I'll make sure you don't regret your decision to stay, Sera." He finished his beer, and then left her with a bright smile on his mouth.

Sera collapsed against the bar, staring at the mouth-watering sight of Valentino's ass in snug dark jeans. She didn't know what had just happened, but she'd stay, if for no other reason than to see what happened next.

To purchase *Captive Fantasy* and other erotic

titles, visit www.thewilderroses.com.